THE MASKED MASTER MIND

George F. Worts

Balata

BY FRED MacISAAC

Bretwalda

BY PHILIP KETCHUM

The Draft of Eternity

BY VICTOR ROUSSEAU

Four Corners, Volume 1

BY THEODORE ROSCOE

Genius Jones

BY LESTER DENT

Gone North

BY CHARLES ALDEN SELTZER

The Sherlock of Sageland:
The Complete Tales of Sheriff Henry, Volume 1

BY W.C. TUTTLE

The Swordsman of Mars

BY OTIS ADELBERT KLINE

When Tigers Are Hunting: The Complete
Adventures of Cordie, Soldier of Fortune, Volume 1

BY W. WIRT

THE MASKED MASTER MIND

GEORGE F. WORTS

COVER BY

PAUL STAHR

ALTUS PRESS
2015

EDITED AND DESIGNED BY
Matthew Moring

PUBLISHING HISTORY
"The Masked Master Mind" originally appeared as "You're Under Arrest!" in the September 4, 11, 18, and 25, and October 2, 1926 issues of *Argosy All-Story Weekly* magazine (Vol. 180, No. 2–Vol. 180, No. 6). Copyright © 1926 by The Frank A. Munsey Company. Copyright renewed © 1953 and assigned to Steeger Properties, LLC. All rights reserved.
"About the Author" originally appeared in the January 25, 1930 issue of *Argosy* magazine (Vol. 209, No. 5). Copyright © 1930 by The Frank A. Munsey Company. Copyright renewed © 1957 and assigned to Steeger Properties, LLC. All rights reserved.

THANKS TO
Joel Frieman, Chris Kalb, Everard P. Digges LaTouche, and Ray Riethmeier

Visit *altuspress.com* for more books like this.
Printed in the United States of America.

TABLE OF CONTENTS

The Masked Master Mind 1

About the Author 249

CHAPTER I

FATE SUMMONS GILBERT DOLLOW

THERE WAS NOTHING in the air of that golden, gladsome summer morning to indicate that the most vibrantly vital hour in the life of Gilbert Dollow was preparing to strike. It was just like any other gladsome summer morning. Birds were caroling in the trees; grasshoppers were hopping about in the grass; and old Constable Jethro Dench was tap-tap-tapping away with his shingle hammer on the roof of his cottage, as he had been doing every morning for a week or more.

Destiny moves on swift, invisible wings. Gilbert Dollow, cradled in a nest of soft, warm sand, his great brown arms and legs asprawl, heard no whisper of her approach.

It was a little after eleven o'clock in the morning on Maple Hollow Beach. It could not be said even that the sky was adventurous. Rather, it was vacuous and blue. Across the lake the Three Neighbors, clad in their armor of tall dark pines, seemed to ride upon a layer of filmy nothingness; but this was an optical illusion. The Three Neighbors were anchored fast to the bottom of the lake, though they seemed to float upon invisible heat haze. It was going to be a hot day. Heat devils shimmered along the lime-colored sand of the beach, and overhead two snow-white gulls wheeled, coasted, tail-spinned, and pancaked.

Gilbert Dollow followed them with eyes half-lidded against the ticklish yellow glare of the up and coming sun, and pondered the profound mysteries of nature.

Had the birds of the air, he asked himself, learned the tailspin and similar tricks from aviators, or had they been doing them since time immemorial? It was Gilbert Dollow's belief that birds had perfected the technique of their flying by observing the methods of stunt flyers. A smart bird knew a good stunt when it saw one, he reasoned.

Sophisticated city people might have smiled at Gilbert Dollow's probings into the baffling mysteries of nature, but here in Maple Hollow, where people lived with nature, his opinions were accepted with respect mingled with downright admiration. Hadn't he answered satisfactorily and for all time the maddening riddle of why woodpeckers bore holes into telephone poles?

Gilbert Dollow had spent days on his back under this telephone pole and that, a tireless searcher after scientific truth, and had watched woodpecker after woodpecker approach a telephone pole and drill away at it, only to fly away with shrill cries of disgust or despair.

It seemed to Gilbert that the woodpecker first put its ear against the pole; then, apparently satisfied that all was well, started drilling. After weeks devoted to this baffling study, the truth suddenly flashed on Gilbert. The otherwise crafty birds were being tricked! The humming of the poles, caused by the electric currents racing to and fro in the wires—this humming the birds believed was caused by living and edible insects inside the poles.

Many woodpeckers, after vainly boring holes to reach insects that did not exist, had flown into the high-tension wires overhead and become electrocuted. With cold bird logic, they had committed suicide, thinking they were losing their reason because they were hearing things.

Gilbert Dollow wrote an account of his scientific findings in an article for the *Weekly Maple Hollow Herald,* and recommended that the telephone companies install a device on the poles that would stop them from humming. But nothing had come of it. And the slaughter of deceived woodpeckers continued.

The woodpecker incident is repeated here to emphasize a fact that residents of Maple Hollow knew well, which was that young Dollow had uncanny powers of observation, penetration, and the ability to make keen deductions. He was often told that he was wasting his talents in Maple Hollow, and that he should pack up and go to Steel City, fifty miles away, where a man of his original turn of mind could find a place for himself.

So far, Gilbert had resisted the faint beckonings of opportunity; for he had, in addition to uncanny powers of observation, penetration, and the ability to make keen deductions, a tremendous sense of duty.

That explained why he was at his post now, hours before the earliest bathers could be expected to appear. Gilbert Dollow was the life guard of Maple Hollow Beach.

Early in the summer Gilbert had won that desirable position against a field of other healthy, virile young men. Before a committee of six judges, composed of the town selectmen, he had dived from rafts, springboards, and elevated platforms; had dragged spluttering fat men from the water; and had resuscitated them according to the rules laid down in the Coast Guard handbook; had swum on his back, on his side, on his stomach, and under water; and had won the hundred yard crawl. He had won the contest handily, and since then not one life had been lost on Maple Hollow Beach.

From where Gilbert Dollow lay in the warm, soft sand, he could hear the busy tapping of Constable Dench's shingling hammer. Some day Jethro Dench would retire. Who would then become constable of Maple Hollow? Gilbert dreamed. He dreamed of himself in the blue uniform of the constable, standing at the intersection of the County Pike and the Yellow Rock Road, controlling with a wave of his hand the streams of Sunday traffic. Power! He would have power! He did not realize how far these day-dreams would carry him.

A crab issued from a hole in the sand near by, and crawled daintily toward him on delicate hairy legs. When the creature was a few feet away Gilbert raised his hand. The crab reared up, darted to one side, and then dashed gracefully backward to its hole and stayed there, half in darkness, its eyes radiant with hatred.

"You can't beat it," said Gilbert, and he was referring, of course, to the wonders of nature. It was wonderful that a crab was so constructed that it could walk forward, sideways, or backward with equal ease.

And wasn't it equally wonderful that Gilbert Dollow was always noticing these trifling things? He used his eyes, that was all. He never forgot a face. He never missed a detail. He was always seeing what the other fellow overlooked, and sometimes he didn't even appear to be looking. At this very moment, indeed, Gilbert appeared to be studying the crab. As a matter of fact, he was perfectly aware that a spot of pale pink had appeared at the far end of the beach, and was quickly advancing toward him.

By a quick recourse to his powers of deduction, he knew that that moving pink spot—no bigger at that distance than the head of a pin—was a girl. He knew that there were seven pink dresses in Maple Hollow. There was a difference in their shadings that the ordinary eye could hardly have detected at a dozen yards. But Gilbert Dollow's eye was not an ordinary eye.

"Annie May Prine," he said, and paid no further attention to the pink spot no larger than a pinhead.

In due course, or many minutes later, a soft, timid, sweet, and rather husky young voice said, with accents of surprise:

"Oh! Why! Hello, Gilbert!"

The life guard rolled over and sat up, blinking his eye with feigned astonishment.

"Annie May!" he gasped. "How you surprised me!"

The girl was blushing with self-consciousness. She even wiggled a little with this devastating emotion, and she clasped her hands, with the small package they contained, behind her. She was an exceptionally pretty girl—by long odds the prettiest girl in Maple Hollow, which is celebrated for its pretty girls. Her eyes were big and brown, her nose was pert, and she had the sweetest mouth! Pink was very becoming to her, perhaps because her skin was so pink. The soft wind from off the lake blew the pink dress against her slim body, and frisked its hem about her round, beautiful ankles.

Almost any young, red-blooded man, looking at Annie May Prine as she stood there, would have said to himself, "Gee! But I certainly would like to fold my arms around her!"

But did this lovely, blushing creature affect Gilbert Dollow in that fashion? Positively not! She left him absolutely cold. All girls left Gilbert absolutely cold. You see, he was girlproof.

"Did I really surprise you?" asked Annie May in her sweet, low, rather husky voice. She looked as if an unkind word would send her flying down the beach like a frightened doe; but Gilbert knew better.

"You certainly did," he agreed.

"I brought you a piece of cake," said Annie May, blushing still more rosily and extending the neatly tied brown-paper package to him. "I baked it myself. It's choc'late—fig filling."

"Won't you sit down?" said Gilbert cordially.

He was always interested, somehow, in cake or cookies or pie, at any hour of the day, and Annie May's chocolate cake with fig filling was a delicacy among delicacies. Yet he was not as grateful for this offering as you might have supposed. Gilbert had fallen into the habit of taking such things for granted.

A day would come when he would look back upon the cakes and pastries, and even the plain home cooking, of Annie May with tears in his heart and a futile excess of saliva in his mouth; even now he vaguely appreciated the fact that Annie May Prine was the best cook in Maple Hollow; but still, all the girls and all the mothers of the girls of Maple Hollow were good cooks, and how can a man who has lived all his life in a valley of diamonds know that the rest of the world is not paved with diamonds?

Annie May sighed as a lovesick girl will, and seated herself beside him. A naughty puff of wind caught the hem of her dress as she was lowering herself to the sand, and for a flickering, thrilling moment the fact was betrayed that Annie May's golden silk stockings were rolled down below her knees, and that those knees were pink, slim, and divinely dimpled.

But Gilbert did not pay any attention to these charming revelations. As a life guard, it naturally followed that he had seen Annie May's knees before—indeed, he had seen all the knees in Maple Hollow, and if any of them had interested him, certainly he had never betrayed any excitement over it. Being a close observer and a keen deducer, he was aware that Annie May had the most beautiful legs in Maple Hollow. But what of it? He was not interested in girls; he was not interested in Annie May Prine.

Here, then, was the most desirable, the most alluring maiden in Maple Hollow. She was the prettiest and unquestionably the sweetest natured. She was the best cook. She was the niftiest dresser. And she had the most beautiful legs. Well, what of it?

That was the way Gilbert Dollow reasoned, if he bothered to reason at all. What of it? What if she was languishing for his arms and his kisses? What if she adored him? What if his every glance thrilled her and made her shiver and go hot and cold by turns?

You may say that Gilbert ought to be shot or drowned or kicked, or all three. But the mystery still remains. Girls left him cold. Perhaps that was why they adored him so.

Annie May sighed, and seated herself beside him with a little shiver. She was still rather a small girl, not much over five feet. She had grown an inch in the past year, and had filled out here and there charmingly, as girls do in their late teens. She would never be a large girl, and, seated there beside Gilbert, she seemed tiny.

He was so big and strong and broad and brown! His legs were like mahogany logs, and so were his arms. He had a broad, deep barrel of a chest, and his hair, bleached by the sunlight, was silvery gold, packed in tight, crisp little curls to his scalp. His brows were bushy and bleached too, and his eyes were the deepest brightest blue imaginable, sapphire blue.

Annie May gazed at his handsome face, and sighed again.

He had opened the package and was devouring the hunk of chocolate cake with slow, dreamy contentment.

"Is it good?" she said timidly.

"Yumph," he grunted.

"I don't think it is as light as the last one I made," she said rapidly in the apologetic voice reserved by all housewives for any and all cooking they do. "Uh—are you going to the dance at the pavilion to-night, Gil?"

"Hadn't thought of it. Why?"

"Oh, I was just wondering," she said hastily. "Bill Sulger's got his new saxophone, and they're practicing a lot of new music up at old man Bemis's barn. It sounded grand from the back porch. I could hardly keep my feet still. I—I was thinking some of going with Hal Hooper."

"Hal's a good dancer," the handsome life guard commented, and he did not see the tears that suddenly filled Annie May's big brown eyes.

"Hal asked me to go, but I told him I wouldn't let him know until this afternoon," said Annie May. "I don't know whether

I'll go or not. One minute I think I'll go, and the next minute I think I won't. There is going to be a full moon to-night, and it ought to be lovely at the pavilion—cool and nice.

"Mame Purdy's going to make some of that grape punch, and grandma's promised me to bake a batch of those cinnamon cookies. But I sort of can't make up my mind whether to go or not."

Gilbert didn't seem to be paying very close attention to what she was saying. As a matter of fact, he wasn't. The truth was, those almost superhuman powers of observation of his had been engaged again by the crab.

The crab, after glaring at him with ill-concealed animosity all this time, had again ventured from its hole. It sidled out eying him balefully, ready to spring back at the slightest move on his part. Having reached the dubious safety of the great open spaces, it hesitated, and then started slowly to move down the beach, away from him.

Gilbert lifted his hand. The crab broke into a full gallop, racing backward, its bright eyes full of hatred for him. It collided against a small white shell, almost sprawled, leaped into the air, and continued its mad flight.

"My Lord," Gilbert breathed, "you're wonderful—wonderful!"

"What?" gasped Annie May, convulsively clasping a hand to her suddenly pounding heart.

She had not seen the crab. All she could see was Gilbert, and she could hardly see him through the rainbow of her tears.

"That crab," Gilbert answered. "The way he can run backward and sidewise and forward. It's wonderful."

He was astonished when Annie May leaped to her feet. Her fists were clenched at her sides. Her small breast was heaving. Her eyes, tear-blurred, were glaring at him.

She stamped one small foot.

"Gilbert Dollow, you give me a great big pain!"

It was the first time he had ever seen Annie May carry on

so; and he climbed quickly to his feet and looked down into her flushed, furious little face.

"I hate you!" she stormed.

"My Lord, what for?"

"Oh, good night!"

"Annie May," he said, bewildered, "for the love of Pete, what's got into you, anyhow?"

"You—you—you and your wonderful crabs!"

"Well, they are wonderful!"

"Oh, so's your old man! Good-by! I'm going! I never want to lay eyes on you again as long as I live."

"But, for Heaven's sake, Annie May, what's the matter?"

Annie May lifted her eyebrows and perked her lips, and planted her hands on her softly rounded hips. This made her look like a little imp, or an elf. Owlishly she gazed up at him.

"Gilbert, are you going to take me to the dance at the pavilion to-night, or aren't you?"

"Why, sure I will!" he gasped. "It will give me the greatest pleasure to take you to the dance—if you want me to."

Annie May's lovely little face still held that impish, elfish, owlish expression. A remark much sharper than the tarragon vinegar she used in her famous French dressing was on her lips, but as chance would have it the remark was never uttered.

At that moment fate came speeding down the beach in the person of Fatty Gillespie. Gilbert's uncanny powers of observation informed him that Fatty was unusually pale—a fact to be gleaned even at that distance. The stout young man came bounding down the sand, emitting faint, gasping cries. His face was drawn with some emotion.

"I wonder if he got mixed up with those hornets in the Widow Fangle's field," Gilbert pondered.

The fat young man came sprinting on, throwing up sand with his agitated feet. When he arrived and stopped before them, he was breathless. The pallor of his emotion suddenly gave way to the pink of superheated blood as his leg muscles suddenly ceased their demands upon that life fluid.

"Kuh-kuh-kuh—" he panted, while his baby-blue eyes rolled wildly.

"What is it, Fat?" Gilbert demanded.

"Kuh-kuh-kuh—" the fat one wheezed.

"Something terrible has happened," Annie May guessed.

"Say it, Fatty, say it!" Gilbert pleaded.

"Kuh-kuh-con-con-constable—"

"Something has happened to the constable!" Annie May wailed.

"Has he had a stroke?" Gilbert cried.

After all, this was not a bad deduction. Constable Dench was eighty-two, and at that age men do have strokes.

But Fatty Gillespie shook his pink, perspiring face.

"He—puff—fell—puff—offen the roof."

"And killed himself?"

"Nuh—nuh—puff—nope! He fell—into—the—onion—bed."

In his impatience Gilbert seized Fatty's shoulders and shook him.

"Has he got internal injuries?"

"Dunno. He—he fell with an awful smack. Wants yuh—you to come a-a-a-a-runnin'!"

Gilbert grasped Annie May's slim, sunburned left wrist. It was ornamented by a small silver wrist watch.

"Good grief!" he gasped. "It's a quarter to twelve, and the constable's due at the corner to regulate traffic at twelve."

"That's why I come so fast. Run!" puffed Fatty.

Gilbert ran.

CHAPTER II

OFFICIAL DUTY

CONSTABLE JETHRO DENCH was lying on his back in bed when Gilbert Dollow loped into the humble cottage of Maple Hollow's guardian of the peace. The old man was very pale; he had a baffled, pained look in his eyes, and he was fumbling with his long white beard which lay on the coverlet when the life guard pushed his way into the room.

All of the constable's surviving relatives and many friends and neighbors were packed into the bedroom with bowed heads, but they quickly stood aside for Gilbert Dollow. Those who did not stand aside Gilbert rather roughly flung aside, and when he had reached the bed he dropped down on his knees.

Mr. Dench gazed up at him from his faded old eyes, and smiled a brave but weary smile. His eyes narrowed slightly, and Gilbert placed his ear close to the old man's lips, because he knew that Constable Dench had a message for him—it might even be a dying message.

"Gil," he said in a gasping whisper as Gilbert bent over him, "they got me this time!"

"I'll spend the rest of my life trackin' them down and slayin' them one by one," Gilbert promised. "Who got you?"

The old man looked a little puzzled.

"Them shinglin' nails it was that got me, Gil," he explained. "All the past week, since I been workin' on that roof I been side-steppin' them nails. But this mornin', with the job just about done, I got lax. I slipped on one, and down I come!"

"Are you hurt bad, constable?" the life guard breathed.

"Don't know. Doc ain't been here yet. But I'm too shocked and shattered by the surprise of it to obey the call to duty to-day. Somebody's got to be at the intersection of the County Pike and the Yaller Rock Road when noon strikes twelve, Gilbert. The traffic must be regulated. The Berryville Boosters are havin' their annual picnic down on the beach to-day, and there is a big ball game on at Wilkin's Corners. It's goin' to be worse than any Sunday traffic jam, and there's only one man in Maple Hollow I can trust to turn over my badge and gun to, Gilbert—only one man with a sense of duty to see that my duties are carried out the way I would carry them out myself.

"That man is you, Gilbert, and there ain't a moment to lose! It's up to you to go out there and regulate that traffic, and to see that the laws and statutes of Maple Hollow are obeyed and respected."

If those who were crowded into the little bedroom thought that the constable was overacting his part a bit, certainly no one betrayed it. Drama came to Maple Hollow so seldom that when it did it was welcomed in any form.

"I'll hurry right home and get into my clothes," said Gilbert nervously. He was at last to have power—at last he was to regulate traffic—but now the prospect of it made him a little uneasy.

"Ain't time, Gil. There's a town ordinance that calls for a police officer to be at that intersection from twelve noon to 8 p.m. You've got just two or three minutes to get over there. You'll find my cap and badge and gun on the hook inside the kitchen door. The keys to the jail are stuck in a hole in the linin' of the cap. Grab them on your way out."

"Very good, constable," said Gilbert, straightening up, and his eyes were bright with the light of duty. "Somebody has got to fill my job on the beach this afternoon."

He wheeled on a tall, anxious young man who stood in a corner of the room. It was Bill Sulger, the saxophonist—Bill

Sulger, who had been a close second in the life guard contest that spring.

"Bill," he snapped, "hop into your bathin' suit, and fill in for me this afternoon on the beach. The Berryville Boosters will be drinkin' a lot of home brew, and they're sure to get careless in the water. Then's when the drownin's happen."

And with that rather somber sentence ringing in the air, Gilbert Dollow hastened into the kitchen where the constable's cap, badge, and revolver belt were hanging. So it happened that motorists approaching the intersection of the County Pike and the Yellow Rock Road as the bell in the tower of the Maple Hollow town hall was tolling off the twelve strokes of noon were edified by the sight of a tall, bronze-skinned young man, who wore a constable's cap on his head, a constable's badge on the shirt of his swimming suit, a pistol belt studded with cartridges at his waist, and rubber-soled sneakers on his feet.

If his appearance was incongruous, certainly his bearing was solemn and dignified.

As twelve thirty approached, the traffic along both roads increased. Down the County Pike came the Berryville Boosters, waving pennants, flaunting banners, banging on dishpans, singing the "Berryville Boosters Ballad," and giving in other ways all the manifestations of serious business men who had put their cares and worries and responsibilities aside for the afternoon of the annual Berryville Boosters' picnic; while down the Yellow Rock Road, proceeding in the direction of Wilkin's Corners, came a long line of cars filled with farmers and villagers in a holiday spirit en route to the ball game between the Wilkin's Corners team and the Milltown team.

It was a busy hour for the handsome life guard. He stopped traffic on the County Pike and let traffic through on the Yellow Rock Road, and *vice versa*. And he suffered stoically an endless stream of taunts.

"Hey, constable, where'd ya get the uniform?"

"Oh, look at the Mack Sennet Bathing Beauty?"

"Ossifer, where's your uniform?"

"What's the matter, kid—can't Maple Hollow buy its police force uniforms?"

"Oh, Elsie, look at the sheik with the gun on his hip!"

"Hey, Adonis, why don't you go home and git dressed?"

From all sides, as the traffic streamed through Maple Hollow, these taunts and jeers were flung at Gilbert Dollow. He blushed again and again, but his head was up, his chin was high, and his eyes blazed with the almost religious light of the Man Who Sees His Duty and Performs It.

Along about one thirty the traffic began to thin down. Most of the Berryville Boosters were at the beach, eating their lunch, drinking home brew, and singing "Sweet Adeline," and most of the patrons of the baseball match were rooting for their favorites at Wilkin's Corners. The time came when not a car was in sight on either road in either direction.

Annie May Prine came briskly down the street with a small hamper, covered with a napkin, over her arm. She came to where Gilbert stood in the middle of the intersection of the two highways.

"I brought you some lunch," she said breathlessly. "I stopped in and saw your ma. She's got another touch of rheumatism, and told me to tell you how proud she is of you."

Gilbert had lifted the napkin, and he gazed with moist, grateful eyes at the hamper's contents. There were meat sandwiches, jelly sandwiches, and cheese sandwiches of fragrant, delicious homemade bread. There were deviled eggs. There was an entire coconut-custard pie. There was a small yellow bowl full of potato salad.

"You hold the basket while I eat," he said. "I can't leave my post except on the call of duty."

So Annie May proudly held the hamper while Gilbert devoured sandwich after sandwich, washing them down with creamed and sugared coffee from a pint milk bottle.

"You certainly can make food fit to tempt a man, Annie May," he said presently.

She glowed.

"Do you really think I'm a good cook?"

"None better," said her hero, sinking his teeth into the heart of the coconut-custard pie.

He had consumed half of the pie in great, man-sized bites when, down the Yellow Rock Road from the direction of Wilkin's Corners purred a yellow Minerva roadster—a long, lean, handsome brute of a car, worth sixteen thousand dollars, if it was worth a cent.

A woman was at the wheel, and beside her was huddled a man, apparently asleep. She was a blond woman, handsome after a certain dashing fashion, with jewels glittering on her fingers and bracelets flashing on both arms. Her eyes were as blue as Delft china, and just about as opaque.

Gilbert lifted his pie hand in a gesture to signal her to go through, but in midair changed the signal. He sprang in front of the car.

"Stop!" he shouted.

The woman quickly applied her brakes, and the yellow Minerva came to a hissing, throbbing stop.

"What's the matter, lamb?" the blond woman chuckled. "I wasn't going an inch over fifteen. The sign outside your town said fifteen, and my speedometer is on the level."

"You're under arrest," said Gilbert firmly. "Pull up to the curb." He hopped upon the running board, pressed the remainder of the pie into his mouth, and was deaf to the woman's ejaculations of dismay and wonder.

It was Gilbert's first arrest, and he did not mean to have the occasion treated lightly.

CHAPTER III

DOUBTS AND DEEDS

THE HANDSOME, BEJEWELED blond woman obeyed his orders, and pulled up beside the curb. It chanced that this maneuver brought the Minerva alongside the Maple Hollow jail. The man who sat beside her was now thoroughly awake, and at sight of Gilbert, he started to climb out of the roadster.

"Stay where you are," Gilbert rasped.

The woman was looking at his broad, brown shoulders admiringly.

"My!" she exclaimed. "But you're a good-looking kid. What are we pinched for, sonny?"

"You're smoking a cigarette," said Gilbert sternly.

Her eyes became round. From the rose-tipped cigarette in her glittering, plump hand she looked at Gilbert's stern, handsome brown face.

"Why, darling, I smoke a hundred of these things a day. It certainly isn't against the law to smoke a cigarette, is it?"

"It's against the law in Maple Hollow," said Gilbert sternly, "for a female to smoke tobacco in any form in public. The law was put on the statute books forty years ago, because there used to be an old lady here who flaunted her clay pipe up and down Main Street. But the law's the law, and the statute is still on the books. I'm sorry to arrest you, ma'am, but you've violated a town ordinance and I have to do it."

The woman looked at him with honeyed reproach.

"Why, you great big handsome thing, you," she purred. "I

16

wouldn't dream of shattering a town ordinance. There! I'll put it right out, and if you catch me smoking another cigarette in this town, you can hang me to the limb of the nearest hickory tree. The minute I laid eyes on you, I knew you were an officer who read the strictest interpretation into the law."

She had squashed the cigarette on the floor under her foot. "And I promise faithfully never to smoke another cigarette in your beautiful village. You aren't going to give me a summons are you, big boy?"

Her eyes were flattering, her voice was flattering. Never in his life had Gilbert Dollow met a woman like her. Her diamonds, and sapphires, and emeralds dazzled him. He felt a little dizzy. And he knew that if he ever fell in love it would be with a woman like this.

All these emotions however, he concealed behind a frowning official mask.

"Where 're you from?" he asked curtly.

"Steel City," said the lady.

"What's your name?"

"Alice Sullivan."

"H'm," said Gilbert. "You own this car?"

"Of course I do, kid, and a half dozen others just as good."

Gilbert was impressed. He suspected that Alice Sullivan was a prominent society woman of Steel City. He was willing enough to let her go, having reprimanded her, but he was unwilling to relinquish this first passing grasp upon the finer and more beautiful things of life.

He glanced sharply at her companion. The man was huddled down still further in his seat than he had been before and he had contrived to pull his cap down over his eyes. He seemed uneasy. He probably owned one of the steel mills in Steel City, Gilbert reasoned. And he studied the man more carefully. His face was pale and rather pasty and it was ornamented by a trim waxed mustache with blunt ends. He had a weak mouth and a weak chin, and dreamy eyes.

Something kept prodding at Gilbert's consciousness as he looked the fellow over: something seemed to be forcing itself upon his attention from the tail of his eye, but the idea, or whatever it was, hadn't quite been born yet.

"Can we roll along, big boy?" the woman asked in her throaty, purring voice.

"If you'll promise me faithfully you won't smoke cigarettes when you're driving through Maple Hollow," Gilbert said.

And then the thing that had been trying to force itself upon Gilbert's attention did so—just as the Sullivan lady touched the accelerator pedal restlessly and the great motor under the hood roared in its eagerness to be on the way.

It was a half-tone photograph, a handbill, pasted on the bulletin board on the wall of the jail that finally effected an entrance into Gilbert's consciousness. In harsh black type across the top of the handbill was the word:

WANTED!

And under that was explained, in smaller type, that the original of the photograph shown below was wanted in six States for bigamy. And the photograph of the bigamist was identical with the face of the man who sat beside Alice Sullivan! A reward of two hundred and fifty dollars was offered for the apprehension and the capture of this monster.

"Wait a minute!" Gilbert roared as the body of the Minerva throbbed.

"What's the matter now?" Alice Sullivan said impatiently.

Gilbert jerked his head in the direction of the man seated beside her.

"You're under arrest!" he snapped.

"Me?" said the man.

"Yes, you!"

"Don't be ridiculous. Alice, let's go!"

"Stick 'em up!" Gilbert snapped, and Constable Dench's blue

six-shooter was lying along the palm of his hand. "Your name's Harry P. Lamson."

"You're full of hop, you hick," the man snarled. "Alice, give her the oats."

"Not with all this artillery staring me in the nose," said the lady named Alice. "What's the matter now, son? Has he been violating a city ordinance by chewing gum in public or something?"

"He's wanted for bigamy," said Gilbert. "His name is Harry P. Lamson, and he's under arrest."

"You're fuller of hop than a hoptoad," the man snorted. "My name is Eugene K. Nichols."

"Get out of that car and keep your hands up by your ears," Gilbert ordered. "One false move from you, brother, and I'll shoot to kill."

"He has that look in his eyes," said the woman anxiously.

Annie May had crept closer and closer to Gilbert's side. Most of the conversation she had missed, and so she asked now:

"Why, Gilbert, what is wrong?"

"This man," Gilbert answered, wagging the revolver, "is Harry P. Lamson, the notorious bigamist that the papers 've been so full of lately. He's wanted in pretty nearly every State in the Union. He's a bad egg of the worst kind. And now—"

"I tell you, officer, you are making a serious mistake," said the alleged bigamist. "I'll have you run out of the county for this."

"Maybe you've made a mistake," suggested Annie May. "That's a perfectly awful thing to accuse a man of, Gilbert."

"You bet your life it is!" the man exclaimed. "I can send him to jail for defamation of character. And what's more, if you don't put that gun away and let us go, I will."

"Keep your hands right where they are," said Gilbert coldly. "Now climb down out of that car, and if you run I am going to shoot to kill." He glanced at the blond woman. "And I'm afraid I'll have to hold you as a material witness."

"Me?" wailed the blond woman. "Be your age, Gilbert! I never laid eyes on this human reptile until half an hour ago. He was walking along the road, and he asked me for a lift and I gave it to him. Did you ever see an act of Christian charity that didn't turn out this way? For all of me, you can shoot him so full of holes he won't be fit for anything but an orange juice strainer. That certainly is his picture, too. Kid, you're good. You've made what I call a brilliant arrest. Now don't let this marriage hound slip out of your clutches."

Gilbert looked slightly bewildered.

"I sort of gathered that you two were old friends. I'm sure I heard him call you Alice."

"You did? Did he call me Alice? Well, I certainly like his nerve! You asked me what my name was, and I told you Alice Sullivan. It was right after that he 'Aliced' me. Say! He's smooth-er than a greased eel, all right. Lock him up, lamb. Chuck him right into the hoosegow!"

"I'm going to," Gilbert said grimly. "Annie May, you run up and tell the constable I've made an important arrest, and that I'm locking him up."

"I'm going to wait right here," said the blond woman, when Annie May had gone. "I want to have a talk with you. Lock up this mustached monster, and hurry back." And she shut off the engine.

Gilbert removed the cap from his head as he walked around the Minerva. He extracted the jail keys, keeping one eye on his prisoner.

"Walk up that path," he said curtly.

The man made some profane comment under his breath, stiffened as if he were about to offer resistance, then looked again at the weapon in Gilbert's hand, and moved slowly up the path to the jail door.

As chance would have it, the Maple Hollow jail was empty. It contained two cells, and these cells would have defied the jail-breaking skill of a Dutch Anderson. The walls were of reinforced concrete a foot and a half thick. The single small window of each cell was high up and guarded by thick iron bars set solidly into the concrete, and the door of each cell was an intricate waffle of stout steel, equipped with a strong, complicated lock.

Gilbert unlocked the door of cell No. 1, and as he did so, the prisoner winked at him.

"Listen," said the man, "how much money do you pick up in a year in this town?"

"What difference does it make to you?" said Gilbert.

"Well," said the man, "how would you like to own a nice snappy roadster, and be able to take a trip to Florida, and buy yourself a whole wardrobe of stylish clothes?"

"What do you mean?" said Gilbert.

"Just this," said the man. "I've taken a liking to you, and even if you have pinched the wrong man, I'm not holding it against you. I want to make you a little present before we part." Thrusting his hand into an inside pocket, he withdrew a dark leather billfold.

The dark corridor of the jail suddenly seemed to burst into golden sunlight. The man's hands were positively full of one thousand-dollar bills. Gilbert, in all his life, had never seen so much money. Once, at the Farmer's National Bank of Maple Hollow, the cashier had called him over and said:

"Gilbert, do you want to have a sensation that you will probably never have again in all your life?" And he placed in Gilbert's hand a thousand-dollar bill. He had permitted Gilbert to hold it there for perhaps fifteen seconds, before his native caution had prompted him to reach for it. The fact that Gilbert had held in his hand a real, genuine thousand-dollar bill was a sensation that supplied Maple Hollow with conversation for days.

Here, now, was a man whose hands were simply spilling over with bills of that awesome denomination.

Mr. Lamson, or whoever he may have been, handled the pack

of bills as casually as if it were a twenty-five-cent deck of cards. Ten of the golden bills he counted off, and these he pressed into Gilbert's surprised and unexpected left hand.

"Great grief!" Gilbert muttered. "What's all this money for?"

The man grinned at him benevolently. "It's to buy you a snappy little roadster, and a trip to California or wherever you please, and swell clothes. I'm a rich man, Gilbert. I won't miss this ten thousand any more than you would miss a nickel."

"S-s-say!" Gilbert stammered. "You aren't trying to bribe me, are you?"

"Bribe you!" the man exclaimed. "Whatever put that idea into your head, Gilbert? I am making you this little present because the minute I laid eyes on you I said to myself: 'Bill, there's a young fellow I'd like to do something for. If I had a boy, he's just the kind of a boy my boy would be. I want to give this young fellow a chance.' And it's going to hurt my feelings terribly, Gilbert, if you don't accept this gift."

"Well," said Gilbert, "it certainly is mighty generous of you to give me all this money, especially seeing that we are perfect strangers and considering that I've brought you into this jail to lock you up."

"No hard feelings at all," said the man affably. "Now do you mind if I take a little walk?"

"That wouldn't do at all," said Gilbert. "If you didn't come back, then where would I be?"

"Well," said the man, looking at Gilbert queerly, "you would be in the price of a roadster, a trip to California, a lot of new clothes, and a nice little bank balance." And he started to walk past Gilbert toward the jail door.

Gilbert brought up the muzzle of the revolver.

"Wait a minute!" he said. "Where do you think you're going?"

"Hell," said the benevolent stranger, "I'm just going. Do you mean to tell me you're still dissatisfied? You think I'm selfish, don't you? Here—take it all." And he thrust the wallet into

Gilbert's hand. "There's fifteen thousand more in that wallet. That means I'm making you a present of twenty-five thousand."

"You mean," said Gilbert, "you're giving me twenty-five thousand—just giving it to me?"

"That's just what I mean," said the man.

"Well, it certainly is mighty generous of you," Gilbert said gratefully. "You must be worth a lot of money."

"Millions," said the man.

"I'm sorry I have to lock you up, after giving me all this money," said Gilbert, and he was genuinely regretful. "And now if you'll excuse me, I have to be getting back to my post."

The man seemed astonished. He started to speak, but words failed him. Only when Gilbert had pushed him into the cell and locked the door did the man find his tongue; then he launched at Gilbert such a volley of profanity that the handsome life guard blushed. He almost ran out of the jail. He was not accustomed to such language.

The blond lady in the Minerva was still waiting, and her slender, tapering eyebrows went up perceptibly as she caught sight of the leather billfold, and the wad of radiant bills in his hand.

"Gilbert," she said earnestly, "I want to have a talk with you. Come in here and sit down." And when Gilbert had done so, she said: "You are wasting your talents in a town of this size. Why don't you come to Steel City where a man with your ability will stand a real chance? Did you leave him his underwear, or have you that, too?"

Gilbert Dollow looked at her blankly.

"His underwear?" he repeated. "What do I want his underwear for? After this, I am going to wear nothing but silk underwear. Look at all the money he gave me!"

"I am looking at it," said the lady, "but if I were you, I would sort of keep it out of sight. That money isn't any more promiscuous than a fist fight in church. I will admit that you are bold and daring, but there is such a thing as carrying it too far. Did you get his entire bank roll?"

"I think he gave me everything he had," Gilbert admitted. "He said he was worth millions and he wouldn't miss this at all. He said he had taken a liking to me, and he wanted me to have it all."

The blond woman had slightly inclined her head, as one will when hearkening to strange, distant sounds.

"That sounds like some one in the jail," she said finally.

"He's swearing," said Gilbert, blushing as a particularly unprintable word came through the wall, muffled, to them.

"You mean," she said, "he's still in there?"

"Sure," said Gilbert, "I locked him up."

The woman turned so that she could look fully into Gilbert's eyes. "You mean, you didn't let him go?"

"Certainly not!"

"After him slipping you his entire bank roll?"

"What has that got to do with it? He wanted to make me a present."

"When," said the woman gently, "are you planning to leave town?"

"Why, I'm not planning to leave town."

"But, what are you going to say when he begins to squeal? You took his money, didn't you? Gilbert, you have no idea how suspicious-minded humanity is. Hasn't it occurred to you that people who aren't as honest-minded as you and I are might suspect that you have taken a bribe from that human reptile?" And she looked at Gilbert sternly.

"It crossed my mind for a minute in there," Gilbert confessed, "that he might be trying to bribe me; but he kept talking about how much he liked me, and he sort of got my mind working along other lines. It just happens that I can use some money right now. I'd like to finish paying off the mortgage and back taxes on our house, so ma wouldn't be worrying about it; and I could buy her that black dress she wants, and a car for myself, and a trip somewhere.

"I got thinking of those things. I guess I was sort of dazzled by the sight of so much money. Say! Do you really think he was trying to bribe me? If I thought he was trying to bribe me, do you know what I'd do? I'd go in there and knock his block off!"

The woman had taken his hand, and now she was gently patting it.

"There, there, lamb, now don't go and get yourself all excited. I know just how you feel."

"This is bribe money!" Gilbert burst out. "I'm going in there and knock his block off!"

"No, Gilbert, no. Remember, you are an officer of the law. Just keep that money as evidence. It proves just how bad an actor he is. It's a criminal offense to try to bribe an officer of the law, and you've got this money as Exhibit A. Keep it, but don't make a secret of it. When he begins to squeal about your accepting money from him, it's best to have a lot of people know that you took it just as evidence.

"If I were you, I'd tell everybody I know about it. I think I'd better be going. Do you know, Gilbert, I've taken quite a fancy to you. I never knew anybody like you before in my life. What's the rest of your name?"

"Dollow," said Gilbert.

"Gilbert Dollow," she murmured. "I guess I told you mine before. It's Alice Sullivan—Mrs. Alice Sullivan. I'm a widow, and I live in Steel City. Have you ever been there?"

"Just once," said Gilbert, "when I was a kid."

She gave his hand a squeeze. "How old are you, Gilbert?"

"I'm twenty-three," said Gilbert.

"I'm just twenty-seven," said Mrs. Sullivan. Gilbert looked at her in surprise. He had really thought she was quite a little older than that.

"I wish you would come to Steel City," she went on. "I'm sure I could find something for you to do. I like you, Gilbert.

I'm a great admirer of men of your type. I want you to come to Steel City. Here is my card. You are too good for this hick town."

Gilbert was blushing with embarrassment. Mrs. Sullivan, with her fine car, her flashing jewels, her scented, rose-tipped cigarettes, her perfect nonchalance, provided a glimpse of a life that he had always longed for.

"You—you wouldn't speak to me if you saw me in Steel City!" he burst out.

"Don't be silly, Gilbert. Just come to Steel City and try! Who knows what might not happen? And now I must say good-by."

Mechanically she had opened a platinum case which lay in her lap, and extracted from it a rose-tipped cigarette. She inserted the rosy end in her mouth, reached to the dashboard, and drew toward her a small steel disk in which was embedded a coil of fine wire that glowed redly. To this she touched the cigarette. She puffed. She exhaled smoke from her nostrils.

It was done before Gilbert could find words to stop her. Now he regarded her in stony silence.

"Well, Gilbert, I really have got to be going. It's been so nice to know—" Mrs. Sullivan stopped. "Why! What's the matter, darling, are you sick?"

Gilbert was, indeed, very pale. His infatuation for this beautiful society woman was engaged in a conflict with his sense of duty. After a short, passionate struggle, his sense of duty won.

"Mrs. Sullivan," he said in a low, tense voice, "I didn't give you a summons when I caught you smoking the first cigarette. When I came out of the jail, you were smoking another, and I pretended I didn't see you grind it under your shoe on the floorboards. It hurts me terribly to do this, but I have got to give you a summons. You will have to appear in court here to-morrow morning to answer to a charge of smoking nicotine in plain public view; and you'll have to give me twenty-five dollars for your appearance bond."

Mrs. Sullivan started to toss the cigarette into the street.

"Gilbert," she said, inhaling the smoke and blowing it out in slender blue quills from her nostrils, "do you know what I would do with that sense of duty of yours? I would take it out and drown it. A sense of duty is all right in its place, but one of these days you are going to trip over it, and fall down and bump your nose. Very well. Here is my twenty-five dollars. I will bring my lawyer, and I will fight this case to the bitter end. Personally, I think it's a crime and an outrage to hand a woman a summons for smoking a cigarette in her own car."

"I haven't anything to do with it," said Gilbert, not meeting her blue bright eyes. "My job is to see that the laws are obeyed, and you have broken the law three times inside of half an hour. Please don't hold it against me, Mrs. Sullivan."

"I suppose you will testify against me in court," sighed Mrs. Sullivan.

"I will have to, Mrs. Sullivan, much as it hurts me."

Gilbert descended from the car. He was more than a little dazed by the events that had been crowded into the past half hour. He wished he could have stayed in that car and ridden with Mrs. Sullivan on and on—forever! Never had a woman moved him so. What simps the Maple Hollow girls were, compared to her! Could this, he wondered, be love? It seemed a shame that he had had to give her a summons.

"Good-by," he got out in a choked voice, as the Minerva purred and hissed like a great yellow cat.

"So long, Gilbert—until to-morrow!" her rich contralto cried, as from a great distance. And she was gone.

And suddenly Maple Hollow became, for Gilbert, barren and bleak and devoid of all romance. In all the gloom there was only one compensating ray—he would see her in court to-morrow. He knew that life had quickened for him. It was as if, beneath the crust of his existence, great rumblings were beginning to be heard. The golden wing of adventure had brushed him, and he would never be quite the same again.

CHAPTER IV

TO THE DANCE

GILBERT WAS STANDING there in the warm noon sunlight, with the forgotten revolver in one hand and the billfold
and Mrs. Sullivan's twenty-five dollars in the other, when a large
crowd of people surrounded him. It was all very much like a
dream to Gilbert. He saw the pale, excited face of Constable
Bench, and he saw Annie May Prine looking at him strangely.
She, too, was very pale. Every one started talking to him at once,
and everybody was shaking him by the hand, clapping him on
the shoulder, and firing questions at him.

Now Constable Bench was shaking his hand, pumping it up
and down vigorously as people will in moments of excitement;
billfold and all went up and down, up and down, and the constable's eyes were moist with emotion.

"Gilbert," he got out in a tremulous voice. "I want to be the
first to tell you how proud we are of you. It's just like I told
everybody. Give you a fair chance, and you'd make good in a
jiffy. You got that scoundrel locked up?"

"Yes," said Gilbert.

"Holy catfish!" the constable exclaimed, looking for the first
time at the hand he had been pumping. "What you got there?"

"Money," said Gilbert. "The woman who was driving the car
he was in was breakin' the ordinance against smoking nicotine
in public. I collected twenty-five dollars for her as appearance
bond. She's to come to court to-morrow morning."

"Gilbert," said the constable uneasily, "we've been sort of

28

ignorin' that old blue law. But it's all right. What's in that bill-fold?"

"That," said Gilbert, "is bribe money. He offered me twenty-five thousand dollars to let him off, and I'm keepin' it as evidence."

The crowd buzzed. Gilbert had refused a bribe of twenty-five thousand dollars! The street which had, a moment before, been deserted, was now full of people. They seemed to come from everywhere. His capture of the bigamist had been executed so quietly that no one was aware until now that the most thrilling event in Maple Hollow history since the big fire of 1877 had taken place.

Every one seemed to be trying to wring his hand, or clap him on the back, or merely to stare at him. Gilbert's bare shoulders became sore under the repeated congratulatory blows, and he became more and more dazed as he heard the story of the arrest being told and retold. It seemed hard to believe that he had been the man who had executed that arrest, and he listened wonderingly to the recital of it from the lips of Sam Egleston, the owner of Egleston's Hardware Emporium. Sam was telling a stranger about it.

"Yes, sir, the boy was just fillin' in for old Constable Bench when this big car come rollin' along with a man hidin' in it. The boy's suspicions was aroused. Quick as a flash he jumped onto the runnin' board, and put his gun down on the feller. Hadn't taken Gil a split second to recognize who he was.

"Y' see, Gil had seen a photograph of this Bluebeard. Around here we call Gil the Man with the Camera Eye. He never forgets a face. Well, Gil slammed his gun on this dangerous character, and marched him into jail. The feller shoved twenty-five thousand dollars into Gil's hands, and Gil just stood there and chuckled at him. Constable Bench's got the money now, holdin' it as evidence.

"There's Gil, standing over there now. Come on over and I'll introduce you. It's all right; he's as democratic as anybody you ever met."

"I'd like to shake hands with him," the stranger admitted.

So Sam Egleston took the stranger over, and he was presented to Gilbert.

"You recognized him right off, did you, Mr. Dollow?" the stranger wanted to know.

"Yes," said Gilbert.

"Did he put up any kind of a struggle when you slammed your gun down on him?"

"Well, he looked as if he wanted to," Gilbert conceded.

"But he sort of looked you in the eye, huh, and changed his mind?"

Every one laughed, and the opinion prevailed that Gilbert was a bad man on the trigger.

"You ought to go into the detective game, son," said the stranger. "You oughtn't to waste your talents in a town of this size."

"Oh, we all admit he's outgrown Maple Hollow," agreed Sam Egleston. "A town like this can't hang onto a go-getter like him."

"What's goin' to be done with the prisoner?"

"The constable had Steel City on long distance a few minutes ago, and they're sendin' out a couple of bulls for him. They'll be here to-night. The Blue Flier's goin' to stop especially to drop 'em off. Some excitement for Maple Hollow, huh?"

Maple Hollow seethed with the excitement. The news of the arrest, and of the attempted bribery spread, and by dusk the village was filled with cars from all over the neighborhood. Crowds surrounded the jail, and tried to get a peek at the prisoner; crowds hunted out Gilbert Dollow; they shook his hand and bombarded him with questions.

Gilbert grew more and more dazed as the afternoon wore on. His right hand ached with handshakings; his shoulders were sore from back slappings, and his voice grew husky with question answering. He refused upwards of thirty-five invitations for dinner, and dined alone in his home with his widowed mother. He ate a simple meal, consisting of a T-bone steak, French fried potatoes, spinach, carrots, beets, a salad of lettuce and tomatoes, and three pieces of apple pie.

He did not forget that he had invited Annie May Prine to go to the dance at the beach pavilion, and punctually at eight he called for her at the little cottage where she lived with her aged grandfather and grandmother.

It was a pleasant, cool summer evening, but not too cool; and Annie May Prine was perhaps prettier than she had ever been before in her life, which is saying a great deal indeed. She was flushed with the excitement of the day, and radiant with pride of Gilbert. She had made a fluffy white dress especially for this occasion; she would have wrung a sigh from the heart of a stone image; but she realized now that all of her efforts had been made in vain.

Not only had Gilbert suddenly grown too large for Maple Hollow, but he had met a woman from the outer world, a woman of charm and fascination, and Annie May with a sinking heart had watched Gilbert as he talked to the woman. Any doubts that may have existed were wiped away in a little conversation carefully engineered by Annie May as she and Gilbert made their way through the fragrant, moonlit evening to the pavilion.

"Did you find out who that woman was?" Annie May asked.

"Her name," Gilbert answered, "is Mrs. Alice Sullivan."

"Oh, is she married?"

"She's a widow," said Gilbert.

"I wonder how old she is," said Annie May.

"Twenty-seven," said Gilbert.

"I would hate to have been hanging since she was forty," said Annie May, and she sensed that Gilbert stiffened. It was all she wanted to know. The woman had made a tremendous impression on Gilbert; and she was, as any one could see, a shrewd, clever woman of the world. Gilbert would be like putty in her hands.

"I think she's a society woman," said Gilbert.

"If she is a society woman," said Annie May with warmth, "I am the Empress Dowager of China. I think she is a common, vulgar creature."

Gilbert stiffened, and said nothing. Annie May, walking along beside him, compressed her lips and gazed with dull, defeated eyes over the lake. A soft, romantic wind was blowing across the lake, and in the moonlight the Three Neighbors looked beautiful and mysterious. Annie May had visited the Three Neighbors on picnics, and on huckleberry parties any number of times, but in the moonlight she could invest them with fantastic people and adventurous happenings. The moon, round and golden, sparkled on the water.

It was, in a word, a perfect night on which to be made love to, and Annie May, tripping along beside Gilbert, for he was walking very rapidly, realized that life stretched ahead of her, empty and sad. Without Gilbert, life was simply not worth living. In her heart of hearts she suspected that Gilbert was not nearly so clever as all these people were saying; but she loved him.

No man she knew was as true and honest and loyal as Gilbert was, and she loved his fine, proud head, and his handsome brown shoulders. She was wise in her generation, and she knew that a woman would be happier in the long run with a man like Gilbert than with one of those brilliant, clever men. Some day she would come into a good deal of money; she didn't have to marry a clever go-getter.

With Gilbert, she knew, she would be perfectly happy, and now that dream would have to be cast aside. She knew she was pretty, and she was aware that she had a quick, agile brain; and she also knew that one of these days Gilbert would suddenly become aware of her, and from that moment until they stood before the altar it would be clear and easy sailing—if nothing intervened. The unexpected had happened.

"But I won't admit that I'm licked," said Annie May to herself as she breathlessly trotted along beside the tall, handsome life guard. "I'll fight to the bitter end. We were made for each other, and I'm going to make him realize it—some day."

This line of reasoning cheered her immensely. By the time they reached the pavilion she was her gay, bubbling self again. She looked over the crowd shrewdly when they went in. A number of strange girls from neighboring villages were there, and all of them were staring with unconcealed admiration at the hero of the hour.

Gilbert was at once surrounded by girls and young men, all babbling, all making fun of his exploit, but underneath the raillery was a note of admiration and envy. Gilbert bore his honors modestly, and when the music struck up for the first dance he pushed his way out of the crowd and came to Annie May.

Another man would have been made so giddy by so much attention that he might readily have forgotten her. It was this trait in Gilbert, his awesome sense of duty, that she relied on as her chief aid in winning her battle. Gilbert would be loyal to any promise, or to the spirit of any promise, he made to her.

The floor was crowded, but Gilbert was an excellent dancer, and for a few minutes Annie May permitted herself to float in his arms in a kind of day-dream. She was awakened rather rudely from this dream by a young man who came pushing across the floor. He was pink, as if from some recent exertion, and his bearing was important. It was Hugh Fuller, who worked in the Maple Hollow garage.

Hugh grasped Gilbert by the arm.

"The two detectives from Steel City have just come," he panted, "and they want you down to the jail right away, Gil."

"Run along, Gil," Annie May urged him as he hesitated. "I'll be here waiting for you. I'll be all right."

"Well, I'll hurry back as soon as I can," Gil promised.

CHAPTER V

CONFRONTING THE PRISONER

GILBERT HAD TO fight his way through the crowd that surrounded the jail. Constable Dench, pale with excitement, unlocked the outer door for him, and locked it after him. Two broad-shouldered men with beefy faces and black derbies were sitting in the anteroom, and across from them sat the culprit.

"Here's the young fellow who nabbed him," Constable Dench introduced Gilbert, and the two detectives said they were glad to meet him. They looked at him from heavy-lidded eyes. One of them was seated before a little table, and on this, under an electric light, was spread the contents of the billfold.

"I'm the chief of the Steel City detective bureau," this man informed Gilbert. "My name's Hobson."

"Oh, yes," said Gilbert.

"And this," said Mr. Hobson, jerking a red thumb at the other heavy-jowled detective, "is Bill Anderson, who runs the finger-print department. Come over here by me, kid, and sit down. I want to ask you some questions."

Gilbert sat down. He felt a little uncomfortable under the penetrating cold scrutiny of the chief of Steel City's detective bureau, and he sat down uneasily on the edge of a chair.

"This is the jack this bird slipped you, is it, kid?"

"Yes," said Gilbert, uncomfortably. Mr. Hobson leaned back in his chair, and looked at Gilbert.

"Did he put up a scrap?"

"No, sir."

"Tell me just how it happened."

"Well," said Gilbert nervously, "I was at the intersection, regulating traffic, when this yellow Minerva roadster came along. And a woman was at the wheel smoking a cigarette. It's against one of the town ordinances for a woman to smoke in public; so I told her to pull into the curb."

"Did you hold the woman?"

"No, sir; she's coming back to-morrow, though. I gave her a summons."

"What's the woman's name?"

"It's Mrs. Alice Sullivan," said Gilbert.

The two detectives exchanged queer glances.

"Are you sure?" said Mr. Hobson.

"That's the name she gave me."

"All right; go on with your story."

"Well, she pulled into the curb, and while we were talking I happened to look at a poster on the wall of the jail, and it was just the same as this fellow here. So I pulled my gun on him and—and walked him into the jail."

"And he tried to bribe you."

"Yes, sir. First he offered me ten thousand; then he gave me his whole roll."

"And you wouldn't let him go."

"No, sir."

Mr. Hobson looked at the finger-print expert.

"What do you think of that, Bill? What would you have done if this bird had offered you twenty-five thousand dollars?"

"Well," replied the finger-print expert, "I have an idea that if he offered me twenty-five thousand, I would have let him go, even if he had been Captain Kidd, Jesse James, Dutch Anderson, and Gerald Chapman, all in one."

"Of course," said Mr. Hobson, "you mightn't have let him go if you had discovered that he had given you a lot of flannel money."

"What do you mean by flannel money?" Gilbert put in.

"You took a good look at this roll, didn't you?" Mr. Hobson answered.

"Of course I did," said Gilbert.

"You knew it was counterfeit, didn't you?"

Gilbert swallowed. "I—I suspected it was. Naturally!"

Constable Dench looked bewildered. "Gil, what was your idea in keepin' this from me?"

"Never mind that," said Mr. Hobson. "The whole point is that this here boy is so lucky he's positively dangerous. If it was rainin' gin, he would have an orange in one hand and a cocktail shaker in the other, and just then an ice wagon would drive up. Am I right, Bill?"

Mr. Anderson only nodded.

"Here's what happens," the chief of detectives went on. "First you stop a woman for smokin' a cigarette. Then you pinch the guy she's with on a bigamy charge because he looks like the picture pasted up on the jail wall. Say, constable, how long's that picture been there?"

"Quite a spell," said the constable vaguely.

"Quite a spell," said Mr. Hobson. "I'll tell the wall-eyed universe it's been there quite a spell. It must've been there goin' on three years, ain't it? That bird was pinched in Seattle in the fall of year before last, and he's been draggin' a ball and chain around ever since."

"What!" groaned Gilbert.

"I'm merely tellin' you, son, that this guy ain't Lamson, the bigamist. It's Carter, the counterfeiter. Ten thousand flat-feet are lookin' for this bird all over this free and untrammeled country this minute. So you pinch a woman for smokin' in public; you arrest a bigamist, and it turns out you've trapped the leader of the biggest counterfeitin' gang in America. A good afternoon's work, I'd say. You're good, kid. I'll have to hand it to you. Now, don't sit there and tell me you recognized him as Carter."

"I got him, didn't I?" said Gilbert.

"Sure, you got him, and it's a wonder to me your toes aren't bein' pointed upward to the roots of daisies right this minute. You must have thrown the fear o' Heaven into this guy. It didn't occur to you to frisk him, did it? Didn't know he was totin' two gats on his hip, and an automatic slung under his arm, did you? How you ever came out of this adventure without bein' let chuck full of daylight is a mystery to me.

"Kid, this guy thinks no more of shootin' strangers like you than you do of eatin' oatmeal. Now I want to get this straight about the Sullivan dame. What I want to know is, what was he doin' in her car?"

"She told me," said Gilbert dazedly, "that she was drivin' along the road, and this fellow signaled her for a ride."

The chief of detectives threw an inquiring glance at the king of the counterfeiters.

"How about it, Carter?"

"The sap's right," he muttered. "I dropped off the Detroit flyer at some hick town and was walkin' down the road, when she came along and gave me a lift. That's on the level. Leave the dame out of this."

"We will," said Mr. Hobson in a relieved voice. "Now, just out of curiosity, Carter, I want to know how you came to let this hick run you off your legs the way he did?"

The master mind of the counterfeiting ring shrugged. "You said it before. If it was rainin' ice cream, that bird would have a pocketful of cones. That's all. I thought I could wiggle myself out of this hoosegow in ten minutes. This jail makes Sing Sing look like a pasteboard shanty."

Mr. Hobson chuckled. He patted Gilbert on the back. "I'll see that you get the lion's share of the reward, kid. It seems to me, though, that Bill and me are entitled to a little of the velvet. If I hadn't spotted that gold tooth of his, and if Bill hadn't brought along the finger-prints, you wouldn't be getting a nickel. Supposing, just to keep peace in the family, we split it four ways—a fourth to you, a fourth to Bill, a fourth to the constable, and a fourth to me. The reward's five thousand dollars. Is that agreeable, gentlemen?"

"It strikes me as bein' fair enough," said Constable Dench promptly. "After all, Gil, you was only spellin' for me."

"I've got a better idea than that," said the finger-print expert. "Supposin' us three take fifteen hundred apiece, and leave the kid five hundred. That agreeable to you, constable?"

"Suits me fine," said Mr. Dench. "All right with you, ain't it, Gil?"

Gilbert was too dazed to realize that this deal was rather unfair. After all, he had arrested the man, and, as events proved, had exposed himself to considerable risk in doing so.

"The main thing," Constable Dench went on, "is that you've given yourself such a fine, big chance, Gil. How about it, Mr. Hobson? Ain't what Gil has done entitled him to favorable consideration if he was to apply for a job on the Steel City police force?"

"Any man," said Mr. Hobson promptly, "who can use his brains the way this boy did this afternoon is just the kind of material we are looking for for the force. He made what I call a brilliant arrest. Flynn himself couldn't have handled the job any neater. Yes, sir, constable, he is certainly entitled to favorable consideration any time he applies for a job on the force."

Gilbert was blushing with self-consciousness and delight.

"Do you really think so, Mr. Hobson?"

"I absolutely do, my boy. You showed ruthless courage and quick brain work in the face of almost overwhelming odds. *Sherlock Holmes* would say the same as I'm saying."

Gilbert leaned eagerly forward.

"Do—do you really think I could get on the Steel City force?"

"When you come to town," said Mr. Hobson, "just look me up."

"I will," said Gilbert.

"And I'll see that you get your share of the reward," said Mr. Hobson quickly. "Five hundred strikes you as bein' perfectly fair and plenty for your share, does it?"

"Oh, sure," said Gilbert gratefully.

"The main thing," put in Mr. Anderson, "is not to say anything to anybody about it, kid. This is all in the family—see?"

"It's like this," Mr. Hobson hastened to explain. "The people who offer these rewards want it kept as quiet as possible how the rewards are distributed—see? If it got around, everybody would want to put his finger in the pie. It's got to be a solemn secret between the four of us—see?"

"Sure," said Gilbert. "I understand perfectly."

"My Lawd," breathed Carter, the counterfeiter, "and they pinch men like me and hang men like Chapman!"

"Another crack out of you," growled Mr. Hobson, "and I'll sock you a good one."

"Take my advice, kid," the counterfeiter chuckled, "and beat it out of this den of iniquity before they get your shirt."

Mr. Hobson sprang up, strode over, and trod heavily upon the counterfeiter's foot. "That'll be enough from you."

Gilbert looked on dazedly. There was only room in his mind for the realization that he had only to apply to Mr. Hobson and he would be given a place on the Steel City police force. To be sure, Mr. Hobson had not said exactly that, but Gilbert was not aware of this until some time later. Just now, anyhow, anything was possible. He was going to get five hundred dollars. He was going to Steel City, where he would be near Alice Sullivan. Oh, what a wonderful, wonderful world it was!

CHAPTER VI

THE VERDICT

LONG BEFORE JUDGE BARLOW appeared next morning the small court room in the Maple Hollow town hall was crowded. It was not enough for Gilbert Dollow to arrest the leader of America's most dangerous and ruthless counterfeiting gang—that alone would have given Maple Hollow enough to talk about all summer—but he must revive one of the town's quaint old blue laws.

The dramatic possibilities that the trial afforded were made doubly exciting by the known personality and prejudices of Judge Barlow. The judge was a man of what is commonly known as the old school. He believed that woman's place is in the home. On the slightest provocation he would extol the virtues of his mother and grandmother, whom every one in Maple Hollow knew had gone to untimely graves because of too much house-work.

He heartily disapproved of short skirts and of bobbed hair. He abhorred drinking, and he had been known to declare that a woman who would smoke a cigarette would pick a man's pocket.

Mrs. Sullivan arrived in a brilliant red Mercedes touring car at about ten o'clock. For this occasion she had donned a short, daring dress of pink crape satin. She wore golden stockings and dark-blue slippers.

Annie May Prine, who sat on the witness bench, estimated that the blond woman also wore—and Annie May was a conservative estimator—two pints of jewelry. Other girls in the court room put the figure as high as three quarts, but two pints was probably much nearer the truth. This jewelry took the form of bracelets, rings, two necklaces, and eardrops. It was a scintillating collection of diamonds, rubies, emeralds, sapphires, and pearls.

The lady was accompanied by a short, square-built, dark-complexioned man with bushy black eyebrows, and eyes that reminded Annie May Prine of oysters—and not very good oysters at that. It was soon whispered about the court room that this man was Mrs. Sullivan's lawyer. He had a grim, efficient look about him that promised interesting developments.

Soon after they were seated Judge Barlow came in. He was a tall, thin man, well along in his sixties, very bald and shiny on top, and the owner of a pair of old-fashioned mutton chops. He had brilliant, hostile blue eyes.

Everybody arose as he entered, and remained standing until he had seated himself. He glared at the roomful of people; he glared at Mrs. Sullivan. Only upon Gilbert Dollow did he bestow a glance that could possibly have been interpreted as friendly.

A court attendant banged upon a desk with a gavel. And presently the first case on the morning's calendar was being heard. Bill Snither's police dog had got into the Widow Fangle's chicken yard and devoured four of her prize Plymouth Rocks.

Bill Snither declared that he had seen the Widow Fangle entice his dog into her chicken yard; that it was all a put-up job. The Widow Fangle had been trying for months to sell those White Rocks; she knew that his dog was a chicken killer, and she had deliberately invited him into her chicken yard.

"Defendant will pay complainant thirty dollars, and keep dog chained up hereafter," decided the court promptly.

No oil painting of the blind goddess was necessary in this court room.

"Next case!"

The clerk droned it off, while the court room held its breath:

"Mrs. Alice Sullivan, of Steel City, given a summons yesterday by Deputy Constable Dollow for smokin' a cigarette on the public thoroughfare."

"Take the stand," said Judge Barlow curtly.

With a lisping of silk, the blond widow took the stand. The court room strained forward. She was smiling with perfect ease.

Annie May Prine darted a glance at Gilbert. Beads of perspiration stood out on his forehead.

"Is your name Mrs. Alice Sullivan?" asked the judge.

"It is, your honor."

"Occupation?"

"I'm a widow," said Mrs. Sullivan, and the room tittered.

"Is that an occupation?" inquired the judge sternly.

The dark-skinned man came to his feet. "It is not incumbent upon Mrs. Sullivan to answer that question further, your honor."

The judge glared at him.

"Who are you?" he snapped.

"I am Mrs. Sullivan's attorney."

"I see. Do you wish to answer her questions, or may I question her directly?"

"I would prefer to have the examination conducted with interpolations from me, your honor, if the occasion indicates that they are necessary."

Judge Barlow looked a little bewildered. "Very well," he said, after a tense pause.

"It seems that you were apprehended by Officer Dollow while flaunting a cigarette in public, Mrs. Sullivan?"

"But I didn't know I was breaking the law, your honor."

"That excuse is inacceptable in a court of law. The ordinance plainly states that it is a misdemeanor for a woman to smoke nicotine in any form in public in this town. You were within the town limits when the violation occurred. You were certainly smoking a cigarette."

"I object, your honor," broke in the lawyer.

"On what grounds?"

"The statute in question plainly states nicotine. It is very questionable if it can be proved that the defendant was smoking a cigarette containing nicotine. Is there a qualified chemist in this court room?"

"You know very well there isn't," said Judge Barlow testily; "and furthermore, this trial is not going to be cluttered up with the testimony of high-salaried experts. We don't need any alienists or insanity experts or long-winded chemical experts to prove whether or not the defendant was smoking nicotine in public. This is a clean-cut case, and I am not going to let any smart out-of-town lawyer get it all fogged up."

The Steel City lawyer planted his feet apart and clasped his hands behind him. He faced the bench with a thin-lipped smile.

"How, then, your honor, can it be proved beyond reasonable doubt that the cigarette the defendant was smoking contained nicotine? I demand that proof be furnished to the satisfaction of my client and myself."

The court room hummed. Judge Barlow banged upon the desk with his gavel.

"Silence in the court!" he roared. "If I hear any more whispering or giggling in here, I am going to have this court room cleared. Officer Dollow, stand up!"

Gilbert arose with compressed lips; he was pale and nervous, but determined.

"Officer Dollow," the judge said, "you were on duty, were you not, at the intersection of the County Pike and the Yellow Rock Road when the defendant drove into town in a yellow roadster?"

"Yes, your honor," Gilbert said in a faint voice.

Mrs. Sullivan was looking at him with a queer smile. It seemed downright treachery to say the things he would have to say against her, but he was prepared to walk the straight, narrow path of duty to the bitter end.

"When you apprehended her," the judge went on, "she had a cigarette in her mouth, did she not?"

"She did, your honor."

"Can you testify positively that the cigarette was lighted?"

"Yes, sir, it was lighted."

"And she was smoking it?"

"Sure, she—I mean yes, your honor; she was blowing the smoke out of her nose."

"There is no question in your mind, Officer Dollow, but what the thing she had in her mouth and that she was smoking was a cigarette, is there?"

"No question at all, your honor."

"Did it smell like cigarette smoke?"

"Yes, your honor."

"Did it look like cigarette smoke?"

"Yes, your honor."

"You are willing to take your oath in this court of law that what she was smoking was a cigarette?"

"I am, your honor."

Judge Barlow glanced with contempt and triumph at the Steel City lawyer.

"May I question the witness?" the lawyer asked.

The judge nodded.

The lawyer turned his cold gray eyes on Gilbert, and Gilbert felt uneasy.

"I should like to know," the lawyer said, "if you have ever been employed in a cigarette factory?"

"No, sir," said Gilbert meekly.

"Have you ever seen a cigarette made?"

"No," said Gilbert, "I never have."

"Do you smoke cigarettes yourself?"

"Oh, now and then."

"What brand do you smoke?"

"Well," said Gilbert, "I smoke different brands. Sometimes I smoke Darnels, sometimes Plucky Strokes, sometimes Beau Brummels."

"I suppose they all taste pretty much alike to you?"

"Oh, no; they all taste different."

"I see. Are you sufficiently acquainted with the taste of them to tell one apart from the other?"

"Sure!" said Gilbert, with a grin. "I could tell a Darnel from a Plucky in the dark."

Judge Barlow leaned forward, frowning. "You're cluttering up a clean-cut issue with a lot of conversation. If you're aiming to get somewhere, get there."

The lawyer bowed. "I am aiming to get somewhere, your honor, but I must object to your constant reference to this case as a clean-cut issue. You have accused me of attempting to befog the issue. I must remind you that the burden of proof does not rest upon my client's shoulders. I am merely obliged to disprove to the satisfaction of this court that the cigarette the defendant was smoking contained nicotine. If you will give me a little time, I believe I can do so.

"This case is much more important than it appears on the surface. The machinery of justice all over this land is hindered and crippled by the appalling number of outworn and ridiculous laws, statutes, and ordinances such as this one."

"Go on with your proof, and cut out the oratory," snapped Judge Barlow. "If it wasn't for all those laws, you'd starve."

"I have here in my pocket," the lawyer obliged, "a cigarette case containing four different brands of cigarettes. One is a Darnel, one is a Plucky Stroke, one is a Beau Brummel, and the fourth is a Harrison. The name of each is plainly printed upon the cigarette. Will you examine them, your honor?"

Judge Barlow looked suspicious. He accepted the cigarette case, which the lawyer handed to him opened.

"Well," he growled, "what of it?"

"I merely wish," said the lawyer, "to test the veracity of Officer

Dollow. He claims he can tell one cigarette from another in the dark. I wish to have him blindfolded and to take as many puffs from each cigarette as he may require?"

"Very well," the judge granted. "Constable Dench, will you blindfold Officer Dollow?"

So Gilbert was blindfolded. A cigarette from the case was placed in his mouth, and the lawyer struck a match. Gilbert took several puffs.

"Plucky Stroke," said Gilbert.

The lawyer removed the cigarette from his mouth and handed it to the judge. It was a Harrison.

Another cigarette was inserted in the mouth of the witness.

A flaming match was applied. Gilbert puffed.

"Darnel," he announced.

This cigarette was taken from his mouth and passed up to Judge Barlow. It was a Beau Brummel.

A third cigarette was placed between Gilbert's lips, and lighted. He puffed and puffed.

"Beau Brummel," he said, smiling.

It proved, on examination, to be a Plucky Stroke.

The last cigarette was put in his mouth, and lighted.

"I'd know that cigarette anywhere," said Gilbert. "It's a Plucky."

The cigarette, of course, was a Harrison.

Gilbert removed the blindfold, and grinned.

"Well," he said, "did I guess them all right, or didn't I?"

"You guessed every one of them wrong," growled the judge, and he glared at the lawyer.

"That was a smart trick," he snorted, "but what of it? What does it prove? What bearing has it got on this case?"

"Your honor," said the lawyer, "I merely wished to prove that the testimony of the witness is unreliable. He could not detect one cigarette from another, in spite of his claim. He swore that the defendant was smoking a cigarette. I maintain that his sense of taste and smell is not sufficiently acute to qualify him as a reliable witness. The defendant may have been smoking cornsilk or a cubeb."

"Nonsense!" snapped Judge Barlow. "A cigarette is a cigarette."

"I object," said the lawyer.

"On what grounds?"

"I maintain that there are cigarettes and cigarettes. There is, for example, the scented cigarette, and there is the nicotineless cigarette."

"I suppose," said Judge Barlow sourly, "that you're going to try to make me believe that the cigarette the defendant was smoking was a nicotineless cigarette."

"That, your honor, is precisely my claim. I admit that the defendant was smoking a cigarette, but it was a nicotineless cigarette. She was not, therefore, violating the ordinance in question. I believe I have proved to the satisfaction of the court that the testimony of Officer Dollow is worthless.

"He cannot tell the smell or the taste of one cigarette from another. Naturally he did not suspect that the defendant was smoking a nicotineless cigarette. I present to this court the plea that the charge against the defendant be dismissed on the grounds of insufficient evidence."

A clear, girlish voice arose from the witness bench.

"Just a minute, please." It was Annie May Prine. She was pale but composed. The lawyer wheeled on her with a frown. Judge Barlow leaned forward with the first smile he had worn that morning.

"Do you wish to introduce new evidence?" he asked.

"I do, your honor. I think I can prove that the cigarette this lady was smoking contained nicotine."

"Were you a witness to the smoking incident?"

"I was, your honor."

Judge Barlow looked pleased. He smiled at Annie May; he

even smiled at the lawyer. For a moment it had looked as if the ends of justice were to be brutally defeated by the clever city lawyer. Judge Barlow knew that Annie May Prine was a bright girl—one of the brightest girls in Maple Hollow.

Gilbert looked at her in bewilderment. He was slightly dazed by the scene he had just gone through, and humiliated because of his failure in selecting one cigarette from another.

Every one, indeed, was looking at Annie May. Here was a modern Portia, her alert mind ready to save the man she loved, not, perhaps, a pound of flesh, but the pangs of humiliation and ridicule.

"I saw the defendant smoking a cigarette," said Annie May, looking brightly at Mrs. Sullivan, who smiled rather coldly in return, "and I must say that I object to the way this lady from Steel City and her lawyer have come out here for no other purpose than to make us all look like hicks. I know there are several reporters in this court room, and I believe that Mrs. Sullivan and her lawyer are out to win this case simply for publicity purposes!"

"So do I!" said Judge Barlow.

"I object!" the lawyer shouted.

"On what grounds?"

"This young lady's testimony is irrelevant, immaterial, and inconsequential. It has nothing to do with the case."

"Objection overruled," growled Judge Barlow. "Go right on, Annie May."

"I think," said Annie May, "this Mrs. Sullivan and her lawyer have come out here to make monkeys out of us. Maybe Gilbert was wrong in dragging in that old blue law about nicotine, but as long as the law is on the books we shall stand by it."

There was a ripple of applause in the court room. When it had subsided the lawyer said:

"May I ask this charming new witness a few questions?"

"Fire away," said the judge. The lawyer looked at Annie May.

His cold, oystery eyes seemed to search out the innermost corners of her soul. His smile was contemptuous,

"Where were you standing when the defendant was apprehended in the act of smoking a cigarette?" he asked.

"Beside Officer Dollow."

"Did you smell the smoke of the cigarette?"

"I did."

"Are you an analytical chemist?"

"I am not."

"Do you smoke cigarettes yourself?"

"I do not."

"Do you consider yourself, in light of your admissions, to be qualified to pass upon a highly technical question concerning a cigarette?"

"I do."

"You do?"

"I think I said I did."

The lawyer made a little sniffing sound. "You're very sure of yourself, aren't you?"

Annie May gave him a smile, but said nothing.

The lawyer and Mrs. Sullivan exchanged glances.

"All right," he said. "You saw the defendant smoking a cigarette, and you saw Officer Dollow apprehend her. Perhaps you are in a position to tell us what brand of cigarette the defendant was smoking."

There was a hush in the court room while Annie May hesitated before replying.

"It was a Magyar," she said. "A Magyar with a rose tip."

"Are you sure?"

"Positive," said Annie May.

"Perhaps," said the lawyer, "you will be so good as to explain to this court room by what steps you arrived at this very important conclusion."

"The lady," Annie May obliged him, "threw one of the ciga-rettes into the road. I picked it up."

"May I ask what your motive was in picking it up?"

"I object!" said Annie May.

"On what grounds?" said Judge Barlow.

"My motive has nothing whatever to do with what I am trying to prove."

"Objection sustained," said the judge. "Go on, Annie May."

"I picked it up, and I kept it," said Annie May.

The lawyer glanced quickly at Mrs. Sullivan. He walked over to her, and they held a consultation in whispers. Presently the lawyer turned, smiling, to Annie May.

"Just when did you pick the cigarette stub from the street?"

"Later in the afternoon," said Annie May.

"About how many hours later?"

"Oh—it must have been three hours later."

"And you're sure you picked up the same cigarette stub that the defendant dropped?"

"Positive," said Annie May.

The lawyer turned to Judge Barlow. "Your honor, the testi-mony that this girl is giving is absolutely absurd. There is con-siderable traffic at the intersection of the County Pike and the Yellow Rock Road. Countless cigarette butts are tossed from cars. She might have picked up a cigarette stub that was tossed from any one of a hundred cars. I request that the testimony be struck from the record."

"Your request cannot be considered," Judge Barlow decided, "until her testimony is complete. Annie May, was there any kind of mark of identification on this cigarette stub you picked up?"

"It had a rose tip," said Annie May. "And I looked carefully. Not only were there no other rose-tipped cigarette stubs in the street, but there were no other cigarette stubs of any description. Last night I looked up an advertisement of Magyar cigarettes in a magazine, and here is the ad. It says: 'Magyar cigarettes are a blend of the choicest Turkish and Egyptian tobaccos. They are manufactured in three strengths—light, medium, and strong. For those who pay homage to My Lady Nicotine, no finer cigarette is made.'"

The court room buzzed. Judge Barlow banged on his desk with the gavel. The lawyer held a hurried consultation with Mrs. Sullivan. He turned and faced the bench determinedly.

"Your honor, I again request, but on fresh grounds, that the testimony of this girl be thrown out."

"What are your grounds?" barked the judge.

"On the grounds that she is a minor. A woman in this State becomes legally of age at eighteen. I question that this girl is older than seventeen."

"I was eighteen this morning!" said Annie May triumphantly.

Judge Barlow gave the lawyer a catlike grin.

"Has the defense any further objections to make?"

"Your honor," the lawyer said angrily, "the testimony of this girl is obviously trumped up. Justice will surely be defeated if her testimony stands."

"Do you put that in the form of an objection?"

"I do!"

"The objection is overruled. It has been proved to the full satisfaction of this court that the defendant was apprehended by Officer Dollow in the act of smoking a cigarette containing nicotine. Has the defense anything further to say?"

"Just this," the lawyer began hotly, "the testimony you have accepted in arriving at your verdict would not be acceptable in any court of law in which I have ever argued a case."

Judge Barlow leaned forward.

"You are stating in so many words that justice is not administered honestly in this court. You are fined one hundred dollars for contempt of court. The defendant is found guilty as charged, and is fined fifty dollars and costs. Next case!"

Dazedly, Gilbert found Annie May squeezing his hand.

"Gil, Gil, you've won your case!" He must realize now how she had his interests at heart.

The eager excitement in Annie May's face drained away. Gilbert was gazing, disconsolately, at the defeated widow.

"How she must hate me!" he groaned.

CHAPTER VII

ON THE MOVE

THE LAWYER PAID his own and Mrs. Sullivan's fines, and hastened out of the town hall. They were climbing into the red Mercedes when Gilbert fought his way out of the crowd. He must have a few words with her; must tell her how sorry he was for her humiliation.

Several young men, strangers, were on the running board. "You really ought to make a statement of some kind," one of them was saying when Gilbert arrived,

"But there really isn't anything to say," Mrs. Sullivan answered. "My sense of justice was absolutely outraged, and I wanted to fight the case on principle. Pinching a woman for smoking a cigarette! In America! In nineteen twenty-six! It's just too thick. I thought we'd come out and shove that silly law down their throats."

"Do you think you were framed?" said one of the young men.

"No," she answered decisively, "I don't think it was a frame, but there is certainly no question about that judge being prejudiced. We were licked before we opened our mouths. Did you notice that he didn't even take the trouble to ask me whether I would plead guilty or not guilty?"

"Are you going to appeal the case?"

"Positively not," said the lawyer.

"Can we say," the reporter asked, "that you believe you were unfairly tried, and that the judge was prejudiced?"

"Do you want us called back here for more contempt proceedings?" the lawyer snapped.

"Of course not!" the reporter hastily agreed. "We'll say simply that you went to considerable trouble and expense to uphold your rights as an American citizen. It is hot stuff, Mrs. Sullivan. The prohibition fanatics are getting so bad that an American citizen doesn't even dare smoke a cigarette in public any more. It will make a hot story. And the editorial writers will eat it up."

"You boys have got me all wrong," said Mrs. Sullivan. "You ought to know by this time that publicity is one thing that I don't want, and can't use. I don't want this in the papers at all. It was nothing but a lark. I was going to have some fun with these hicks, and I got stung."

The reporters murmured a protest in indignant chorus.

"Oh, but Mrs. Sullivan, we came up here to get a story, and this is a bear. You wouldn't want us to—"

The lawyer leaned forward.

"Let me put you boys straight on this," he said sternly. "If one word of this trial or any of the events leading up to it finds its way into any Steel City paper, whoever is responsible might just as well pack his suit case and take the first train out of town. Tell that to your city editors, and tell them I said so; and if they won't take your word for it, tell them to phone me.

"Let's get out of this hallowed spot, Alice, before they arrest you for wearing earrings in the daytime. It's a lucky thing for you that the penalty for smoking nicotine in public wasn't the ducking stool or the whipping post. That dear old anti-nicotine ordinance says 'Fifty dollars fine and costs, or ten days in jail, or both'; so let's get out of here before that old nightmare sends a constable after us and changes the sentence."

Gilbert edged through the clustering reporters, and Mrs. Sullivan saw him. She made a little grimace.

"Well, Gilbert, what am I pinched for this time?"

"Mrs. Sullivan," Gilbert said earnestly, "I just want to tell you how sorry I am that all this happened. I wouldn't have had you

embarrassed this way for anything in the world, honestly I
wouldn't; but it was my duty and I just had to do it. After the
kind way you acted yesterday, and all, I just feel sick about
everything."

"It's all right, Gilbert," she said, and she really did soften as
she looked into his sunburned, handsome face, "and I won't
hold it against you; but for the love of Mike, the next time we
meet, will you send that sense of duty of yours for a walk around
the block? A conscience like yours is a real menace to a young
man. I'm not joking, Gilbert. If I didn't have a generous, forgiv-
ing nature, I would certainly like to say some strong things to
you."

Gilbert was perspiring, but his face now broke into a smile
of relief. She didn't hate him, after all! Suddenly the birds
seemed to be singing again, and the sunlight became golden
and clamorous.

"I am taking your advice," said he eagerly, "and I am going
to Steel City just as soon as I can get things arranged. I have
to find somebody to fill my job as life guard on the beach, and
then I am going to Steel City and join the police force. The
detectives who were here last night said positively they would
get me a job on the force. I think it's a great opportunity, don't
you?"

"Listen to me, Gilbert," said the lawyer. "You keep away from

Steel City. If you took that sense of duty of yours on the police force there, everybody in town would be a nervous wreck before you had been on your beat an hour."

"Well," said Gilbert doggedly, "I have made up my mind, and once I make up my mind—"

"Yes, yes," the lawyer agreed hastily, "I know your type perfectly, Gilbert. Once your mind is made up, the San Francisco earthquake, the Chicago fire, the Johnstown flood, and the eruption of Mount Vesuvius couldn't swerve you. All right. Come to Steel City if you must, and if you do, look me up. I know I can give you some very sound advice."

"Welcome to Steel City, Gilbert!" Mrs. Sullivan cried. "Don't forget to look me up. Now if you boys want a real story, here it is." And she waved a flashing, plump hand at Gilbert. "This is the boy who captured Carter, the counterfeiter, single-handed. I'll bet you can get a whale of a story out of him; but you must promise to leave my name out of it. Good-by, Gilbert! Good-by, boys! Good-by, dear old Maple Hollow!"

In a burst of laughter, she was gone, and the great red Mercedes was roaring down the road.

Annie May, a witness and an auditor to all of this, gazed with narrowed eyes from the vanishing car to Gilbert's enraptured face. Then she looked at the reporters. They were closing around Gilbert, and something about them reminded her of pictures she had seen of wolves closing about a ewe-lamb. She had an agile, bright little mind, did Annie May—as we have said before and will doubtless say again and again—and she was suspicious of these news gatherers.

"So you're the young fellow who captured Carter?" one of the reporters was saying. "The morning papers all said that he walked up to your constable and surrendered, because the chase was getting too hot for him."

"That's a lie," said Gilbert indignantly. "He came along in a big yellow Minerva roadster, and I—I slammed my gun down on him!"

"Wait a minute," said one of the reporters gravely. "Let's get this straight. Where were you standing when it happened?"

"Right over there," said Gilbert, pointing. "That's the intersection of the County Pike and the Yellow Rock Road. The regular constable was sick—he'd just fallen off his roof into his onion bed—"

"What was he doing up on the roof?"

"He was up there, reshingling it, and there's a town ordinance that says an officer must be on duty at the intersection between noon and eight p.m. to regulate traffic. He told me to fill in for him, and I did. And this yellow roadster, this Minerva, came along—"

"Who was driving it?"

"Mrs. Sullivan, but she said you mustn't say so."

"All right, we won't. And this fellow Carter was in the car, huh?"

"Yes, he was sitting in there, huddled down. He'd been walking down the Yellow Rock Road just this side of Wilkin's Corners, and she'd given him a lift without knowing who he was. So I slammed my gun down on him—"

Two of the reporters exchanged solemn glances.

"Wait a minute. Did you recognize him right off?"

"Well, not exactly."

"Yes!" said Annie May. That quick brain of hers already perceived trouble ahead for Gilbert.

"No!" shouted Gilbert. "How can you say that, Annie May, when it isn't true? I didn't recognize him right off. It happened like this. I told Mrs. Sullivan to pull up alongside the curb—that was because she was violating the ordinance about smoking nicotine in public. Well, she stopped the car just alongside the jail over there, and while I was talking to her I thought I recognized the fellow as a man wanted for bigamy—his picture was pasted upon the wall. See it over there?"

"Ah, yes," breathed one of the reporters. "So you slammed your gun down on him."

"Yes," said Gilbert.

"Gilbert," interrupted Annie May, "I wouldn't say any more if I were you."

"Why not?"

"Well, I just wouldn't. I don't think you ought to say any more."

Two of the reporters gave her a look that was not kindly.

"You were just saying," one of them prompted Gilbert, "that you slammed your gun down on him. Then what happened? Did he put up a fight?"

"Well, he looked as if he was going to," said Gilbert. "And he was armed—a gat on each hip and one under his arm. Well, I walked him into the jail, and—"

"You mean, after you slammed your gun down on him you walked him into the jail."

"Yes, after that. And when I started to lock him up, he tried to bribe me."

"I know," said one reporter, "but your sense of duty wouldn't let you take a bribe. How much did he offer you?"

"Well," said Gilbert, "he offered me ten thousand dollars to begin with, and then he gave me everything he had—it was twenty-five thousand dollars. He said he had taken a liking to me. But I was wise. I—I knew it was flannel money."

"You did?" a reporter exclaimed admiringly.

"Sure I did! Don't you suppose I know the difference between flannel money and real money?"

"Sure you do! They can't fool you!"

"You bet they can't! Well, I guess that's about all. I just locked him up, and last night, Hobson, the chief of the Steel City detective bureau, and Anderson, the finger-print expert, came out and took him away."

"I like the part best," said one of the reporters, a tall, thin fellow with gray eyes, "where you slammed your gun down on him. That must have been real drama. Listen, Mr. Dollow, do you mind if we take a picture of you? I'd like to run a picture of you in the Steel City *Star,* in some good, dramatic pose. If you're going to Steel City to get a job on the force, it ought to be fine publicity for you."

"Gilbert," said Annie May, "I don't think you ought to let—"

But Gilbert was being escorted across the street to the three-year-old poster of Lamson, the bigamist. One of the reporters had a camera. One of them went to borrow Constable Bench's revolver, and the reporters posed him in various attitudes.

It was the *Star* man who hit upon the happy idea of having Gilbert leveling the revolver at the poster of Lamson, the bigamist. One of the reporters tried to ascertain what part Annie May had played in yesterday's sensational arrest, but Annie May would say nothing. She bristled whenever one of them approached her, and they finally left her alone.

Presently the reporters left in the motor car in which they had come; the crowd thinned, and Annie May and Gilbert strolled off toward the beach. It was almost time for Gilbert to appear on the beach and guard lives.

"It certainly is funny," Gilbert soliloquized, "how a little thing like what happened yesterday will all of a sudden make a fellow prominent. You wouldn't have thought yesterday morning, when you came down there to the beach with that piece of choc'late cake, that to-day I would be interviewed and had my picture taken for the Steel City papers."

Annie May looked up into his eager, good-looking brown face with anxious, motherly eyes.

"When a fellow gets into the public eye this way," Gilbert went on, "it certainly is a good thing to take advantage of it, isn't it? Now you may have thought I was kind of conceited, or immodest, or something, talking that way to those reporters, but I had an idea in my head all the time, Annie May.

"When that story gets into the papers, everybody's going to know who I am. The chief of police is going to know who I am. It's going to make it just so much easier for me to get a job on the Steel City police force. Say, Annie May, why were you butting in all the time when they were interviewing me? What was the idea, anyhow?"

"Oh, I don't know," she muttered, avoiding his eyes. "I guess maybe I was wrong. You—you're pretty innocent, Gilbert."

He stopped and turned on her indignantly.

"What do you mean—innocent?" he demanded.

"Oh, I don't know, Gilbert. You're brave and strong and fine, but—but you don't realize how people can take advantage of you. You—you're just like a kid who hasn't grown up. Oh, Gilbert, I think you're making such a mistake to get mixed up with these Steel City people. You oughtn't to go to Steel City. I know you, Gilbert."

"I don't know what you're driving at," he said stiffly. "I guess I can handle myself. I'm not so dumb. I'm simply grasping my opportunity. You haven't seen these Steel City people slip anything over on me yet, have you? Well, you won't, either!"

They had reached the low picket fence in front of the cottage where Annie May lived, and he stalked on with his head in the air.

She did not see him again until that evening. She was alone on the front porch of the little cottage, rocking slowly in her grandmother's rocker, a copy of the Steel City *Star* clasped tightly in her hands, her eyes staring unseeing into the purple dusk, when Gilbert came stumbling up the walk.

He, too, had a copy of a newspaper rolled up and clutched in one hand, and before he was through the gate he was moaning:

"Annie May! Annie May! Are you here? Where are you?"

She met him at the top of the steps; and she knew that he had come to her instead of to his mother for sympathy and guidance.

He grasped and squeezed her hand until it hurt, and his hand was wet with perspiration.

"Did you see that write-up of me?" he groaned.

"Sit down," she said.

Gilbert sat down and buried his face in his hands, and his big body rocked slowly from side to side. A man acts like that only when his pride has been struck to the core, and Annie May knew that Gilbert's pride had all but been disemboweled.

SMALL-TOWN SLEUTH SLAMS
GUN ON FLANNEL MONEY KING!

"I slammed my gun down on him," the boy constable confessed.

Then the pictures—those ghastly pictures—of Gilbert with glaring eyes and lips skinned back from teeth, leveling the revolver at the portrait of Lamson, the bigamist. It was so terribly funny! The reporter had not overlooked a laugh, or a chuckle, or a giggle, or a titter in the whole dreadful episode. And the caption under the photograph:

> Gilbert Dollow in act of slamming down gun on photograph of Bigamist Lamson, who was arrested two years ago in Seattle.

From every part of the article that sickening phrase stood out:

"Then I slammed my gun down on him!"

The article had been concluded by the statement that the Sherlock Holmes of Maple Hollow was expected shortly to apply for a position on the Steel City police force.

> The ruthless young officer is expected to slam down his gun on every item of vice and corruption within our city limits. The old, old dream of our foremost citizens, that Steel City would some day become pure, clean, and wholesome, is soon to be realized.

"Did you read it all?" Gilbert groaned.

"Yes, Gilbert." She wanted to take his poor, aching head into her hands. "Would you like a piece of cake, Gilbert?"

"Oh, my Lord, no! I never want to look at food again as long as I live."

"Well, I'll get it anyway."

"Well, I might eat just a little piece."

"And a nice glass of milk."

"Annie May, you're mighty good to me."

When she returned to the porch with a ten-inch pile of sandwiches, a pitcher of milk, the half of a huckleberry pie, and a large chunk of choc'late cake, peace was at least superficially restored. Gilbert was sitting just as she had left him, but he was no longer swaying from side to side, and moans were no longer being emitted by him.

Annie May placed the food on one side of him, and seated herself on the other. A glow over the treetops gave promise of a beautiful moonlight night, and Annie May believed that Gilbert's senses were on the way to be restored. She had made real progress in the past twenty-four hours, and in his hour of greatest need he had come to her for solace—to have his bruises kissed, as it were.

"After all," Annie May said softly, "Maple Hollow is pretty nice. The people may not be as smart as they are in the big-towns, but they are pretty honest and true and dependable, and in the long run, it seems to me, that those things count for the most. I'm glad in a way that this happened, Gilbert. It shows you where your friends are, and you know you can live a life just as full and useful here as you can in a big city, and it is so much nicer."

Gilbert looked at her in silence, except for the deep crunching sound made as he masticated the sandwiches, and the swashing sound as he gulped down milk.

"Do you suppose," the girl went on, "that it's anything like this to-night in Steel City? Smell the honeysuckle, Gilbert. Isn't it sweet? Listen, and you can hear the waves on the beach. What do you suppose you can smell and hear in Steel City at this hour? Smoke from the blast furnaces, and smoke from the automobiles; and the clatter of street cars and trucks, and that awful rumble, rumble, rumble."

Gilbert washed down a mouthful of sandwich.

"Do you think for a minute I'm going to stay here?"

She was startled. "Why, aren't you?"

"Do you think I'd stay here another day, after the way that dog-goned reporter made a fool out of me? Do you think I'd show my face around here, having everybody laughing at me behind my back? Gee whiz, Annie May, I couldn't. And I don't want to. No, sir! By gosh, I'm going to Steel City!"

"Oh, Gil, you aren't!"

"Huh! You wait and see! By this time to-morrow I'll be in Steel City. They don't know me there. Oh, I'll get a laugh when I go around to apply for a place on the police force, but they won't laugh long. Hobson, the chief of detectives, promised to put me right on the force, and that lawyer of Mrs. Sullivan's told me to be sure to look him up. Say, do you know who he is? Did you hear what that reporter said? He's Shark Ferris, the political boss of Steel City! He's the power behind the mayor and everything."

"Gilbert, you—you mustn't go."

"I'd like to know why."

"Oh, you don't belong there."

"I belong in this hick town, huh?"

"You belong in Maple Hollow. I won't have you or anybody else calling it a hick town. It's a nice town, and we're mighty fine people. Look here, Gilbert," she argued earnestly, "suppose you got in trouble in Steel City, and got your feelings hurt, the way you did to-night, who would you go to? Would you go to Mrs. Sullivan?"

Gilbert munched on in silence.

"Gilbert, would you have gone to her to-night?"

"I don't see what you're getting at."

"Why did you come to me, anyhow?"

"Why?" he repeated gruffly. "I don't know why. I didn't know I was coming here until I was here. Well, what about it? What are you getting at?"

"Oh, gee, I don't know," said Annie May in a voice of defeat.

"I'm going to Steel City on the morning train. Bill Sulger's going to take my place as life guard. I'm going to show those city smart alecks that I'm no hick. I put over a clever trick when I slammed down my— I mean, when I pinched that counterfeiter, and I guess I can put over other tricks just as clever."

"Well," said Annie May, rising, "I wish you luck, Gilbert. I—I hope you make good." She extended her hand, and Gilbert engulfed it in his big brown paw.

"You certainly have got determination."

His head dropped down a little. For a moment she thought he was going to kiss her, and her heart beat a frantic tattoo against her ribs; but he only looked at her vaguely, as if he wanted to say something but could not quite recall what it was; and, giving her hand a little farewell squeeze, he turned and strode to the gate. He did not hesitate. He did not look back.

Annie May watched his shadowy figure until it was lost from sight. She knew that if they ever met again, things would never be the same. She felt terribly unhappy. His going would leave Maple Hollow absolutely empty, as far as she was concerned.

The moon came up, and she stared at it disconsolately. It seemed to her that life was very unfair, very cruel. She had done so much for him; she was willing to do anything. She would, she believed, be willing to lay down her life for him. She loved him more than she could ever love another man. She had planned, and schemed, and sacrificed herself for him—to what end?

She was still too young to know that women do not really love men unless they plan and scheme and sacrifice for them, and that, once they have planned and schemed and sacrificed, it is difficult to withdraw their love, no matter what the men may do. She knew that some one ought to go to Steel City, to protect Gilbert from the sharp edges. His mother, with her rheumatism, could not go. Some one ought to go.

"I ought to go," said Annie May. The idea made her feel a little faint, "I will go!" she said determinedly.

CHAPTER VIII

GILBERT GETS ADVICE

GILBERT DOLLOW'S FIRST day in Steel City could not be described with entire accuracy as a chapter of delights. He had not been in the city in years, since he had been a boy of ten or eleven, and in the interval the manufacturing town had grown up. It was now a community of some ninety thousand souls. The crowds, the noise, the traffic congestion dazed him; and Gilbert, as we know, was rather easily dazed at the best of times.

He did not go to the police station that day at all. His first act was to seek out an inexpensive boarding house, which had been recommended to him by a man he had talked to on the train. It was cheap, and the food was terrible. It was either undercooked or overcooked. The vegetables were boiled or fried or stewed until all taste was extracted from them; the meat was tough and stringy, and the desserts were simply impossible to describe, they were so awful.

He spent all afternoon and all evening in his room, poring over a map of the town. Late at night he ventured forth with the map in his hand, and wandered from one end of Steel City to the other, familiarizing himself with streets, sections, parks, and spots of historic interest.

He knew that a policeman must know the topography of a town as a man knows the palm of his hand, or an egg knows the inside of its shell; and he was going to be prepared when he consulted Chief of Detectives Hobson. He had two adventures that night. Neither was particularly exciting, but each was interesting in its way, and both were illuminating.

He was passing through the business district when he came unexpectedly upon two policemen who were standing outside a motion picture theater. It was so late that the theater was in darkness, and Gilbert's approach was so noiseless that neither policeman was aware of it. They were discussing something earnestly, and as Gilbert was intensely interested in all matters pertaining to the activity of the Steel City police force he stopped and listened.

"Well, he guarantees that it's prewar stuff," one of the policemen was saying, "and he only charges me forty a case for it, which is fair enough. It hasn't got much of a bite, and it certainly has plenty of kick."

"Let me have his name and address," the other policeman said, "and I will try him out. I have a friend who knows a steward on one of the big transatlantic boats, and he gave me a taste; and I am not kidding you, Mike, it went down like so much perfumed velvet. But this steward is asking highway robber prices for it—a hundred and ten a case."

"Let me write down this fellow's telephone number for you—" the other policeman began, when he saw Gilbert standing there a few feet away. He gave Gilbert a friendly grin.

"Hello, there, buddy! What's on your mind?"

"Nothing—nothing at all," Gilbert said hastily. "I was just taking a little walk before going to bed."

"Nice night for a walk," the officer said pleasantly. "By the way, Mike, how did that batch of wine turn out you started last fall?"

"Simply elegant," the other policeman replied. "It's going to be ripe in another week or so, and we want you and the missus to come over when we tap the barrel."

Gilbert waited to hear no more. He was pale and trembling. He was so shaken by the revelations that had just been made to him that he presently lost his way. He was in the factory district, and on every side loomed the rusty steel cupolas of the mills. He turned a corner and came upon a policeman who leaned against a telephone pole, twirling his night stick and looking rather bored.

Gilbert accosted him with a pleasant good evening, and the officer stopped twirling his night stick, but did not audibly reply.

"How do you like it?" Gilbert pleasantly asked him.

"How do I like what?" the minion of the law growled.

"Your job—being a policeman."

"Say," said the cop, "are you trying to be funny? If you are, take that load of jokes and dump them on somebody who will appreciate them, will you?"

"I wasn't trying to be funny," Gilbert hastily explained. "You didn't seem to be especially busy, and I came to Steel City to-day to try to get on the force myself; and I was just wondering if I could ask you a few questions."

The policeman looked at him owlishly.

"Yeaa-a-a-h? Where'd ya come from?"

"Oh, a little hick town up in the country. You probably never heard of it."

"What's the name of the place?"

"Maple Hollow," said Gilbert.

The policeman straightened up and looked at him intently.

"Say," he breathed, "you aren't the guy who slammed down his gun on Carter, the counterfeiter, are you, by any chance?"

"I arrested Carter," Gilbert stiffly admitted.

"You did? Are you the guy—honest? No kidding?" the cop gasped.

"Why, yes," Gilbert said warily, "I'm the fellow." He looked intently at the cop, but there were no signs of mirth in the man's face; nothing but surprise and great interest. Gilbert was beginning to loathe that heroic episode.

Without making any explanation, the policeman began to beat vigorously upon the pavement with his night stick. Pres-

ently the drumming of feet was heard, and a tall, portly policeman came loping down the middle of the street. He arrived
almost out of breath.

"What's up?" he puffed.

"Emmett," said the policeman whom Gilbert had accosted,
"I want you to take a good look at this bird. Can you place him?
Have you ever seen his pitcher anywhere?"

The newcomer, Emmett, scrutinized Gilbert in the glaring,
startling beam of an electric torch.

"Do you get him?"

"He just skips my memory. Who is he?" said Emmett, still
panting a little from his run.

"It's the guy from up in the sticks who slammed down his
gun on Carter!"

"No! You're kidding me!"

"Ask him for yourself."

The policeman named Emmett looked closer at Gilbert.

"Are you that fellow?"

"Yes," said Gilbert, "I'm the one."

"Say," demanded Emmett, "is it true what the papers said,
no kidding? Are you goin' to join the force and clean up Steel
City?"

"I'm going to join the force if they will let me on," Gilbert
coolly admitted. "But what the papers said about me gives me
a great big pain in the neck—all that stuff about how I slammed
down my gun on Carter."

"But you did pull a gun on him?"

"Sure I did! He was armed, wasn't he?"

"Yeah! Certainly! And you're goin' to get on the force?"

"That's why I came to Steel City," Gilbert affirmed. "I stopped
to have a talk with your friend here and to try to get some advice
from him."

"Listen, kid—we will simply be tickled to death and highly
honored to give you our advice. It's a mighty good thing you

stopped to have a word with Terry, and not some other cop. He will steer you right, and so will I. A lot of cops in this town would try to pull some low-down practical joke on you, if you had happened to fall in with them. We don't go in for that sort of stuff, and any advice we give you you can bank on to the limit."

"Emmett is telling you the absolute truth, kid," said Terry earnestly. "There are a lot of kidders on the force. They are mostly Irishmen, and you know how the Irish are. It's a lucky thing for you you fell in with a couple of serious-minded German policemen, and not a couple of those Micks. You can say what you want about us Germans, but we don't go around playing practical jokes on innocent strangers."

"I've always liked the Germans," said Gilbert. "A lot of people knocked them on account of the atrocities and so on they did during the war, but I've always said that the whole German nation can't be like that and there must be some good in them."

"Did you hear that, Terry?" said Emmett.

"I certainly did, Emmett, and I'm telling you right now there is hardly anything I wouldn't do for a boy who says such nice things about us Germans."

Gilbert looked from one to the other. Something deep down inside of him warned him that all was not as it should be, but this faint alarm was silenced by the grave, kindly expressions on their faces.

"I always thought Terry and Emmett were Irish names," he said.

"Oh, not always," said Terry. "His last name is Schwartz, and my last name is Schultz. We're German through and through. Now I guess we had better hurry up and give you what advice we can, because Emmett has to hurry back to his beat before the sergeant begins sniffing around. Tell us just what you were figuring on doing, and make it snappy, and we will steer you right."

"Well," said Gilbert, "Mr. Hobson, the chief of the detective bureau, told me to be sure to look him up when I came to town, and he would fix things up for me to get right on the force."

"Did Hobson say that?" Terry gasped.

"He said practically that."

"Why," Emmett cried. "Hobson was just kidding you! You can't rely on a word that big slob says. What has he got to say about who goes on the force and who doesn't? He isn't anything but a flat-foot. Don't waste your time with the likes of him, kid. The best man for you to see is the police commissioner—Police Commissioner Hayes."

"I was thinking of the mayor myself," Terry put in; "but, after all, I guess Hayes is the best bet. Now, I'll try to tell you something about Hayes, son. Hayes is a sort of a peculiar fish, see? He has one of these temperaments that you have got to know about before you see him or you might just as well stay away, especially when you are trying to get on the force. What he likes is a man who isn't afraid to come right out in the open and say what's on his mind. If there's one thing in the world he hates, it's one of these timid guys—these yes-men."

"He likes a man to talk back to him," Emmett added. "The timid stuff doesn't get anywhere with Hayes at all. My advice to you in all earnestness, kid, is to walk into his office, right past his secretary in the outer room, and go up to his desk and bang on it with your fist and say: 'Commissioner, I'm the man who nabbed Carter. I think I'm good enough for a place on the force.' The thing you must remember is, talk back to him. That's what he likes best in a man. Don't be afraid to talk up to him."

"No," Terry affirmed, "don't be timid. If he roars at you, roar right back at him, and the louder you roar the more he will respect you. Get his respect by roaring at him, and you will have the job cinched. You know what I mean. He likes a man who fights back."

"Don't forget that," Emmett broke in. "It's the way he tests a new man. He'll roar at him, and if the new man roars and fights back Hayes will fall for him. Don't let him scare you. Go in there with a chip on your shoulder. We know his ways, and what we are telling you is the absolute truth. Remember, he likes a fighter. I don't know but what he might make you a sergeant right off the bat."

"I was thinking," said Terry, "that he might even make the kid a captain, seeing what he's done."

"Oh, shucks. I wouldn't want him to do that," Gilbert interrupted. "The way those dog-goned reporters made fun of me, Mr. Hayes is just as apt as not to laugh at me when I tell him who I am."

"Don't you believe it," Terry said earnestly. "Mr. Hayes is a man who can read between the lines, and he knows you have got the stuff. No, sir—the more I think of it, the more I think you ought to *tell* him you want to be made a captain right off."

"Oh, I'd really rather start in as an ordinary policeman," Gilbert said modestly. "I don't know enough to be a captain."

"Listen, kid, anybody who takes a dangerous egg like Carter single-handed is good enough to be a captain right off."

"You mustn't forget to go into his office with a lot of energy," said Emmett. "Don't forget to bang on his desk. Show him you've got a lot of pep. If there's one thing he hates, it's a pepless policeman. Do you think you get what we mean?"

"I think I do," said Gilbert after a moment's consideration. "I'll be just as energetic and peppy as I can. Listen—you aren't kidding me, are you?"

"For the love of Mike!" Terry moaned. "Do you think we would kid you after what you just got through saying about the German nation? Don't you think we Germans have any gratitude at all?"

"I'm sorry I mentioned it," Gilbert apologized, "but I've been kidded a lot lately, and I am pretty sensitive about it. It certainly is nice of you fellows to give me all this advice."

"Oh, forget it. All we ask is that if Hayes makes you a captain right off the bat, be a little bit easy on us if we ever happen to get into any kind of trouble in your district."

"I'm mighty grateful," said Gilbert "but I can't promise that. I think duty ought to come before everything else, and if any of the men in my district need disciplining I am afraid I will have to discipline them."

The two officers looked at each other; then both turned a gaze of honest admiration on Gilbert.

"Did you hear that, Terry?" said Emmett.

"I did," said Terry; "and I want to tell you that I didn't think that boys like this one existed any more. I for one am certainly glad to know that the force is going to be snapped into line. Things have been getting pretty sloppy and loose lately, and I think this boy will be chief of police before we know it. There are a lot of cops in this town who don't take their jobs seriously, and it ought to be stopped."

"Listen," said Gilbert eagerly. "You may not believe it, but a little while ago I was down town, and I overheard a couple of cops talking. They were absolutely shameless about it. They were talking about where they were buying their liquor, and one of them said as plain as I am talking to you that he was getting liquor for forty a case."

"You heard a policeman in this town saying that?" Terry gasped.

"I did."

"Where did he say he was getting it?" Emmett demanded. "I certainly intend to look into this."

"I didn't stop to hear," said Gilbert. "And one of them told the other he had made a barrel of wine last fall."

Terry shook his head. "I can hardly believe it, but it just shows how the force is going to the dogs. You didn't catch the name of the fellow, by any chance, who had the barrel of wine, did you?"

"No," said Gilbert; "I wasn't interested. It was a sort of a shock to me. I've always had the idea that a policeman had standards. Of course I don't think much of prohibition, and I think we ought to have light wines and beer, but at the same time it's a bad influence for the community when a policeman encourages that sort of thing. Well, I want to be getting to bed so I can see Mr. Hayes bright and early in the morning. I thank you kindly for your advice."

And he started to move away.

"Don't forget to bang on his desk," Terry called.

"Hard!" Emmett added.

"I won't," Gilbert said gratefully.

"Emmett," said Terence O'Rourke to Emmett Casey, as the figure of the Maple Hollow life guard vanished down the street, "if you had told me there was one of them still in existence I certainly would have called you a bare-faced liar."

"Terry," Emmett replied, "has it struck you that maybe that hick has just been stringing us along?"

CHAPTER IX

INTERVIEWING
THE COMMISSIONER

GILBERT DOLLOW DID not sleep very comfortably that night. Uneasy lies the head below which is a stomach full of indigestible boarding house victuals. Gilbert was not aware that the discomfort in the neighborhood of his stomach was a mild attack of indigestion, a protest being registered by his alimentary canal against the tasteless vegetables, the stringy meat, and the awful dessert. Whenever his stomach called itself to his attention he always repaired to the nearest pantry and ate until the signals ceased. To-night, as he awoke from time to time and tossed uncomfortably about the bed, images of pies, heavily frosted cakes, toppling piles of sandwiches, and other edibles passed tantalizingly through his mind.

At breakfast the eggs did not taste exactly right, and the coffee was muddy; but his mind was so preoccupied with the forthcoming interview that he hardly realized what he was putting into his mouth. He wasted a great deal of time getting down to police headquarters, stopping along the way and looking into this shop window and that. He was really quite nervous. It was the first time he had ever applied for a job, and he was full of the usual qualms. By the time he reached the shabby, worn old building it was almost eleven o'clock.

Policemen were going in and out, and the corridors were full of little groups of men who stood around smoking and talking. These, Gilbert supposed, were detectives. Gilbert asked a heavy-lidded, fat old man in rusty black clothes the way to the police commissioner's office, and presently found himself in a sort of anteroom beyond which was another room. On the ground glass panel of the door, which was slightly ajar, was painted:

POLICE COMMISSIONER

In one corner of the anteroom was a typewriter table and a group of filing cabinets, and along the opposite wall was a line of badly worn kitchen chairs. All of these were empty save one, and this was occupied by a policeman who had a worried look in his eyes. There was nobody at the typewriter desk.

Voices were issuing from the door. Gilbert bowed slightly to the seated policeman, and sat down on one of the chairs with his hat on his knees.

"Another word out of you, Brown, and I'll throw you off the force," a harsh, irritable voice said from the inner room.

The policeman seated near Gilbert winced slightly, but Gilbert leaned forward and listened intently. That must be the voice of Mr. Hayes, the fight-loving police commissioner, he thought.

"But—" a faint, meek voice began.

"There isn't anything more to say. You were sound asleep in that hallway. Three witnesses saw you. It means your stripes, Brown. You'll report to Captain Gilroy for duty in the factory district. That's all! Send Delehanty in on your way out."

The harsh, irritable voice stopped. The door opened, and a tall, broad-shouldered policeman appeared. He had sergeant's stripes on his sleeve, and a look of anguish on his face. Gilbert felt sorry for the fellow, but after all, a man who went to sleep while on duty, deserved to have his stripes removed.

Ex-Sergeant Brown said nothing to the policeman. He only made a grimace at him as if he had just tasted something sour, and jerked his thumb over his shoulder.

The seated policeman cleared his throat, stood up, made quite an affair of adjusting the collar of his uniform, and went into the commissioner's office on tiptoes.

"Good morning, commissioner," Gilbert heard Delehanty saying in a mild, ingratiating voice.

"Delehanty!"—a bark.

"Yes, sir?"—almost a whimper.

"Are you, or are you not a policeman?"

"Why, I—uh—um—er—"

"Delehanty, do you know what I called you in here for?"

"Why, uh—um—" the policeman stammered.

Gilbert fidgeted uneasily. Why didn't the fellow fight back at the commissioner? Didn't Delehanty know that the commissioner loved a fighter?

"Were you or were you not shooting pool in Tony Costello's last Friday night between the hours of nine and ten thirty when you were supposed to be on your beat?"

Silence. Why, Gilbert wondered, didn't Delehanty bang on the commissioner's desk?

The harsh, disagreeable voice went on: "Delehanty, you're relieved of further duty for a month. When you get back on the force, think twice before you get into another pool game. If I ever catch you again in a breach of duty, your suspension is going to be permanent! Get out!"

The policeman came slinking out. He was pale. Even his eyes were pale. He did not see Gilbert as he slunk out of the office, but walked unsteadily toward the corridor, his eyes glazed, his manner that of a sleep-walker.

Gilbert arose briskly, walked to the commissioner's door, and strode in. He slammed the door. He was glad that he had been a witness, or an auditor, to the failure of the two men before him—men who didn't know that the commissioner liked a man who fought back.

The commissioner jumped slightly as the door slammed. The window was behind him and his features were not clearly revealed, and in this uncertain light, Gilbert saw a smallish man with gray hair and a foxlike face, and eyes that were brighter than diamonds.

As he slammed the door, Gilbert experienced a moment of misgiving. Then his courage returned, and he strode to the desk and stretched out his hand.

"Good morning, commissioner!" he boomed.

The commissioner leaned back in his chair, and stared up at him coldly.

"Who let you in here?" he rasped.

"Why! I just walked in, commissioner!"

"Wasn't my secretary out there?"

"Nope! Nobody was out there. I thought I'd just come in and introduce myself."

"All right," the commissioner barked. "Hurry up and introduce yourself. Who are you and what do you want?"

"I am the fellow who nabbed Carter, the counterfeiter, in Maple Hollow!" Gilbert exclaimed, and doubled his right fist. He had selected the spot on the desk he was going to bang, and all he required now was the legitimate opportunity.

"I read about it in the papers," said the commissioner. "What do you want?"

Gilbert's fist crashed down on the desk.

"I want to get on the Steel City police force." Again Gilbert's fist descended, and again the commissioner jumped.

"Stop banging on this desk!" Mr. Hayes shouted.

Gilbert uttered a hearty laugh. "You can't kid me, Mr. Hayes. I've come to Steel City to get on the force, and I'm going to get on. My handling of Carter entitles me to favorable consideration." And he banged on the desk again.

"Get out of this office!" the commissioner roared.

"I will, Mr. Hayes, the minute you tell me in so many words that I am a member of the Steel City police force."

Bang! went Gilbert's fist.

The police commissioner pressed a pearl button which was set into one leg of his desk.

"You like fighters! You hate yes-men! Well, I'm a fighter, and I'm not a yes-man. And I certainly think I'm entitled—"

Gilbert's voice died in his throat. The police commissioner had relaxed in his chair, and was looking up at him with eyes that were bright with hatred.

"Are you going to get out of this office, or must I have you thrown out?" the rasping voice said.

Feet pounded in the outer office. The door burst open, and two burly policemen crowded into the room.

"I'm a fighter!" Gilbert reiterated. "I'm not a yes-man! I've got plenty of energy, and I've got plenty of pep, and I—"

"Did you ring for us, commissioner?" said one of the policemen.

Gilbert looked at them. He smiled faintly.

"Oh! Are they going to fix me up with a uniform and so on?"

"Take this simp," said the commissioner in a voice gentler than Gilbert had hitherto heard him employ, "and run him rapidly into the street."

It dawned on Gilbert that Police Commissioner Hayes was employing unfair methods.

"Look here!" he shouted. "I'm the fellow who arrested Carter, the counterfeiter, and I'm entitled to some consideration. I want a place on the force!"

With an almost audible swish, Gilbert's right fist cleaved the air, but it did not reach its mark. One of the policemen seized his shoulders as the fist descended and jerked him backward, and the fist traveled on downward. Gilbert would have been carried to the floor by the momentum of that blow if the policeman had not been holding him so securely. "Take him away," snapped Mr. Hayes.

Gilbert straightened up, and flung off the policeman.

"You won't take me anywhere!" he shouted. "I'll go. The first one of you who touches me is going to be turned into mince meat! I can lick both of you!"

He glared at them. He backed slowly out of the room.

As he went down the corridor toward the open air he blushed, and through the daze that cloaked his mind there penetrated the suspicion that the two policemen with whom he had talked last night had tricked him. It flashed on him with theatrical suddenness that they had not been Germans at all.

CHAPTER X

THE DETECTIVES OFFER HELP

OUT OF THE aching depths of his humiliated pride emerged an impulse; he wanted to creep away somewhere and hide. And in all the world there was only one person to whom he wanted to creep for sympathy and understanding. How sweet and comforting Annie May had been the other night! It occurred to him that he might look up Mrs. Sullivan and tell his troubles to her, but he dismissed the idea without even considering it. He wanted to go to her with head high—and in brass buttons!

In the shade of a dusty little maple tree he brushed off his clothing, and then started to walk aimlessly. It presently occurred to him that he had better look up Chief of Detectives Hobson without any further delay, and putting this impulse into action he approached the first policeman he saw.

The policeman was standing beside a mobile peanut stand, one of those affairs that advertises its presence with a thin, shrill, pertinacious whistle. He was in a deep, pleasant discussion with the swarthy-skinned foreigner who evidently owned the stand, and whose interest was not on the conversation, but on the practiced hand of the policeman which at intervals deftly reached into the revolving roaster and returned with four or five hot peanuts. These the policeman enjoyably munched as he conversed.

"I beg your pardon," Gilbert intruded himself, "but I wonder if you can tell me where I can find Mr. Hobson, chief of detectives."

The policeman jovially considered him while he munched. He tossed a shelled and skinned peanut into the air, threw back his head, opened his mouth, and caught the nut easily. His smile, considering the difficulty of that trick and the years that had doubtless gone in perfecting it, was quite modest.

"You a friend of his?" he affably inquired.

"Well," said Gilbert, "yes and no. I met him in a business way a few days ago, and he told me to look him up next time I came to Steel City."

The policeman stopped munching, and looked at him intently. Gilbert's heart skipped a beat. Was he going to be asked if he was the guy who slammed down his gun on Carter, the flannel money king?

"Where you from?" the officer asked.

"Pittsburgh," said Gilbert.

"Oh," said the policeman respectfully. "Why, you'll find Hobson down at headquarters, corner of Spruce and Main, Room 112."

He retraced his steps to headquarters, went in the Main Street entrance, and presently opened the door of Room 112. It was a dirty, shabby room with a yellow paint scaling from its walls, and light sifting in through unwashed windows. It was a large room, with chairs scattered all about it, and a battered flat-top oak desk at the far end, under the windows.

A number of men, all smoking cigars, were clustered about it, and as Gilbert's senses focused, he became aware that they were all concentrating their attention on a short, thin, pasty-faced young fellow with ratty eyes and a ratty air.

"Aw, for the luvvamike, I did not," he was whining when Gilbert entered and softly closed the door behind him.

One of the detectives, a big man, seized the youth by the shoulders, and slowly shook him. And Gilbert saw, for the first time, that the ratty youth had handcuffs on. This gave him a big thrill. Here, doubtless, was one of the city criminals of whom he had read so much in the papers.

"We haven't got much time to waste, Spider," said one of the other detectives in a growling voice. "If you know your onions, you'll spill your stuff now."

The ratty one only hung his head sullenly.

Gilbert softly crossed the room. Mr. Hobson was seated behind the desk, and he looked up blankly at Gilbert. Then his expression brightened.

"Hello, Gilbert!" he called. "Stand over there a minute, will you, kid? Sit down. Make yourself at home. I'll be right with you."

Gilbert sat down.

The big detective slowly shook the youth named Spider.

"I didn't see nothin'."

"You're a lousy little liar!"

Still the pasty-faced youth held his head down in sullen silence.

"Listen," said Hobson. "You aren't goin' for another sleigh ride until you come through. Do it now! Spill—and you walk right out of here into God's clean fresh air. Don't spill—and back you go to your cell—and *no more snow!*"

"No more snow," reiterated one of the detectives.

"My Lawd!" wailed Spider, "I'd spill if I had anything to spill. I didn't see that stick-up. I'm tellin' you, on my word of honor, I was down in Mop's drinkin' beer all evenin'. I can prove it by twenty witnesses. I swear I'm tellin' you the truth, chief."

"Take him back to his cell," said Hobson curtly, "and see that he gets no dope. When he gets ready to talk, bring him around. That's all."

Two of the detectives walked out with Spider between them, and two remained. Gilbert got up and walked over to the desk. Mr. Hobson grasped his hand.

"Gilbert, I'm certainly glad to see you! Shake hands with Mr. Downey and Mr. Soppel."

Gilbert smilingly shook hands with the two detectives, and

he suddenly felt happy again. It was almost like coming home—
to meet a man who was so friendly and cordial as Mr. Hobson.

"This is the boy," Mr. Hobson explained, "who pinched Carter
the other day up in Maple Hollow."

"Oh," said Mr. Downey.

"Hah!" said Mr. Soppel. "I read about you in the papers, Mr.
Dollow. It was certainly fast work, the way you slammed down
your gun on—"

"Listen," Gilbert interrupted with a tired but patient smile.
"Honest, I am getting so tired of hearing about how I slammed
down my gun on Carter that I am almost seasick with it. A
joke's a joke. The laugh was on me all right. We live and learn."

The detectives chuckled, and Gilbert breathed more easily.

"Speakin' of jokes," said Mr. Soppel, "I just heard a swell one.
Some guy from out of town crashed the commissioner's office
a few minutes ago, and started bangin' on his desk and tellin'
him he wanted a place on the force. The commissioner rang for
Burke and Laughlin, and they gave the guy the bum's rush.

"You know how Hayes hates to have anybody say anything
but a real polite 'Yes, sir,' or 'You're quite right, sir,' to him. This
bird kept yellin' like a mad bull, 'I know you like a fighter, commissioner. Well, I'm a fighter. I got plenty energy!' And he kept
bangin' away on the old man's desk until Burke and Laughlin
slipped in and gave him the bum's rush!"

Gilbert joined heartily in the general laughter, and when it
had subsided he said:

"Well, some guys are born saps. We live and learn."

Mr. Hobson said: "I suppose you've come to town to burn a
little red fire and looks the gals over." And he winked point-
edly.

"Good gosh, no!" Gilbert hastened to correct him. "What I
came to town for was to see you about getting on the force. You
said something the other night about fixing it for me to get on,
and I thought I'd come on down and take you up on it. I'm all
ready to go to work. When do I begin?"

The chief of detectives scratched the back of his head, and looked puzzled.

"Gilbert, did I tell you that?"

"Sure! Don't you remember? Just when you were taking Carter away? You told me any time I wanted to get on the Steel City police force—"

"Gilbert," said Mr. Hobson with a worried air, "are you sure I said that, in so many words? It seems to me I told you to be sure to look me up when you came to Steel City, and I would be glad to give you any advice I could. I couldn't have told you I would get you on the force. I didn't have any authority to say that."

"But don't you think the way I nabbed Carter entitles me to favorable consideration."

"Sure, Gilbert, the fairest kind of consideration. The way you slammed down your—I mean, the way you tackled that fellow, armed the way he was, and desperate and all that, would entitle you to favorable consideration on any police force in the country, New York or anywhere."

"They made a lot of fun about it in the papers," said Gilbert earnestly, "but the way I look at it, not everybody would have spotted who he was and got the evidence on him, and so on."

"Oh, I admit you're a clever young fellow, Gilbert, and the slick way you acted when you recognized who he was from that poster of Lamson, the bigamist, or however you made the deduction—I'm sort of confused on it all, Gilbert—but anyhow, you did act quick, and if I could get you on the force I certainly would."

"I think he deserves a place on the force," said Mr. Soppel determinedly. All this while he and Mr. Downey had been exchanging looks. When Gilbert had first started to talk they had seemed a little bored. Suddenly both of them had seemed to be visited by a startling idea.

Behind Gilbert's back, Mr. Soppel had pointed with vigorous gestures at him, and Mr. Downey had nodded vehemently and pointed in the general direction of the commissioner's office. Then they had both looked at one another and nodded violently; and now Mr. Soppel said with great earnestness and determination: "I think he deserves a place on the force. The kid is clever, there is no doubt of it. And if he admits he's clever, well, why not? If you don't blow your own horn, who is going to blow it for you?"

"Maybe we can make a suggestion," put in Mr. Downey, who was a stout man with a thin, rather sad mouth.

Mr. Hobson looked up at him and then at Mr. Soppel, and the evasive, defensive air that he had worn since Gilbert began to talk was replaced by one of alert interest.

"Go right ahead and make your suggestions," he invited them. "We are all here to help Gilbert get on the force."

"You do think, don't you," Gilbert put in, "that the way I handled Carter entitles me to a place on the force?"

"There is absolutely no question about it," Mr. Soppel firmly agreed, "and the only question in our mind is how to go about it. The situation at the present moment is like this: the force is full, right up to the last vacancy, and to get you on will require a little engineering."

"Let me make a suggestion," put in Mr. Downey.

"Let me make mine first," said Mr. Soppel. "Now I am a great friend and very close to the commissioner of police. He is the man you heard us talking about a minute ago, Gilbert."

"Oh, yes," said Gilbert, with a distinct feeling of nausea in the pit of his stomach.

"Well," went on Mr. Soppel, "my suggestion is that you let me take you upstairs and introduce you to him. Let him hear your story about Carter, and I am pretty sure that he will put you on the force without a moment's delay."

The handsome life guard had lost almost all of his color. He looked uncomfortable; he looked as if he might even be feeling a little sick.

"Let's all go up and talk to the commissioner about it," suggested Mr. Hobson.

"Come on!" urged Mr. Downey.

"Ho-hold on a minute," Gilbert gasped. "I—I—I—really don't think that idea is so good. I mean, I certainly appreciate your kindness, but I would rather not get on the force by applying to the commissioner."

They stared at him in apparent astonishment.

"Why not?" Mr. Hobson demanded.

"I—I—I don't know, but I'd rather not. I don't think it's a good idea. Isn't there some other way I can get on?"

"But this would be a cinch," Mr. Soppel pointed out.

"Well, I don't know," said Mr. Downey thoughtfully. "Maybe the kid is right. A hunch is a hunch, and maybe his hunch is right. Now I've got another idea. We all know that Gilbert is certainly entitled to favorable consideration."

"I did nab Carter," Gilbert reminded them.

"That's what I mean," Mr. Downey agreed, and both Mr. Hobson and Mr. Soppel nodded. "You got Carter, but there are some people narrow-minded and mean enough to say that it was a piece of pure luck, do you see what I mean?"

"I hadn't thought of that," Gilbert admitted.

"Well, in this game you've got to think of everything, and we don't want to go off half cocked, see? Now, my suggestion is that we give Gilbert a good, fair chance to prove that brains and guts and not luck were responsible, and that he has got the makings in him of a policeman."

"That's a good, sound idea," Mr. Hobson agreed, "but just what is your plan for doing it?"

"Well," said Mr. Soppel, "you know that badge that is in the middle drawer of your desk there—the one we got off that fellow last week who was detained on a lunacy charge? And that gun we got off of him—that's there with the badge, isn't it?"

"Sure, I still have them," said Mr. Hobson, "and as that fellow turned out to be absolutely crazy there's no chance that either the badge or the—the pistol will be needed for evidence. Go ahead with the rest of your idea, Soppel."

"Well," obliged Mr. Soppel, "my idea was to let Gilbert wear the badge and carry the pistol, and go around town looking for criminals on his own time, see? And if he pinches any, why, it will certainly prove that the Carter thing wasn't luck, and the commissioner will make room for him on the force without any question."

Gilbert looked doubtful, but Mr. Hobson nodded.

"I think that idea is good and sound," he said at length. "We could take Gilbert through the Rogues' Gallery, and let him study closely the photographs of all the fresh ones. He would have just as good a chance of grabbing off criminals as regular detectives would have."

"Would you let me wear a uniform?" Gilbert asked.

"No, you couldn't wear a uniform, but this badge will give you all the authority you need."

"And, of course, you would have the pistol to back up your authority if it came down to making an arrest," put in Mr. Downey.

"Is it a real badge? I mean, the kind you men wear?" Gilbert wanted to know.

"Good Lord, Gilbert!" Mr. Hobson said impatiently, "how in the world could we let you wear a real badge? Be reasonable, Gilbert. It looks enough like a real badge to fool anybody. Look! Look at it for yourself."

And, opening the middle drawer of the desk, Mr. Hobson took out a large but neat nickel-plated badge. Gilbert picked it up and inspected it. Across the middle of it in large letters was the word:

DETECTIVE

And underneath that, in smaller letters, it said:

Issued by the Star Correspondence School
Scranton, Pa.

"Wear it on your vest, out of sight," said Mr. Hobson, "or, if you don't wear a vest, wear it on your left suspender strap. When you make an arrest, flash it quickly, and who will know the difference?"

CHAPTER XI

THE TEST OF HIS COURAGE

GILBERT GLANCED DUBIOUSLY from the face of one detective to the other, but they were all regarding him with grave, kindly interest. That faint voice, deep down within him, was talking to him as it had talked last night when he was listening to the advice of the two spurious German policemen, Terence O'Rourke and Emmett Casey.

Certainly they had played a dirty trick on him, with their talk of walking in on the police commissioner, banging on his desk—hard—and demanding to be made a captain on the force. But this was something else again. His intelligence told him that Mr. Hobson, chief of detectives of Steel City, was above such low pranks.

"How about the pistol?" he asked, as he pinned the badge on his left suspender strap.

"Let me explain about that pistol," Mr. Soppel put in hastily.

"We'll get around to that in a minute," said Mr. Hobson. "I think we ought to seriously discuss just how you are going to go about finding these criminals, Gilbert. My advice to you is to spend all the rest of to-day in the Rogues' Gallery. The fellow up there will let you look at all the photographs of men we are especially anxious to lay our hands on, and he will give you the records of all of them—I mean the particular crimes they are wanted for.

"I will have him show you photos only of men we especially want, and they will range all the way from pickpockets to murderers. You won't need warrants for any of these men, and if you should run into one of them, simply stick your gun into his ribs, march him to the first policeman you can find, and go along with him and see how he is run in. It will all be useful to you later in your work. Just slam down your—I mean, just point your gun at him, and—"

"Well, but where's the gun?" Gilbert asked breathlessly. "I'm anxious to see the kind of gun I'm going to carry. Is it a West & Nisson or a Volt?"

"We'll get around to that in a jiff, Gilbert. Just be patient. As I was saying, you can have free access to the Rogues' Gallery any time of day or night you want, and I think it would be a good idea for you to report to me every morning at just about this time and let me know what luck you've had. I will gladly give you all the advice I can, and so will Soppel and Downey here. They have never in all their years on the force made any arrests as brilliant as the one you made when you got Carter, but they are pretty good when it comes to plain, ordinary, everyday arrests."

"If I make good," interrupted Gilbert, "that is, if I bring in any of the crooks you want, there won't be any question, will there, about my getting on the force?"

"Absolutely none. Now just for instance, Gilbert, did you have a good slant at that hophead we were buzzing when you blew in?"

"Yes," said Gilbert. "Just what is a hophead?"

"A hophead is a guy who goes on sleigh rides," Mr. Soppel explained.

"Sleigh rides?" Gilbert repeated, mystified.

"Yeah. He's a snowbird."

Gilbert's brow was crisscrossed with lines of complete misunderstanding. He looked rather dazed.

"A cocaine fiend," Mr. Hobson explained, "or a dope, or a hophead. Well, we have pretty reliable information that this guy was the lookout man on a stick-up job that was pulled off night before last in a cigar store way out on Maple Avenue.

"The gang that pulled it off went in and stuck up the proprietor, and when he started to yell, one of them socked him on the nut with a billy, see? And he is in the hospital now with concussion of the brain, and they say he probably won't pull through. So we want to get the birds that did it, get me? There were three in the gang, and we are pretty sure who they were, as all three of them haven't been seen around town since.

"If they are hiding and can be brought in, we have all sorts of ways of making them let go of any information that we want. I will show you the photographs of these three eggs in a minute when we go upstairs. We are very anxious to land those babies, as there has been a whole series of stick-up jobs lately just like that one: we think the same gang has been doing it, and the newspapers are beginning to razz us, see? It would be a real feather in your cap if you could land that trio.

"Of course, Gilbert, you have been reading about the crime wave that's swept the country. Only last night, over in Springfield, a gang plundered the Springfield First National. There was four in that gang, and they killed the watchman and shot a cop through the lung, and he isn't expected to pull through.

"Anybody who lands that bunch of crooks is going to attract a whole lot of favorable attention.

"Then there are a few murderers we would like to lay our hands on. In a few words, Gilbert, Steel City is just crawling with fellows we want to find and can't. In the whole history of crime I don't think there ever was a better opportunity for a courageous, quick-thinking young fellow like you."

"Now, about the gun—" said Gilbert determinedly.

"I will get around to the gun in just a minute, Gilbert, if you will only have a little patience. I was saying that that gang that pulled off the First National job in Springfield and got away with over half a million may be right here in Steel City, and I'll have to explain why I think that. Steel City has always been a hangout for crooks from all over, see?

"The reason, as near as we can dope it out, is that this is a mill town, and people come and go by the hundreds all the time. We have what they call a big floating population, and wherever you have a big floating population you are almost certain to find a lot of crooks, because they know it is hard for the police to keep tabs on everybody, see? The main thing I want to impress on you, Gilbert, is that there are plenty of crooks in Steel City if you will only take the trouble to find them."

"It's just as easy as looking for a raisin in a loaf of raisin bread," Mr. Soppel explained.

"Gee, it certainly sounds easy," said Gilbert with enthusiasm. How interesting it was to be on the inside like this, and to be actually getting ready to go out looking for wanted men, even if he wasn't wearing a uniform!

"Easy!" Mr. Downey exclaimed. "With your brains and your nerve, Gilbert, you ought to be wearing brass buttons by tomorrow night!"

"Gee!" said Gilbert, and his trustful eyes were shining with eagerness. "I certainly am anxious to get started."

"I'll take you right up to the Rogues' Gallery and let you fix some of these mugs on your memory," said Mr. Hobson, rising.

"Oh, you forgot to give me the gun I'm to carry."

"Now, let me explain about that gun," Mr. Soppel began anxiously.

"Here it is," said Mr. Hobson rather breathlessly, and he tossed upon the desk what appeared at a first hasty glance to be a small pistol. It was shaped like a pistol, or rather a revolver; in fact, it had a very close resemblance to a revolver, but a closer examination revealed that it was really made of two hollow iron castings fitted and riveted together, the ensemble nickel-plated, but not polished.

"Say!" Gilbert gasped. "That thing isn't anything but a cap pistol! I used to use those things on the Fourth of July when I was a kid. They cost a dime in any hardware store. What is this—a joke?"

"A joke?" barked Mr. Hobson. "Gilbert, do you think for a minute I would permit you to carry a loaded revolver in Steel City? Don't you know you have to have a permit to carry a genuine revolver?"

"And didn't you know," put in Mr. Soppel in a voice that sounded rather choked, "that the only way you can get a permit is by applying personally to the commissioner?"

"But my good Lord," Gilbert burst out indignantly, "how can I shoot anybody with this?"

"Gilbert," said Mr. Hobson patiently, "you aren't supposed to shoot anybody with anything. You are supposed to carry that around in your hip pocket, and to pull it out only in cases of absolute emergency—to flash it on a crook when you find one. Do you think a murderer, or a bank robber, or a stick-up man, or any of these birds you are going to catch will suppose for a second that it is nothing but a cap pistol?"

Mr. Soppel placed his arm affectionately around Gilbert's shoulders. "Don't be ashamed of carrying that around in your pocket, Gilbert. Every one of us started out by carrying one of them before we earned our place on the force. If we hadn't, we would have gone around just shooting anybody who looked like somebody who was wanted, see?

"Bring it down on your man, and he will surrender quick enough. I don't think Mr. Hobson wanted to mention it, because he is so big-hearted and sentimental, but that cap pistol you have there in your hand was carried by Mr. Hobson himself when he was trying to earn his place on the force."

"I thought you said," Gilbert suspiciously took him up, "that it had been found on a fellow they sent up last week for being a lunatic."

"Oh, you got us wrong, entirely, Gilbert. What we took off him was a *water* pistol. There isn't any connection at all. This is a *cap* pistol."

"Oh," said Gilbert feebly, but he still hesitated. He was still preyed upon by the suspicion that all was not as it should be.

"Say!" Mr. Downey growled at him, and Gilbert turned his head and looked at him wonderingly. "You aren't afraid, are you. Gilbert? You aren't looking for a knot hole to crawl out of, are you? Because if you are—"

"No," said Gilbert, "I'm not afraid. It isn't that. But I've been kidded so much in the past few days that I'm getting kind of sensitive."

"My Lawd!" groaned Mr. Soppel. "Do you think for a minute that we are kidding you, Gilbert?"

"If you do," said Mr. Downey sternly, "give the badge and that pistol right back to Mr. Hobson."

Gilbert hesitated only a moment longer. Then, with a gesture of decision, he picked up the cap pistol and slipped it into his right hip pocket.

"I am ready to go to the Rogues' Gallery now, Mr. Hobson," he said in a voice that was low, but firm and determined.

CHAPTER XII

ANNIE MAY HUNTS GILBERT

ANNIE MAY PRINE disembarked from the train which had brought her from Maple Hollow, and, grasping her straw suit case firmly, walked through the crowds in the Steel City Union Depot. She was presently standing on the sidewalk on River Street, looking at the sights and listening with some awe to the sounds about her.

It was Annie May's first visit to the big city, and her heart beneath the simple blue serge suit was pounding rapidly. Automobiles, motor trucks, and drays purred and rattled and clattered past her; people came and went, all hurrying.

Where, in this noisy, stuffy city, was Gilbert Dollow? She had come to protect him from the sharp edges, and now she must set about finding him.

A taxicab rolled up to the curb beside her, and the driver leaned out with a genial grin.

"Hello, kid! Where can I take you?"

"Nowhere," said Annie May firmly. She had heard that the drivers of taxicabs were lineal descendants of Captain Kidd, Jesse James, and other well-known robbers, and she wanted no dealings with them.

She was certain that she would find Gilbert wearing brass buttons on a blue uniform somewhere in Steel City. A few blocks away she saw a tall, slender policeman in the middle of the street regulating traffic. At that distance he resembled Gilbert, and with a suddenly agitated heart Annie May hastened down the street, the straw suit case, with its burden of cookbooks, bumping heavily against her knees.

But the policeman was not, of course, Gilbert. He was, however, a nice, pleasant young policeman, and when Annie May came to him he stopped traffic in both directions, and gave his entire attention to her brown eyes. Motorists soon began blowing their horns, and truck drivers, growing more and more impatient, shouted various kinds of advice to him, after the manner of their kind. But to all of this commotion the good-looking, polite young officer was oblivious. He stood there, slightly bent over, giving an attentive ear to Annie May's questions.

"No, miss," he said, "I don't know of any such officer, but, of course, there are a good many policemen in Steel City. The best thing for you to do would be to go down to headquarters and tell your story to the pay roll clerk. He has a list of every man on the force, and while he doesn't generally like to give out that kind of information, I think he is apt to make an exception in your case."

The tooting of horns was now almost deafening.

"If you don't find him down there," the policeman suggested, "why not come back here, and we'll think of some other way."

Annie May thanked him, and was presently trudging along the sidewalk with the heavy, bumping suit case.

Eventually she reached the shabby old building on the corner of Spruce and Main Streets. And at this point in her quest, fate became capricious. It is, apparently, one of the pranks that fate likes best of all to play—to permit us to walk time and again within hailing distance of riches, or happiness, or our manifest destiny without realizing that it exists. Annie May got lost on the second floor of headquarters.

Presently she found herself confronted by two doors. On one of them was painted the words:

ROGUES' GALLERY

And on the other:

POLICE COMMISSIONER

If Annie May had entered the first door, her search would have been over; for she would have seen Gilbert sitting at a table covered with photographs; and if she had, this story would certainly have had a different outcome. The words "Police Commissioner" doubtless had a pleasanter sound than the words "Rogues' Gallery." At all events, after only a few seconds of indecision, Annie May turned the knob of the door labeled

POLICE COMMISSIONER

and she timidly went in.

Gilbert, at that moment of Annie May's indecision, had just made a rather dismaying discovery, which we will return to in due course; but it is certain that if Annie May had walked into the Rogues' Gallery at that moment, he would have been so happy to see her that he would have wrapped her in his arms, and they would have doubtless gone straight from the Rogues' Gallery to the marriage license bureau, and— But why speculate?

Annie May did not open the door at that vital moment. Instead she opened the adjoining door, and found herself in a bare, ugly anteroom with battered kitchen chairs along one wall, and a typewriter desk in a corner, where a pale young man sat busily tapping the keys.

Two harassed-looking policemen were seated against the wall. They looked up with unhappy eyes as she entered, and through the thin partition at the end of the room she heard a hard, rasping voice. The words came to her very clearly.

"I don't know why you are at the head of the detective bureau, Hobson," the harsh voice was saying. "Heavens knows, you haven't done enough in the past three months to entitle you to a job as an office boy in this building. Has it occurred to you, by any chance, Hobson, that the purpose of the police force of this city is to apprehend and capture people who commit crimes? Have you, by any chance, been reading the newspapers?"

"Yes, sir"—very meekly.

"Then you have chanced to read what the people of this town think of their police force. They think it is a great big laugh, Hobson. Just consider the past month.

"In the past month the outstanding crimes have consisted of two murders, five street holdups, six store robberies, and one bank robbery. To date, how many of the perpetrators of these crimes have you rounded up? Not one, Hobson. I am sick and tired of having the newspapers laugh at my force. You have plenty of men. There are more policemen and detectives per capita in Steel City than in many large cities."

The harsh, rasping voice went on, but Annie May heard no more of the conversation. The pale young man at the typewriter had risen.

"I am looking for the pay roll clerk," she said.

"Yes, madam," the young man said courteously. "You'll find him in Room 217, just down this hall."

Annie May shivered a little as she went out. The building had depressed her; the harsh, rasping voice of the police commissioner disturbed her still more. She knew that Gilbert was not constituted for this sort of life, and she hoped that she could persuade him to return to Maple Hollow.

The pay roll clerk was curt but agreeable. He went through his card file, and in less than twenty seconds she was out in the corridor again with the distressing information that Gilbert Dollow was not on the Steel City police force.

Where, then, was she to look for him? Was he sick somewhere in a hospital, or languishing away in some grubby little boarding house? Had he fallen into evil company?

Then the name Alice Sullivan came to Annie May's mind. If Gilbert was still in Steel City, she could doubtless find his whereabouts from the gaudy widow.

On the ground floor of police headquarters Annie May found a public telephone, and on a shelf beside it a dog-eared telephone book. She turned to the S's, and found a solid page of Sullivans, but the name Alice Sullivan was not among them. How was she to go about finding Mrs. Alice Sullivan?

Annie May left her suit case at a drug store, and started walking the streets. Steel City, she reasoned, was not so large that she did not have a fair chance of seeing either Gilbert or Mrs. Sullivan if she walked long enough.

She walked miles. She walked until she was exhausted. Late in the afternoon she recovered her suit case, and went to a cheap hotel, where she took a small room without bath. Early next morning she started out again on her search. It was almost noon when she saw a bright yellow roadster, and she recognized it as Mrs. Sulivan's.

The car was stopped at the corner of Maple and Center Streets, waiting for the traffic policeman's whistle. It was about half a block away when Annie May saw it, and she ran toward it, making her plans as she ran. She would leap upon the running board and simply ask Mrs. Sullivan where Gilbert was.

But before she had covered half the distance the traffic policeman blew his whistle, and the yellow car shot ahead. Annie May hastened after it, but it soon turned a corner, and when she reached the corner it was lost.

Once again that day she saw the yellow roadster, but it was

far away and going rapidly. By evening she was too tired to eat any dinner. She went to her room, poured warm water and witch hazel into a hand basin, and sat with her feet in the felicitous solution until she fell asleep.

Annie May's third day in Steel City was more successful. Out of her meager savings she hired an automobile with a driver for the day, with instructions to drive slowly here and there about the town. Shortly before noon she espied the yellow roadster with Mrs. Sullivan at the wheel, and eagerly instructed her driver to follow it. Her driver looked at her queerly, but said nothing and obeyed.

An elderly man was in the car with Mrs. Sullivan, and evidently she was taking him on a sightseeing trip. She drove slowly from one end of town to another, eventually dropped her passenger at an office building, drove on, and presently stopped the car before an interesting-looking brick house on Cherry Street. The shades were drawn at all the windows, and before the house an electric sign hung, which read:

IDAHO ALICE'S NIGHT CLUB

"Who," Annie May inquired of her driver, "is Idaho Alice?"

"It's that dame right there who we've been following for the past two hours," said the driver, looking at Annie May more queerly than before.

"But did you know who she was and where she lived all the time?" Annie May demanded.

"Sure I did, and I'd 've told you if you'd asked me. Why, everybody in town knows Idaho Alice."

"But her name is Mrs. Sullivan," Annie May faintly protested.

"Sure its Mrs. Sullivan. She's a landmark."

It dawned on Annie May that she had on two days walked until she was too tired to stand, and on the third day had spent fifteen dollars on the hire of this automobile, when she could have secured the information she wanted by putting a question to any policeman.

She paid off the driver. There was a row of maple trees across the street, and under them Annie May spied a bench. She wanted to sit down and think out some plan of procedure.

She had been seated there perhaps ten minutes when the door across the way opened and Mrs. Sullivan came out. She was hatless, and she wore a simple black dress and no jewels.

Annie May was afraid that Mrs. Sullivan had seen her; then she was quite sure that Mrs. Sullivan had seen her. Mrs. Sullivan was waiting for a motor truck to pass, and when it had passed she crossed the street with a smile and a bright-eyed look of curiosity.

Annie May did not quite know what to say; but she needn't have worried, because Mrs. Sullivan always knew what to say, and she was not one to beat about the bush.

"Hello, there!" she cried cheerfully, as she approached the bench. "Aren't you the little girl from Maple Hollow?"

Annie May looked up at her and silently nodded.

"You're the little girl who brought in that verdict of guilty against me in the celebrated cigarette trial, aren't you?"

"I'm the one," Annie May faintly admitted.

"And haven't you been following me around town all day in a Buick touring car?"

"Y-y-yes," Annie May faltered.

Mrs. Sullivan sat down beside her, and beamed upon Annie May. Here was a woman who bore malice toward none.

"And what's become of that good-looking young fellow who arrested me? Wasn't his name Wilbur?"

"You mean Gilbert?" Annie May answered with a sinking heart.

"Oh, that was it—Gilbert! What's become of Gilbert?"

"Don't you know?" said Annie May. Mrs. Sullivan stopped smiling and looked at her gravely. "Am I supposed to know?"

"Why—why—why, hasn't he—haven't you seen him?"

"Me?" said Mrs. Sullivan, indicating herself with a plump thumb.

"He came to Steel City three—four days ago," Annie May said breathlessly. "He came to get on the police force."

"Oh, my Lord!" said Mrs. Sullivan. "Darling, tell me everything."

"He left Maple Hollow the day after those articles came out about him in the Steel City papers."

"I saw them. They were murderous."

"And he was so ashamed that he wanted to leave Maple Hollow, and he wanted to come here and make good. And he did come."

"And he didn't get on the force?"

"No. I went to police headquarters the first day, and there wasn't any one by his name on the list. I was sure he would have—have come to see you. Mrs. Sullivan, I've got to find Gilbert."

"Of course you have, dear. Don't cry."

"He's—he's so—so helpless without me, Mrs. Sullivan. He doesn't realize how much he depends on me. You see, we grew up together, and ever since he was a little boy I've always helped him. And he's nothing but a boy now, and people are always taking advantage of him. I'm so afraid that something's happened to him."

"Well, don't you worry, honey. We'll find Gilbert."

"I'm sure he'll come to you, Mrs. Sullivan, sooner or later. That's why I followed you. I thought if I could—could sort of watch your house, I'd find him when he came to see you."

"You poor little kid. This is getting kind of complicated, isn't it? Where are you staying?"

"At the Palace Hotel."

"That dump? It won't do at all, not for a nice kid like you. Now, look here. I don't know whether you're right or wrong about Gilbert wanting to see me, and all that, but my suggestion is that you come here and stay with me. It isn't supposed to be a very respectable place, but the rough stuff is only on the surface. People like to come to a place that has a reputation for being wicked, and I let people think my club is pretty wicked."

"Do—do you sell liquor?"

"Darling, I buy my liquor by the truck-load. Now, here was what I was getting at. While you are waiting for Gilbert to come around here and see me, come and stay with me, and at the same time you can do me a big favor. You are young and you are very pretty, as dozens of men have probably taken the trouble to tell you. I am badly in need right now of a pretty girl to sell cigarettes.

"My cigarette girl got despondent over the futility of life, and a handsome young bootlegger who wasn't quite as crazy about her as she was about him; and she took a dose of veronal, from which she is slowly recovering in the hospital.

"It leaves me without a cigarette girl, and if you will take the job you will be doing me a big favor, and I will pay you ten dollars a week and your room and board, and you ought to make a couple of dollars a night in tips. Does that appeal to you, or doesn't it?"

"I—I'd love to help you," Annie May said sweetly.

"You're just a dear, and now, if you like, I'll show you around my dump. It's dead now. Doesn't come to life until around eleven or twelve, and from then until dawn it's just a riot."

They crossed the street and entered Idaho Alice's Night Club. Annie May had heard a great deal about these notorious places, and she was as curious as a kitten in a strange garret.

On the ground floor were the cloakrooms, and a real bar. On the second floor was the restaurant, and a small area of polished hard maple for dancing; and on the third floor were quarter and half-dollar gambling machines, and several roulette and poker tables. Above that were Mrs. Sullivan's living quarters.

It was in Mrs. Sullivan's luxurious, but comfortable living room that Annie May asked the question that had been in her mind since they started to inspect the building.

"What kind of costume do I wear?" asked Annie May.

"Oh," cried Mrs. Sullivan, "it's the cutest costume you ever saw. You're just about the same size as Miriam was, and I am sure it will fit."

She clapped her hands, and a French maid appeared in the doorway.

"Yvette, run down to the restaurant floor and bring up Miriam's costume. It's hanging in that closet by the musician's stand."

Yvette curtsied and departed.

"You can try it on if you like," Idaho Alice suggested. "Take off everything but your undies, dear."

She showed Annie May where her bedroom was, and Annie May undressed. The girl from Maple Hollow was ready when Mrs. Sullivan appeared a few minutes later with the costume.

Annie May was seated on the edge of the bed, blushing. She wasn't accustomed to disrobing in the presence of any one, not even her grandmother.

"Stand up, dear, and try this costume on."

When Annie May stood up, clad only in her step-ins and stockings, Idaho Alice uttered a faint "Good Lord!" Then she said in tones almost reverential: "My dear child, has any one told you that your figure has a cash value of approximately eight billion dollars?"

Annie May blushed more rosily than ever.

"Annie May, you must go on the stage. Haven't you ever thought of going on the stage?"

"Well," said Annie May modestly, "I suppose every girl thinks at one time or another that the stage can't get along without her. Yes, I've thought of going on the stage."

"My dear, you're going to. I would be committing the crime of treason against all of the tired business men in this country if I didn't make it possible for you to go on the stage. Have you ever sung? Have you a voice?"

"Oh, I've sung a little in the church choir."

"With that figure it doesn't make any difference if you have the voice of a crow with the croup. Do you know what I am going to do? I am going to send you to New York. I am going to send you to a good theatrical school. What's the matter with that, honey?"

Annie May was slowly and deliberately shaking her head.

"Mrs. Sullivan, what would happen to Gilbert?"

"Gilbert!" Idaho Alice exclaimed, and into her pronunciation of that innocent name she compressed the profanity of any five violent swear words. "That soft-boiled egg!"

"Gilbert," said Annie May severely, "is not a soft-boiled egg. He needs me, and I love him. Gilbert is one of the truest, finest, most upstanding men in the world."

"Do you mean to say you would sacrifice an opportunity to be sent through a dramatic school, and a chance to go on the stage for—for him?"

"Yes," said Annie May, "I would sacrifice everything for him."

Idaho Alice gave forth a tumultuous sigh.

"Love," she said, "is wonderful. All right, lamb, the chance is here any time you want to take it. Now, let's try on this costume."

She held up what appeared to be a pair of long silk bloomers. They were pale yellow. The other part of the costume was a small bright-red jacket.

Annie May slid into the jacket, and buttoned it. It seemed to her that the jacket exposed an unnecessary amount of back, shoulders and chest. She stepped into the long bloomers.

"You wear bright blue slippers with them, and they are turned up at the toes. These elastics hold the bloomers to your ankles. They won't work up."

Annie May turned with misgivings to a pier glass.

"Why!" she gasped. "You can see my legs right through them!"

"My dear, my customers are not going to object to that in the least."

"Don't I wear anything under them?"

"No, Annie May. You have beautiful legs, and I see no reason why you should conceal them forever from the admiring gaze of the public. You don't realize how this sort of thing adds to the attractiveness of a dump like this," Idaho Alice explained.

"There are three other night clubs in town, and the competition is something terrific. There are men in this town who will come here and spend hundreds of dollars in a night simply because they can buy cigarettes from a fresh, lovely thing like you. All girls are appealing in this harem get-up, but you are positively a knock-out."

"What would Gilbert say if he should see me in this costume?" Annie May gasped.

"Darling, he would bump his forehead on the floor three times and worship you."

"Hmph! I'm afraid you don't know Gilbert!"

"No," said Mrs. Sullivan, "and I don't want to know Gilbert;" but she said this under her breath in so soft a voice that Annie May thought she was mumbling to herself.

CHAPTER XIII

STICKING TO HIS QUEST

THOSE FIRST FEW days in Steel City were fascinating ones for Gilbert Dollow. He studied hundreds of photographs of men wanted for or suspected of this crime and that. He was particularly interested in murderers, and he was thrilled when, that first afternoon, in the description of one man he read:

> Warning! This man is a killer. He is a dead shot, and has a reputation for shooting on little or no provocation. Also is an expert knife thrower.

Mr. Soppel selected several dozen photographs of murderers, and Gilbert seated himself under a window at a little table and concentrated on them, trying to commit the faces to memory. By late afternoon he had a headache, but this did not deter him from returning to the Rogues' Gallery after supper.

The man who kept the files and took the photographs was a genial, obliging fellow, and Gilbert would no sooner finish inspecting one pile of photographs than Mr. Bayliss would fetch him another.

And one morning Gilbert came upon a photograph that looked familiar. The longer he looked at it the more familiar it became. He was sure he had seen the man somewhere. He had an intelligent face, with dark eyes set rather far apart, and he wore a trim, dark mustache above a sensitive, somewhat petulant mouth. Where, Gilbert wondered, had he seen this fellow before?

He laid the photograph aside, to return to it again and again, and on that almost fateful morning when Annie May stood out in the corridor, wondering whether to open the Rogues' Gallery door or the police commissioner's door, the truth flashed upon him.

Then it was that Gilbert felt very sick indeed; for in that moment the truth dawned on Gilbert that he was being made the butt of a cruel, practical joke.

The man in the photograph was the same man whose picture was pasted up on the outside of the Maple Hollow jail. It was Harry P. Lamson. There were so many aliases under which this man traveled, that in the accompanying description of him, Gilbert had not before noticed that name. Harry P. Lamson was the bigamist who had been arrested two years ago in Seattle and was now serving time in some penitentiary in the West.

Mr. Bayliss had been giving Gilbert nothing but old photographs to look at, photographs of men who were now serving time! It was, Gilbert thought, a mighty dirty trick. And if Annie May had opened the door at that moment, instead of going into the commissioner's office, he would have returned to Maple Hollow with her without a single word of argument.

He said nothing of his discovery of this trickery; he wanted to check up, to be sure that Lamson's photograph was not there by accident. So he wrote down the names and aliases of several men, picking them at random, and then went to the room where the records were kept. And the record of each man contained the statement that he was at the present moment serving time in some jail or penitentiary.

It was dark when Gilbert had finished checking up, and he returned to the Rogues' Gallery with violence in his heart.

The Rogues' Gallery was empty save for Mr. Bayliss.

"Well," said Gilbert, "I suppose you think that this is mighty funny, don't you, letting me go through all these stale old photographs. I want to tell you, dog-gone you, that—"

"Listen," said Mr. Bayliss after a quick look into Gilbert's blazing sapphire eyes, "I want you to know, kid, that I am only carrying out orders. I was telling my missus last night that if the detectives would spend a little more time trying to catch these crooks instead of cooking up practical jokes to play on innocent, harmless kids like you, this town would be a sight better off.

"A joke is a joke, and it has made my heart bleed to watch you going through these old photographs. I am sorry I had any part in it, and if you will come home to dinner with me, why, there is going to be a fricasseed chicken, and dumplings, and apple pie with plenty of cinnamon in it."

Gilbert's ire faded before the kindliness of Mr. Bayliss's words and manner.

"No, thanks," he said wearily. "I—I don't feel very hungry. You've been mighty kind to me. Well—good night. I'm through being kidded. Well, we live and learn."

Outside headquarters, on the steps, Gilbert encountered Mr. Soppel. Mr. Soppel was standing there, chewing a cold cigar, and his big heavy shoulders were sagging.

"Oh, hello there, kid," he said in a dull voice. "Say, are you sure you want to be a detective? I just had a little interview with the commissioner, and I kind of wish I had gone into the plumbing business as I had a chance to and ought to have. I am kind of sick of my job."

"You are going to be a lot sicker of your job in about five minutes," said Gilbert wrathfully. "You thought you were being mighty funny, having Mr. Bayliss show me all those stale pho-tographs, didn't you? Well, if you are a half a man you will take off your coat and come back with me to the gymnasium and have it out with our bare fists!"

"Gilbert," said Mr. Soppel in a pained voice, "the calendar says I am forty-two years old, but I know that I was ninety-seven a few minutes ago. To-morrow morning I will put on the gloves with you gladly. I positively am not in the mood for fighting to-night.

"What are you bellyaching about anyway? Are you a sore-head, just because we have pulled off a little joke on you? Say, what do you think the life of a cop is—a bed of roses? Don't be a sap, Gilbert. Come on along with me now, and I'll take you home to dinner. We are having spare ribs, sauerkraut, and—"

"No, thanks," said Gilbert coldly. "I never want to see a cop or a detective again as long as I live."

"If you feel that way about it," said Mr. Soppel, bristling, "you had better go back to where you came from. I'm trying to tell you that we are all boobs in this game when we start, and every one of us has been kidded pink at one time or another. So if you can't stand the gaff, my advice to you is to go back to the sticks. This is a man's game, and cry babies don't belong in it."

"I'm not a cry baby," said Gilbert angrily, "but I never did anything to you fellows, and I don't see why you make me waste my time looking at a lot of dead pictures when Steel City is simply crawling with crooks."

"Just as long as you're a fall guy," Mr. Soppel explained, "there will always be somebody to make you trip and spill. You will get hardened to it."

"Well, I'm sensitive, and—"

"Oh, hell, so is everybody. The truth of the matter is, Gilbert, we don't think you have the stuff in you to make a good cop. You are too innocent."

"We live and learn," said Gilbert, "and all I want is a fair chance. The way I nabbed Carter, the counterfeiter—"

Mr. Soppel said something under his breath that Gilbert did not catch. They were walking down Spruce Street under the trees, and Mr. Soppel suddenly seized Gilbert's arm.

"If you want to be a detective, you can begin right now. You see those two old birds ahead of us there?"

Gilbert looked. Two men, somewhat stooped with age, were walking along perhaps fifty feet ahead of them. They seemed to be slinking. There was something suspicious in their air.

"What do you suppose he has in that black box under his arm?" Mr. Soppel said in a low voice.

Gilbert's pulses were quickening.

"It may be a false lead," Mr. Soppel went on in the same hushed tones, "and again we may have stumbled on something. There are so many crooks in this town it's safe to suspect almost anybody. How do we know that those two old birds haven't just got through robbing a store or something and are carrying the loot somewhere to divide?"

This struck Gilbert as a plausible explanation, but he was suspicious of Mr. Soppel. If events kept on at their present pace he would soon be suspicious of everybody.

"Is this just another one of those jokes?" he said.

Mr. Soppel snorted. "Gilbert, I'm afraid you've got a single-track mind. If you don't want to trail these two guys, don't do it. I may be slipping you something on a silver platter. My years of experience tell me that those two guys are acting suspiciously. See how they slink along? And what have they got in that box?"

"That's right?" Gilbert agreed, weakening. "What can they have in that box?"

"If you want to trail them, maybe you can find out. This is my corner. Go after them, Gilbert."

Mr. Soppel turned and went heavily down the side street, and Gilbert followed the two old men. If this was just another of Mr. Soppel's practical jokes, he was going to go back to Maple Hollow tomorrow.

The two old men *did* seem to be skulking along. What, Gilbert wondered as he slunk along after them, was in that black box? His fancy filled it with money that had been stolen from a till, with jewels that had been robbed from some store.

One of the old men looked back, and it seemed to Gilbert that they quickened their pace. They were approaching the older section of Steel City. The streets were lined with brick houses, mostly fine old residences that had been converted into boarding houses.

Suddenly the two men with the black box turned into one of these houses. Except for a light burning faintly on the ground floor, it was all in darkness.

There was a large black truck, a moving van, parked at the curb. The driver was not in sight, and Gilbert hovered close to it so that he would not be seen.

The door closed, and presently a light came on at an upstairs window. A head appeared, and Gilbert recognized the man as the one who had been carrying the box.

He crossed the street and tiptoed up the front steps of a house that was marked "For Sale," but the porch was not elevated enough for him to see in the window across the way. He could see the heads of the two men. Seemingly they were seated and facing one another across a table. Gilbert's suspicions, prompted by Mr. Soppel, became a certainty. The old rogues were opening the box, and preparing to divide the loot!

But he must make sure. He must climb upon something from which he could look into the window and see the table. His roving glance fell upon the moving van. He crossed the street, and climbed and scrambled to the top of it.

He thought he heard muffled voices, and he listened, but the voices, wherever they were coming from, stopped.

Unseen by him, a young man hastened out of an areaway across the street and approached the truck.

A sensation almost of nausea occupied Gilbert's stomach as he looked into the window. He had been tricked again. Mr. Soppel's irresistible sense of humor had induced him to betray Gilbert into another humiliating predicament.

The two old men were facing each other across a table, as Gilbert had shrewdly guessed. They were now arranging upon the black and white squares of a board the bishops, castles, kings, queens, and pawns of a chess set.

"I'm through," said Gilbert to himself. "I'm going to take the early morning train back to Maple Hollow, where I belong."

Suddenly the roof on which he was standing commenced to throb. The truck driver had cranked the engine. Now he leaped into his seat behind the wheel. Before Gilbert could move, the truck was lurching along the cobblestone street, and Gilbert, saved by a miracle from a fall to the pavement, was on his hands and knees as the van rolled and pitched.

In the midst of his previous excitement Gilbert had not discovered that the van, or at least its roof, had been recently painted. The paint had not had time to dry. It was still wet and sticky, but not slippery. It was so sticky that he could hardly free his hands of the adhesive surface.

He knew that his suit—the only good suit he possessed— would be ruined. But he didn't care. He was like a fly on a sheet of fly-paper. He was ridiculous. He was more ridiculous than he had been at any time since his arrival in Steel City, and it remained only for Mr. Hobson or Mr. Downey or Mr. Soppel to see him to complete his humiliation. But he didn't care.

It was the lowest hour in Gilbert's life. He had been the butt of one practical joke after another, and as he stuck to the wet paint of the moving van's roof the practical jokes of which he had been made a victim in the past few days passed before his eyes as they say the events of a man's life do when he is about to drown.

The van's front wheels dropped into a hole in the pavement, and when they bounded up Gilbert was thrown flat upon his face. Black wet paint was smeared liberally upon his forehead, his cheeks, and his nose. If Mr. Hobson could see him now he would get a *real* laugh out of Gilbert. How ridiculous he must look!

Gilbert clung to the sticky roof of the bounding, pitching van, and considered all this quite calmly. His brain was exceptionally clear. He was a fall guy, just as Mr. Soppel had said.

What a fool he had been to dream of becoming a policeman! And suddenly Gilbert realized that he loathed Steel City.

He wanted to be back in Maple Hollow, where life was not so complicated. He wanted to lie on his back under telephone poles and ponder upon the mystery of woodpeckers. He wanted to lie in the warm sand on Maple Hollow Beach and study the crabs. No, he didn't want to be a policeman. He wanted to be home. He wanted to eat good food once more; he wanted to sit on Annie May's front porch in the evening and eat cake and sandwiches. How glad Annie May would be to see him!

A great revelation was made to Gilbert as he clung to the roof of the lurching, pitching, bounding, rolling motor van. He loved Annie May. He had always loved Annie May. How blind he had been! And how he needed her sympathy now!

Yes, he would go back to Maple Hollow and Annie May— if she would have him.

"Oh, my Lord, she's got to have me!" Gilbert groaned.

Bitter tears spurted into his eyes as he recalled the happy hours they had spent together. What a wonderful cook she was! What a smooth little dancer she was! What a fine little pal she was!

He would explain everything to her—wouldn't keep back a thing. He would even tell her about the correspondence-school detective badge, and the cap pistol that he had trustingly carried for so many days. At this moment the badge was upon his left suspender strap, and the cap pistol was in his right hip pocket. How she would laugh! But she would understand. He felt almost happy again.

His smile was stricken from his face abruptly. The truck had dropped into another hole and rebounded, and again Gilbert's face was rudely slapped by the roof of the van and more fresh paint smeared upon it.

That blow almost stunned him. Street lights were reeling. The red light of a filling station was swinging toward him. The truck was slowing down. In a moment it had stopped, and on the left loomed the open door of a public garage.

In his daze Gilbert heard men talking. He wanted to climb down. Here was his chance, but he was too weak from that last blow to move for a few seconds.

"I want to fill her up with gas and oil," one voice was saying. "And I guess I'd better check up on my transmission."

"Better run her inside," another voice said. "Going far?"

"Got a load of furniture from Mill Center to Jamesville. Got to be delivered at the guy's house before nine. Ten bucks bonus for me if I'm there on time. All right, I'll run her inside. Want to check over my ignition anyhow."

The truck was rumbling again. Gilbert tried to move, but he could not move fast enough. The gaping door of the garage was approaching. He would have to flatten himself down or he would be scraped off.

"Will my roof clear?" the truck driver shouted.

"Ya got nine or ten inches to spare," the garage man yelled back.

Gilbert did some rapid calculating. Did he constitute more than nine or ten inches? He wondered what the diameter of his head was. He made himself still flatter.

The truck rolled slowly into the garage, and Gilbert was spared the humiliation and the possible danger of being scraped off. But it had been a close shave, and Gilbert lay quiet for a moment to catch his breath and to steady his shaking muscles.

"Might as well shut this door," the truck driver muttered.

Gilbert saw the huge door slide closed. He heard muffled whispers; then all was silent again.

"I'll bring you the six hundred and one," the garage man said, and the driver answered: "All right. Let's make it snappy."

Gilbert peered over the edge. The wall was perhaps ten feet away, a whitewashed brick wall. Near the door was a telephone. As Gilbert looked and prepared to descend, the door slid softly open a few feet. Two men with felt hats pulled down over their eyes slipped inside, and one of them pushed the big door shut again.

The truck driver had the hood over his engine lifted.

Abruptly each of the two newcomers removed a pistol from his pocket.

"Stick 'em up!" said one of the men.

CHAPTER XIV

CROOKS IN CROWDS

THE TRUCK DRIVER sprang back from his engine with hands elevated. At that moment the garage man returned with a can of black oil in one hand.

"Put down that can," snapped one of the newcomers, "and stand over there with your hands above your head and your face against the wall."

The garage man put down the can with such haste that it spilled over the floor. When he was standing against the wall the tall man, who was evidently the spokesman, turned to the truck driver.

"What have you got in this van?"

"Household furniture," said the driver.

The two men looked at him and grinned.

"Do you know any more jokes?" the tall one asked. "We happen to be Federal enforcement officers. Let's take a look inside."

"It's locked," said the driver, "and I ain't got the key."

The tall man considered him thoughtfully.

"Where you goin' with this load?"

"Jamesville."

"All right. It's goin' to cost you twenty-five hundred bucks to take this truck out of this garage. Have you got it?"

"No," said the driver. "But I can get it; my boss is right here in town."

"Can you reach him by phone?"

"Sure. He ought to be home eatin' supper now."

"All right. You go over to that phone, and you tell your boss it's going to cost him twenty-five hundred bucks to get this load of booze out of this garage. Tell him if there's any monkey business we'll pinch the load and him and you too. Get me?"

"Sure, I get you, and there won't be any monkey business," said the driver nervously.

"All right, hop over to that phone and do your stuff."

The truck driver, eying them uneasily, went to the telephone on the wall and called a number. Presently in a low voice he was explaining the situation to some one at the other end.

"There's a couple of prohis up here at Audrey's Garage, and they won't let me go until you bring twenty-five hundred bucks. They mean business. For Heaven's sake, bring the jack and don't come here with any idea of startin' trouble, Jim. You get me, Jim?"

He hung up the receiver a moment later, and turned to the men with the black pistols.

"He says he'll be right up with the jack."

"All right. Now you stand over there against the wall, too. I killed one man up in Mill Center last week, and my partner here don't think any more of letting lead into a man than you do of—"

The truck driver was staring at him. "Are you the guy who croaked that traveling man—"

"Shut your mouth," the other interrupted him, "and stand over there like I told you. No monkey business."

"Let's take a look at this truck," his companion suggested.

Gilbert heard them walk to the rear of the truck, and heard them fingering a heavy padlock. And he heard them whispering.

One of them said: "You big boob, why in hell did you have to let the whole world in on that killing you pulled off in Mill

Center? Next thing, you'll be broadcasting to everybody that I'm Sweeney, the guy who pulled off that mail truck job in Cleveland last Saturday. Learn to keep that trap of yours shut, will you?"

Evidently the two men were on edge, for they immediately began to quarrel, at first in whispers, then more loudly; and it was firmly established in Gilbert's rather dazed mind that the name of one was Gorley and the name of the other was Sweeney, and that one had killed a traveling salesman in Mill Center last week, and the other had held up and robbed a mail truck in Cleveland only a few days ago.

His senses swam. What was he going to do about it?

His ponderings were cut short by the arrival of an automobile outside. He heard the engine stop; then footsteps could be heard approaching the door.

Two tall, tough-looking men came in. They were confronted by Gorley and Sweeney with leveled guns.

"You got the twenty-five hundred?"

"Put them guns down, will you?" one of the newcomers snarled. "We ain't aimin' to start any trouble. All we want to do is get this truck out of here and on the way. Here's your twenty-five hundred. Count it and let this guy get started, will you?"

"Fork over," snapped Gorley, "and stow the grouch. We are business men."

Peeking over the edge of the roof, Gilbert saw one of the newcomers pull a wad of bills out of his pocket. They were held together by a rubber band.

Gorley passed the wad of bills to Sweeney.

"You count it, Jack," he said, "and I'll keep my eye on these two babies."

The smaller of the two men took the money, sat down on the front wheel of the truck, and started counting.

"One hundred—two hundred—three hundred—" He looked up presently. "Say," he growled. "I don't make it twenty-five hundred. It's only twenty-three."

"It's twenty-five," snapped the man who had parted with the money.

"I'll count it," said Gorley. He lowered his gun, and reached for the money.

In that moment the two newcomers acted more swiftly than Gilbert had ever seen any man act in his life. Pistols seemed to drop into their hands from the air.

"Drop those gats!" snarled one.

"Stick 'em up!" roared the other.

Gorley and Sweeney dropped their revolvers to the greasy floor. They elevated their hands.

"You lousy double-crossers!" Gorley snarled. "I know you two guys. I knew you the minute you stuck your head in that door!"

"Shut your mouth!"

"Banana oil! You're Slim Gibson, and you're Mike Hefflin."

"What of it? Mike, I'll hold this gun on 'em while you are friskin' 'em."

In a daze Gilbert saw Mike Hefflin go through the pockets of the two spurious prohibition officers; and saw Mike Hefflin deprive them of their watches, their stickpins, and their money.

"Now," said Slim Gibson, "you two birds stand over there against that wall, and if one of you moves you're all goin' to be shot."

Sweeney and Gorley joined the garage man. The truck driver was grinning at Slim Gibson and Mike Hefflin.

"Boys," he said, "that was certainly one narrow squeak. Don't you reckon you'd better ride along with me the rest of the way?"

"No," said Slim Gibson; "it would look suspicious. You beat it along, and we'll follow you in the car. If we are stopped again, lead is goin' to fly, and I am not kidding. Open that door, Mike."

Mike Hefflin obeyed. He gave the door a tug and it rolled back on it wheels.

Gilbert was peering down as Mike Hefflin did so. Three men

were standing side by side in the open doorway. In the right hand of each was a revolver.

"Stick 'em up!" snapped the chunky, red-faced man in the center.

Slim Gibson and Mike Hefflin let their firearms drop to the floor. They raised their hands over their heads and cursed as they did so.

The three men came in, and one of them shut the big door after him.

"My Lawd!" Slim Gibson exclaimed. "If this ain't worse than bein' run over by a flivver!"

Gilbert's eyes were bulging. Events were taking place almost too rapidly for him.

"Mike," Slim Gibson groaned, "do you know who these babies are?"

"Their faces are certainly familiar," said Mike.

"It's the gang that has been stickin' up cigar stores. And we get stuck up by pikers like them! My Lawd!"

Perhaps the trio were small fry in the criminal world, but it must be said for them that they worked efficiently. They stood Slim Gibson, Mike Hefflin, and the truck driver against the wall with Gorley, Sweeney, and the garage man, and they expeditiously went through the pockets of them all. One of them looted the cash register.

"Now," said the fat, red-faced man who was evidently their leader, "you guys are to stand right where you are while us three pikers make our get-away—see?" We may be pikers alongside of you guys, but we ain't afraid to blow the everlastin' daylights out of any of you. We're goin' to take our time leavin' and if one of you moves a muscle inside of ten minutes—"

He did not finish that threat, but Gilbert shivered at what the man implied.

Carefully Gilbert moved himself to the edge of the truck. No one was looking in his direction. He swung his legs over the edge, and cautiously he drew the cap pistol from his pocket.

The backs of the three men were toward him, as were also, of course, the backs of the six men against the whitewashed wall.

It was shadowy where Gilbert sat, and he was sure that no one would identify the real nature of the pistol in his hand.

"Stick 'em up, you birds!" he roared. "You're under arrest!"

CHAPTER XV

THE ROUND-UP

THREE REVOLVERS FELL to the floor of the garage with a simultaneous thud. Three pairs of arms flew into the air, and three men turned about and looked up at Gilbert with startled terror.

Now the six lined up against the wall turned and stared up at Gilbert, and as they stared terror crept into their faces likewise, for Gilbert, perched up there on the roof of the van under the garage rafters, would have struck consternation into the heart of the bravest man—not because of the pistol in his hand, which at that distance looked deadly enough, not because of the nickeled badge on his left suspender strap.

It was Gilbert's face that caused all of these dangerous characters to turn paler than even these circumstances called for. Only here and there did a patch of white skin show. It was as if Gilbert were wearing a hideous mask. Perched up there near the rafters, he resembled some evil bird of prey; he was not a man, he was a ghost, an apparition, a specter—a leering terror.

"Line up against the wall!" Gilbert commanded the trio, and when they had done so he said snappily: "You over there—the guy who runs this garage—pick up one of the guns off this floor and come over this way. Shoot the first man between the ears who moves."

The garage man obeyed him. Gilbert scrambled down from his perch, shoved the cap pistol into his hip pocket, and went to the telephone.

He called police headquarters, and asked for Mr. Hobson.

"Mr. Hobson," said Gilbert, "please bring a patrol wagon full of cops up to Audrey's Garage right away. I've rounded up a whole mess of criminals."

"Are you kidding me?" gasped Mr. Hobson.

"Listen here, Mr. Hobson," said Gilbert, "if you use that word kidding to me once more I am going to knock your block off. Now you hurry up here with that patrol wagon."

He hung up the receiver, and as he did so Slim Gibson began to talk earnestly.

"Look here officer," he said, "I want to make a business proposition with you, and I won't waste a moment of time. If you will let me and my partner here, and this truck driver and the truck, out of here, I will fix things for you so you won't have to do another day's work as long as you live.

"I'm talking big money, fellow. You've done a big night's work rounding up the rest of this gang here. We won't even be missed. You let us go with the truck, and I'll give you more actual cash than you can earn on the force in fifty years. A hundred thousand cash, fellow."

"Don't make me laugh," said Gilbert.

"Two hundred thousand cash!"

"Banana oil," said Gilbert.

"Listen, fellow; I'm not kidding you. Think of your wife and the kiddies, will you?" he said earnestly and rapidly. "Think of all you can do for them—fine clothes and diamonds for the missus, and swell educations for the kiddies."

A clanging was heard approaching. The volume of it swelled and swelled. Sweat began pouring down the necks of the eight against the wall.

"Let me and my pal go, too," burst out Gorley, "and we'll boost it to a quarter of a million."

The clanging drew nearer and nearer.

"We'll chip in twenty-five thousand," cried the stout, pink-faced man who was the leader of the trio.

"The first man who moves," said Gilbert sternly, "is going to have the everlasting daylights blown out of him."

The clanging stopped. There was a trampling of many feet outside. The door was thrown open. Mr. Hobson strode in with a revolver in each hand. Two detectives followed him. Behind them was a solid pack of blue-coated, brass-buttoned figures.

"Gilbert!" Mr. Hobson cried. "What in hell have you been doing?"

"Oh," said Gilbert, "just rounding up a few criminals. Turn around, you guys. That fellow over there is Gorley. He murdered a traveling salesman up in Mill Center last week. That bird next to him is Sweeney. He stuck up and robbed a mail truck in Cleveland a few days ago. Those three at the left end of the line are the gang that's been pulling off all the cigar-store robberies lately. I don't know who the other three are, but they just offered me two hundred thousand bucks to let them go; so they must be pretty bad."

"My Lord!" breathed Mr. Hobson. "Gilbert, did you do this with that cap pistol?"

"Cap pistol!" cried eight voices in chorus.

"Yes," said Gilbert.

"What have you been doing to your face?"

"My face?"

"Look at yourself in that mirror."

Gilbert looked at himself. He was almost as startled as his captives had been.

"Oh, that," he said. "Why—" He was about to say that he had rubbed the paint off the roof of the track, but he would not give them another chance to ridicule him. "That," he explained, "is the disguise I decided to wear. I am the man in the black mask."

"You're a masked marvel, all right," growled Mr. Hobson. "What's in this truck? Liquor, I suppose."

"I think," Gilbert answered, "there are some men in there,

and if there are you'd better be kind of careful when you open it."

One of the policemen brought a crowbar to pry off the padlock. Mr. Hobson shouted:

"Is anybody inside this van?"

There was no answer.

"Here, you," said the chief of detectives briskly, and he poked one of his revolvers in turn at five policemen. "Each of you five men stand a few feet apart facing this side, and begin shooting through when I give the word."

"Wait a minute," a muffled voice inside the van pleaded. "Don't shoot. We surrender."

"How many are there of you?"

"Four," said the muffled voice.

"Knock off that padlock," Mr. Hobson ordered, "and you five stand back there ready to shoot the first guy who's enough of a sap to start anything."

The padlock was pried off, and the doors of the big black van were flung open. The beams of several flash lights were thrown inside, and at the sight which met their eyes the five policemen, the two detectives, and even Mr. Hobson himself, who should have been inured to shocks of any description, uttered cries of disbelief and amazement.

Four men with hands above heads were standing shoulder to shoulder just inside the doors, and beyond them, scattered about on the floor, were bundles of currency, bundles of bonds, and rolls of gold and silver money.

"For the love—" a detective started to say.

"Well, I'll—" a policeman began.

"It's the stuff from the Springfield First National!" Mr. Hobson exclaimed in a shrill, excited voice. "There's a cold million in cash here, and another cold million in bonds—if it's all here!"

"It's all here—every last damn dime of it," one of the captors growled.

"Gilbert," Mr. Hobson panted, "you've got the whole gang—all seven of them! What a round-up! Which of you guys bumped off that watchman?"

"Slim Gibson," snarled all four of the new prisoners.

"You don't tell me! My, my! And who shot that cop through the lung?"

"Mike Hefflin!" chorused the four outraged van passengers.

"Chain 'em together," Mr. Hobson snapped.

The four were herded with the eight, and all twelve were manacled, the wrist of one to the wrist of another.

"Gilbert," said Mr. Hobson enviously, "it is the greatest round-up I have ever heard of in the history of crime. A murderer, a mail truck driver, seven yeggs, and three cigar store stick-up men! Gilbert, you are a regular Sergeant York. How did you do it?"

"With my cap pistol," said Gilbert sullenly.

For a few seconds all was so still in the garage that you could have heard a king-pin drop, if any one had chanced to drop a king-pin. The detectives, the squad of policemen, and the twelve prisoners stared at Gilbert's strangely blackened face. Two or three men swore softly under their breath. But Gilbert was not joking. Nor was he bragging. The secret of how he actually engineered the wholesale arrest would go to the grave with him. He was tired of ridicule, tired of being laughed at. But it seemed that Gilbert was doomed to be laughed at.

The startled silence of the garage gave way at the moment to laughter. The policemen started it. Then the detectives started to laugh, and the twelve assorted criminals were not far behind. The word "cap pistol" popped upon the air, and the policemen, the detectives, and the twelve prisoners roared. The garage fairly shook with their laughter. They became pink, and breathless, and limp, and Gilbert turned paler and paler.

"Gilbert," Mr. Hobson said in a weak, gasping voice, "if it was raining w-w-waffles you would be caught out in the shower with a p-p-pitcher of maple syrup in one hand and a p-p-pound of butter in the other!"

CHAPTER XVI

BACK IN HIS HOME TOWN

BUT GILBERT WAS not there to hear that cruel summing up of his heroic capture of the twelve bad and dangerous men. His eyes were staring straight ahead of him. His ears were ringing and burning with the shame of it. And he was stumbling down the road under the reeling stars as fast as his legs would carry him. He was through forever with Steel City. Never again would he look upon a man in a blue uniform with brass buttons without wincing.

There was now no place for him to flee from ridicule except to strange, far-away lands. He was the laughing stock of Maple Hollow because of the brutal way those reporters had quoted his description of the capture of Carter, the counterfeiter.

Boy Sleuth Slams Down Gun on Flannel Money King

And to-morrow morning's papers would scream with the tidings:

BOY SLEUTH SLAMS DOWN
CAP PISTOL ON CRIMINAL GANG

No, there was no place to go to now. Wherever he went the finger of scorn and derision would be pointed at him. Nowhere in the world where newspapers were read would he be safe from ridicule. It occurred to Gilbert that the heart of darkest Africa or China might afford relief, but he didn't want to go to Africa or China. What he wanted was understanding and sympathy, and he didn't believe the natives of Central Africa or China were much given to sympathizing with the wrongs done to white men.

In all the world there was but one person from whom he could be sure of getting sympathetic understanding, and he would go to Annie May without any more delay. He would tolerate the wise cracks of his friends in Maple Hollow. No; he wouldn't mind that. He wanted Annie May to put her arms around him, and he wanted to lay his head upon her gentle, understanding breast.

The mental picture of Annie May folding him in her arms and crooning over him heartened Gilbert considerably. That would compensate for everything. The lights of the Steel City union depot were blurred by the tears that spurted into his eyes—tears compounded of furious resentment against the Steel City police force, of pity for himself, and of joyous relief over the decision he had made.

He slunk through the station to the ticket window, and thence slunk out and aboard the accommodation train, fearing that the press, with its lightning magic, would already have flung his shame before the greedy eyes of the world.

He found himself a seat in the smoking car, and there he sat down and stared sightlessly out of the window over the green and red and white lights of the switchyard.

Presently the train started to move, but Gilbert was only vaguely aware of this. His face was radiant with an inner light. He was walking down the lane toward the house where Annie May lived with her aged grandparents. It was dawn. The sky overhead was still the deep miraculous blue of night, but the horizon all around was pink and gold. A gentle breeze blew from across the lake and softly stirred the trees under which he passed, and in these trees birds sweetly warbled. It was going to be a beautiful summer day. It was so early that no one was up. The world was a beautiful empty desolation.

With his head up and his arms swinging, he strode down the board sidewalk to the low picket fence surrounding the cottage. He opened the gate and walked around to Annie May's room. The pink glorious light of dawn filled the room, and fell on the sweet curly head on the pillow.

"Annie May!" he whispered. "Oh, my love!"

Her eyes opened. They gazed upon him sleepily, while slowly a rapturous smile illuminated her lips. With a faint delighted cry, she sprang from bed, slipped into a pink négligée, and hastened to him.

"Gilbert!"

"Darling! I have come back to you. Dress! Hurry! I'll meet you at the gate. I must talk to you!"

"My dear, my dear!"

"Tickets!" snapped a harsh voice.

Gilbert returned to reality with a start. He looked up and saw a man bending over him, a man in blue with brass buttons.

Gilbert uttered a moan, as if an old wound had been prodded. He relinquished his ticket to the man, and after a little while the bright threads of his fancy were again assembling into the pattern that he had been knitting when the conductor aroused him—in her freshly starched pink dress, Annie May met him at the gate. With a soft, happy glance upward at him, she took his arm, and they strolled down to the beach. It was glorious here. The sand was touched with the gold of the rising sun. Blue wavelets whispered at their feet.

He placed his hands gently on her shoulders, and she looked up questioningly into his somber face.

"You have waited," he said.

"I would wait forever," she whispered.

"I hoped you would understand. You know, I am not very demonstrative."

"I know, Gilbert."

He could say no more. Her eyes were shining with tears. Her lips were trembling. With a happy little cry she came into his arms. He held her tight. How soft she was! How warm! How delightful to hold her thus!

His lips found hers. How fresh, how sweet was that kiss!

The pattern of the dream abruptly changed. Looking over her shoulder, Gilbert saw a crowd of policemen with Mr. Hobson at their head marching up the beach. He was no longer wearing his blue serge suit, but his bathing suit. In small electric lights across the chest of it blazed the word:

DETECTIVE

The column of policemen advanced until they were abreast of him. Then they lined up facing him, marking time. To his dismay he saw that each policeman was armed with a cap pistol. From marking time they changed to a queer slow dance. Suddenly the policemen slammed down their cap pistols on Gilbert, and with a brittle snapping they all went off.

All of the people that Gilbert knew were standing about him, pointing their fingers at him and laughing. Every one was laughing. Constable Dench was fairly doubled over with convulsions. Mrs. Sullivan and her lawyer were looking on and laughing. So was Judge Barlow. And Bill Sulger. Annie May was now standing some distance away, no longer in her fresh pink dress, but in her pink négligée. She was bowed with grief. Her head was in her hands. She was sobbing.

One of the policemen grabbed him by the shoulders, and started to shake him. Slowly this policeman merged into the distasteful face and shoulders, and brass buttons of the train conductor. He was shaking Gilbert vigorously.

"You're goin' to Maple Hollow, ain't you?"

"Yumph," said Gilbert.

"Well, we're pullin' in."

Gilbert rubbed his eyes, and looked out the window. It was raining. Where was the pink golden dawn of his fancy?

The train pulled in to a dark, deserted station. If dawn had come, the world was still unaware of it. Maple Hollow was all in darkness, and the rain came seeping down from a black night sky.

Under the shelter of the station roof, Gilbert pondered. Should he arouse Annie May at this unseemly hour? He decided, after a few minutes of concentration, that she would be delighted to see him—so happy to see him that she would not mind the unseemliness of the hour. He felt like a burglar as he crept through the village to the lane on which stood the cottage where Annie May and her aged grandparents lived. Not a light was burning. Every house was dark. Even the street lights were out. They were turned out, he knew, at two in the morning.

He stumbled along the board sidewalk.

A faint, gray smear appeared on the eastern horizon about the time he reached the front gate. Stealthily, he let himself into the yard and crept about the house to Annie May's room.

Her window was closed. He softly tapped on the pane. To this summons there was no response. He tapped again. He felt uneasy and frightened. The rain dripped from the gutter pipe to his head and shoulders.

"Annie May!" he called plaintively.

There was no answer. Again he tapped on the pane and again he called, but Annie May did not answer him. In despair Gilbert leaned against the side of the house.

"Stick' em up!" a hoarse voice snarled. "Who's there?"

In his startled confusion, Gilbert recognized the voice as that of Grandpa Prine.

"It's only Gilbert," he moaned. "Don't shoot."

"Gilbert Dollow?"

"Yes, sir. Just Gilbert,"

"What are you doin' snoopin' around here this time o' night?"

"I—I've got to see Annie May."

"Annie May ain't here."

"What!" Gilbert wailed.

"Annie May ain't here. She's gone, and the Lord knows where she is—thanks to you, consarn you!"

"Me!" Gilbert gasped. He crept toward the voice, which issued from the general direction of the front porch.

And in the gray greasy light of the rainswept dawn, Gilbert faintly saw Grandpa Prine standing at the rail in his short-tailed nightshirt.

"Yes, you!" the old man snarled.

"But—but—but I thought she was here. She—she must be here. Oh, my Lord," Gilbert groaned, "she's just got to be here!"

"I tell you, she ain't here," Grandpa Prine rasped. "She went to Steel City to look you up, against my best advice, you can be sure, dog-gone you. I hope you're sufferin'. I hope you're goin' through the tortures of the damned the way grandma and me are, and have been the past few days."

"I can't believe she isn't here." Gilbert sagged down to the steps—whipped. The old man regarded his shadowy figure with keen disapproval.

"Yes, I hope you suffer just like her and grandma, and me suffered."

"Did she suffer?" Gilbert asked.

"Did she suffer? She cried her heart out all day, the day you left. And you ain't seen her. No! You're too damned dumb to see anything!"

"She—she went to Steel City?"

"She did, like I told you a dozen times. And we haven't had so much as a picture post card from her. She went there to find you, and where is she?"

"Steel City!" Gilbert groaned. And his dazed, poor, aching brain was promptly filled with pictures of what had happened to poor little innocent Annie May. He knew what happened to innocent and beautiful country girls who went to the great cities. Often they vanished and were never heard of again, dragged down into fates worse than death by the fiends of the underworld.

He sprang up.

"Where're you goin'?" the old man snarled.

"Back to Steel City!" Gilbert cried. "I'm going to find her and bring her home! Oh, my Lord! Poor little Annie May!"

"Yes," growled the old man. "Go on and suffer, and the more you suffer, the more I'll like it."

But Gilbert did not hear the old man's parting wish. Far away he had heard the whistle of the milk train. He must return to Steel City. He must find Annie May and save her from a life of shame.

"Run, you fool!" a harsh voice bellowed after him.

Gilbert ran.

CHAPTER XVII

TELLING THE CITY

THAT NIGHT WHEN Gilbert fled from Steel City vowing never to return, the capricious fates that had been working so hard in his behalf, put their heads together and devised still new forms of excitement for the handsome and harassed young life guard.

These fates, so determined to electrify Gilbert's future, took the form of the department heads of the Steel City police force. To be sure, they—these shrewd hounds upon the trail of crime—were not taking Gilbert's future into consideration out of any wish to make Gilbert's life full and complete. Looked at in one sense, he was a monkey wrench that had been dropped into a maze of delicate machinery; and looked at in another sense, he was a pawn in a great, exciting game, namely, that eternal game of organized law versus unorganized lawlessness.

The meeting took place in Commissioner Hayes's inner office, and there were three men present: Chief of Detectives Hobson, Chief of Police Martin, and Police Commissioner Hayes. Soon after the twelve captives whom Gilbert had arrested single-handed at the point of his cap pistol had been placed in individual cells in the Steel City jail, these three men who comprised the directing brains of the police force went into conference.

"Who is this fellow, and where did he come from, and how did he do it?" Commissioner Hayes wanted to know.

Mr. Hobson supplied him with a thumbnail biography of

Gilbert, taking pains to omit the part he had played in harassing the young man.

"He didn't say how he had rounded them up," said Mr. Hobson, "and he beat it before I could get a word in edgewise."

"You shouldn't have let him get away," said the police commissioner sternly. "This whole thing is shaping into a farce that's going to make us the laugh of the town for weeks to come, if we can't head it off. You saw that story the newspapers carried about that hick when he pinched Carter up in Maple Hollow. Well, that story is going to sound as funny as an obituary alongside of what they'll write if they get the low-down on this round-up. They will laugh us out of our jobs."

"I don't get it," said Mr. Hobson.

"There are a lot of things you don't get," said the commissioner bitterly. "Not getting things is one of the best things you do, and when it comes to not getting bank robbers and burglars you are absolutely perfect. Here these twelve criminals have been circulating around in this town with as much impunity as if they were Salvation Army captains. They've been doing their stuff under your nose for weeks on end, and in all those weeks you haven't made one important arrest.

"It took a hick armed with a cap pistol to round up practically every big criminal in town in one fell swoop. You don't think there's a big front-page laugh for the papers in that, huh? These reporters are going to corner that fellow, and by the time he gets through bragging about how he did it, the reporters are going to have enough laughs to keep Steel City in hysterics for a month.

"This is the biggest story that's broken since the salt docks burned down. It will stay on the front page for three or four days. It's our chance to put ourselves right with the public, and you've spilled the beans by letting that hick get away. Did you warn every man who went out on that job to keep his mouth shut?"

"I did, sir," said Mr. Hobson. "Every man."

"They won't talk," put in Chief of Police Martin. "They don't want to be laughed at any more than we do. If this story gets out, the streets of this town are going to be full of people having hysterical convulsions every time they lay eyes on a cop. Every cop on the force will be laughed right off his beat."

"How about those twelve?" asked Mr. Hobson. "We've got them all in solitary now, but you've got to let them see their lawyers sooner or later, and it will come out."

"It will never come out, as far as they are concerned," the commissioner disagreed. "They're so ashamed of letting themselves be caught by a hick with a cap pistol that they'll never peep. A big crook takes as much pride in his work as a big detective does—a big detective like you, for instance, Hobson."

Mr. Hobson winced under this thrust, and just then some one tapped on the door. Mr. Hobson unlocked the door. One of his detectives was standing there. It was Mr. Soppel.

"Listen, chief," said Mr. Soppel nervously, "this building is fairly crawling with reporters. They've just got time to get their stories in for the city editions; and they say if you won't come across, they are going to say anything they feel like."

"Well, what are they saying?" snapped the commissioner.

"They're all worked up, commissioner, over a rumor about some detective who wore an iron mask. They say they'll make a kidding story out of it if you don't give them the straight dope."

The commissioner leaned back in his chair, and his foxy eyes were glassy with some dream. Suddenly he sat up.

"Soppel," he said crisply, "send in Fogarty of the *Star*, Burns of the *Tribune*, and Mason of the *Herald*."

Mr. Soppel withdrew, and Mr. Hobson and the chief of police looked at the commissioner expectantly.

"Keep your mouth shut, you two," said the commissioner. "Let me do all the talking."

"What are you going to tell them?" the chief of police asked anxiously.

"I don't know," said the commissioner, "I am going to let something work itself out. Let's find out first what these fellows know."

Mr. Soppel returned with the three reporters, and their eyes were bright, too, with expectancy.

"It was a great raid, commissioner," said Fogarty of the *Star*. He was known as the sharpest reporter in Steel City. He was a young man with shrewd gray eyes, a sharp, pointed nose, and curiously outstanding ears. He had helped the police in more than one crime mystery.

"Yes, Fogarty," said the commissioner with his brief, cold smile, "but it looks as if the attacks you've been staging lately on the police force have borne a little fruit."

Fogarty grinned. "You ought to know, commissioner, that I will go just as far with praise as with blame. All I want is the chance. We haven't got much time to get this story in. Let's get down to business. Who is the man in the iron mask?"

"Where did you hear about a man in an iron mask?"

Fogarty looked mysterious.

"Have you talked to him?"

"Nope."

"Have you seen him?"

"Nope."

Mr. Hobson and the chief of police exchanged relieved glances.

"How do you know he isn't a myth?"

"Is he a myth?" asked Fogarty bluntly. Again the commissioner flashed his cold smile. "What do you think?"

"If my assumptions are worth anything," said Fogarty, "here they are: There is no doubt in my mind but that the fellow who executed this wholesale arrest is one of the cleverest men on your force."

"Clever is no word for it," murmured Mr. Hobson, but he was heard by no one.

"So clever, in fact," went on Fogarty, "that I might almost go so far as to suspect that he wasn't on this force."

"Maybe he was imported from some other town," put in Mason of the *Herald*.

"That's an interesting guess," said the commissioner.

"Is this a guessing contest?" said Fogarty with some warmth.

"All I can do," said the commissioner, "is to answer your questions. The fact of the matter is, you've stumbled upon a mystery that we firmly intended was to remain a mystery. Can't you leave the man in the mask out of the story? Isn't it enough that we grabbed off twelve of the worst criminals in this section in a single round-up?"

Fogarty shook his head vehemently. "Nope; it isn't enough, commissioner. I'll admit that that's a whale of a story, but the town is soon going to be buzzing about this man in the mask. Was it an iron mask?"

"No," said the commissioner, "plain black cloth."

"Why did he wear it?"

"To conceal his identity."

"Why should he want to conceal his identity?"

The commissioner only smiled.

"It wasn't you, was it, commissioner?" blurted Burns of the *Tribune*.

Commissioner Hayes laughed, and shook his head.

"All right," snapped Fogarty. "Now, let's see how this thing pieces itself together. You admit that the man was imported, not a member of the Steel City force. Any one with half the brains of an idiot could draw the conclusion that he is probably one of the few great detectives in the country."

"And he would still be an idiot," Mr. Hobson muttered, but in a voice so low that no one overheard.

"What the man in the mask did," went on Fogarty, "was to bring brilliant head-work to the problem of rounding up the greatest band of criminals ever captured in the history of Steel

City. He wore the mask to conceal his identity. It's a great publicity stunt to drive the crooks out of Steel City, commissioner! That is really the idea behind his wearing the mask, isn't it?"

Commissioner Hayes only smiled.

"I want to tell you," said the reporter enthusiastically, "that I think you have hit upon a crackerjack idea, commissioner. Every crook, every lawbreaker, is deathly afraid of the moment when a hand will be laid upon his shoulder from behind and a voice will say: 'You're wanted!' He's afraid of the dark, deathly afraid of mystery. The man in the black mask—"

"The masked marvel," suggested Mr. Hobson.

"Yes! The masked marvel will throw the fear of God into the criminal element in this town. Of course, you don't care to reveal his identity."

"No, Fogarty."

The reporter's eyes were shining with his enthusiasm.

"Commissioner, I want to shake your hand for originating this brilliant idea."

"So do I!" exclaimed Mason of the *Herald*.

"So do I!" cried Burns of the *Tribune*.

Mr. Hayes with modest murmurs permitted them to shake his hand. Then they hastened to their respective city editors. Unquestionably, it was the biggest story that had broken in Steel City since the salt docks burned down.

CHAPTER XVIII

ANNIE MAY AT IDAHO ALICE'S

THE DOOR OF Idaho Alice's Night Club was opened shortly after nine o'clock but that was really nothing but a gesture. The musicians did not arrive until ten forty-five, and most of the waiters did not appear until eleven. But the other employees were in their places by nine sharp, so that parties dropping in unexpectedly would not be disappointed. The doormen were at the door; the two hat-check girls were at their posts; the croupier was at his station behind the roulette wheel; the bartenders were behind the bar.

For several hours before the crowd began to arrive, Annie May wandered about the scene of her future labors. She did not change to the harem costume until the first sprinkling of patrons came up the stairs to the restaurant. Then she went upstairs to Mrs. Sullivan's luxuriant apartment, and, with trembling fingers, removed her suit and slipped into the costume Mrs. Sullivan had prescribed for her.

Annie May crept timorously down the stairs, secured the tray of cigars and cigarettes, and began to make her rounds, going from table to table as they filled with patrons, and singing in a lilting voice, as Mrs. Sullivan had coached her:

"Ciga-a-a-a-arr-rrs? Cig'rettes?"

Business for Idaho Alice's new cigar girl was brisk, and tips were plentiful. Shortly before midnight she heard two waiters excitedly discussing an arrest that had been made.

"Twelve of 'em," one of the waiters was saying. "Biggest round-up of criminals in years."

"Who pulled it off?"

"Don't know. Bill just blew in and said the whole town's buzzing."

"I'll bet it wasn't that fathead Hobson."

"Don't know who did it."

Annie May was anxious to hear more, but just then a young man at a table of noisy young men called her over, and in another few seconds her mind was too busily occupied to deal with arrests.

She found herself gazing down into a pair of blurred, hot brown eyes. The young man who owned them was staring up at Annie May with a wet, loose smile.

" 'Lo, kid. What kind o' cigarettes you got?" he wanted to know.

"All kinds," said Annie May with her bright smile. Inwardly she was by no means comfortable. Drunken men always frightened her.

This drunken young man was, she saw, dressed loudly. He wore a blue shirt, and a violent necktie, and his suit was a vivid affair of black and white checks.

"Got 'ny Darnels?"

"Yes," said Annie May.

"Got 'ny Beau Brummels?"

"Yes," said Annie May.

"Hamertons? Pluckies? Harrods? Rajahs? Bal Maccans?"

"Yes, I carry all of those," said Annie May.

"Well, I guess I don't want some of either," said the young man. "All I want in the world is you."

"Slissen, Jack," one of his companions broke in, "don't be such a hawg. Who's your little girl friend?"

The young men at the table were now all looking at Annie May from head to foot, slowly, carefully, admiringly.

"How d'you like my new sweetie?" the young man in checks inquired; and he stood up.

Annie May sensed trouble and started to go, but he grasped her elbow and swung her around so sharply that several packages of cigarettes spilled from the tray to the floor.

Then he put his arm around her waist, and gave her a squeeze that was by no means gentle. His hot, moist, alcoholic breath was in her face, and she saw that his chin was covered with pimples. Never in her life had she been so terrified, or so disgusted. And she was aware that people all over the restaurant were looking at her.

The orchestra was playing. Should she scream? She wanted to cry, and she wondered how a more experienced girl would have handled the situation. She knew that she should be able to handle this intoxicated young man without help from any one.

"Let me go," she said.

"Lissen, baby, you look mighty good to papa. Do you know what time it is? It's time for you to be kissed."

Another of the young men had stood up, and he was pawing at Annie May, too.

"Let go of her! I saw her first!"

One young man, the first one, had Annie May around the waist, and the other one had her around the neck. Cigarettes and cigars spilled to the floor unheeded, and the two drunken young men pulled her this way and that.

Oh, if Gilbert were only here!

A wet kiss was planted on the back of Annie May's neck and she squealed with distaste and fright.

Then some one came rushing down on the swaying trio, and Annie May saw, to her immense relief, that it was Idaho Alice.

Mrs. Sullivan's hard blue eyes were blazing with wrath.

"I'll teach you young pipsqueaks to lay a hand on any girl in my place!" she panted.

She thrust a muscular hand inside the shirt collar of each of the two contestants. She ran with them, stumbling and sliding, across the dance floor; and in the same formation she ran with them downstairs to the street door. To the doormen she said: "If either of these brats comes here again, don't let him in."

Returning upstairs, she found Annie May, aided by the remaining young men and the head waiter, recovering cigars and cigarettes from the floor and rearranging them on the tray.

Annie May was pale, and trembling, and scared.

"Listen, honey," said Idaho Alice, "if any man in this place so much as looks cross-eyed at you, yell for me. And if I don't come quick enough, you have my free permission to hit him with the first piece of furniture you can lay your hands on, including the piano. You are doing beautifully, and I am just beginning to get an idea. You are too good for this cigarette job. I'll see you in a minute when I'm not so busy.

"Have you heard about the big pinch? Some bull pulled in twelve of the worst criminals who ever hit town. I'll bet if your Gilbert was on the force, honey, it would have been him. There hasn't been any sign of Gilbert yet, has there?"

"Not yet," said Annie May sadly.

"Don't worry, darling. He'll be around. I've told both doormen to keep an eye peeled for him. They'll rush him right up to me the minute he comes in. You have to have a membership card, you know, to get in this place, but it's all fixed for Gilbert."

Annie May, with eyes rounded with curiosity, wandered about the night club, pausing beside the roulette wheel, peeping into the bar, and watching the dancers. Every department of Idaho Alice's was now crowded, and still people continued to come.

The head waiter, who had struck Annie May at first as being a cold, haughty person, asked her how she was getting along.

"I am sorry I wasn't around when those two dumb-bells got fresh with you," he apologized. "I would certainly have enjoyed socking them good, and the next time a thing like that happens I only hope I am handy. Have you known Mrs. Sullivan long?"

"Not very," Annie May admitted.

"Well, believe me, Miss Prine, she is the salt of the earth, and she is the cleverest woman in this town. Three other night clubs are running in competition against her, and you see how this place is crowded. It's because she has a full set of brains, Miss Prine. She is all the time pulling new stuff and good stuff, and people come here because they are afraid of missing something.

"You stick to her, Miss Prine, and you will travel far, and believe me, I am not kidding you. She has taken a big liking to you, and she will shove you along fast. A girl is playing in real luck to have a woman like her for a friend.

"Maybe you think she is hard-boiled, but she's only that way on the surface. I have known her for years, and I would lay down my life for her without a minute's hesitation, and so would everybody else who knows her well. She is solid gold and a yard wide. You know what I mean, the salt of the earth. A table for five? *Oui, m'sieu.*"

Annie May recovered from her trembling and went her rounds, going from the dining room to the gambling room, and from there to the bar, singing her song of cigars and cigarettes, and amassing a small fortune in tips, because she was so young and fresh and sweet and pretty.

Along about three thirty a boy came in with the morning papers, and Idaho Alice's was at once plunged into the throes of the greatest excitement. In a big black banner stretched all the way across the front page of the Steel City *Star* shrieked:

MASKED MASTER MIND
NETS 12 CROOKS IN COUP!

At least half of the front page of every paper was given over to an account of the brilliantly executed round-up of murderers, mail truck bandits, bank robbers, and holdup men. There may have been some vagueness in the description of the steps leading up to this spectacular wholesale arrest, but it was all as thrilling as it could be; and Fogarty, who could really write like a streak, had turned loose the full battery of his largest caliber literary artillery.

He gave you the impression that the mystery man, the man in the black mask, who had been imported to cleanse Steel City of its crooks, its thieves, its burglars, its yeggs, its stick-up men, and all the lesser fry of crookdom—Fogarty gave you the impression that the masked marvel combined the genius of *Sherlock Holmes* and *Lecoq,* of Burns and Flynn, of all the great detectives, indeed, who have ever lived in fiction or reality.

Police Commissioner Hayes, said Fogarty of the *Star,* had decided to employ drastic methods in ridding the community of its undesirables. He had imported this master mind from some distant metropolis, and Fogarty hinted at New York, and Chicago, and even at Paris and London. Steel City was going to be swept clean. Fogarty congratulated the commissioner on his audacity and the imagination he had employed. There was no question but what the evil element of Steel City would be terrified, would flee. Said Fogarty in his signed article:

> If there is one thing a crook fears more than anything else,
> it is the unknown, the mysterious. The man in the black mask,

backed up by this brilliant and daring exploit, instantly obtains a power to inspire awe that verges closely on the supernatural. It is safe to say that every evildoer in Steel City is at this moment shaking in his boots.

The other papers discussed the masked marvel, the master mind of detectivedom, in much the same vein, and Idaho Alice's buzzed with the excitement of it. At one table, in a corner, three men had just been served with a great, thick, juicy porterhouse steak. When one of them had finished reading aloud Fogarty's article in the *Star*, all three seemed to have lost their appetites for the delicious steak. They toyed with their French fried potatoes, and the rest of the night they sat with heads together talking in low, earnest whispers.

Our interest, however, is not with this anxious trio. They were only rather unimportant burglars anyway.

Shortly after the papers were circulated, Annie May got her promotion. She was in the bar when Mrs. Sullivan, with eyes agleam, sought her out.

"Listen, kid, can you cook?"

"Yes," said Annie May.

"Can you use a chafing dish?"

"Oh, yes. I've used one lots of times."

"Can you scramble eggs?"

"Anybody," said Annie May modestly, "can scramble eggs."

"Indeed they cannot, my dear," the blond woman disagreed. "Only a true artist can scramble an egg. There are scrambled eggs, and scrambled eggs. If you can scramble eggs, you are going to become the talk of Steel City, because I have a stunt in mind for you. Let's go up to the kitchen and we'll scramble a few eggs."

They went upstairs, and into the kitchen.

Twenty minutes later Idaho Alice walked out into the restaurant alone. She went to the center of the dance floor, and clapped her hands to attract her patrons' attention. Idaho Alice always announced, or introduced her stunts with great gusto. Now every one stopped talking and paid attention to her.

"Everybody give a hand to the little butter-and-egg girl!" Idaho Alice shouted. "She's coming in to serve scrambled eggs and hot buttered rolls the way you used to get 'em back on the farm! She'll pass among you, going from table to table, scrambling eggs and buttering hot rolls for anybody who cares for 'em. How she can scramble an egg! How she can butter a roll! A big hand now, boys and girls, for my nice little butter-and-egg girl!"

CHAPTER XIX

THE MAN BEHIND THE MASK

AND WHILE ANNIE May went from table to table, scrambling eggs and buttering hot rolls, Gilbert Dollow was returning to the scene of his shame. It was raining in Steel City when the train pulled in—a dour, gray, dismal day. The outlook was exactly the way Gilbert felt.

He slunk through the union depot. The street seemed to be choked, glutted with newsboys, all shouting about some arrest that had been made. He shuddered as he heard their shrill, eager voices.

"Paper, mister?"

"No," Gilbert snarled.

"Well, ya don't hafta bite me, do ya?"

No; he did not want that ridiculous episode reproduced before his tired eyes in cruel black print. He knew what the headline said—the black headline screaming across the front page of the papers. It said:

HICK SLEUTH SLAMS DOWN
CAP PISTOL ON OUTLAW GANG

He started walking down the street toward headquarters. He was prepared to swallow the tattered remnants of his pride. He must find Annie May; must find her and save her from the horrible depths to which she might sink in this wicked city. And to find her he must enlist the services of his enemies, the police.

On a corner a couple of blocks from the union depot, he heard some one shouting his name. A man in a blue serge suit and a black derby was sprinting toward him, dodging the early morning traffic, and Gilbert recognized him as a detective, although he did not know the man's name.

The detective rushed up to him; grabbed him by both arms.

"Say! Ain't you Gilbert Dollow?"

"I am," Gilbert snapped. "What of it?"

"Where in hell have you been all night?"

"What's it to you?"

"Say, don't be so cocky. We've been scourin' this town for you. Th' commissioner wants you down to headquarters. Have you seen him yet?"

"I'm on my way now."

"Well, listen. Have you seen or talked to any reporters?"

"No," said Gilbert.

The detective seemed tremendously relieved.

"That's good. That's fine! You mosey right on down to headquarters, and if any reporter tries to talk to you, shove him aside, see? Have you seen the morning papers?"

"No," said Gilbert.

"Well, for the luvva—all right, all right! Hurry right down to headquarters, bo. Listen. You still got that cap pistol on you, kid?"

"It's none of your damned business," said Gilbert furiously.

"Gee, you cert'n'y are touchy this mornin', ain't you?"

"I guess I've got a good right to be," snapped Gilbert. And he strode on down the street toward headquarters, leaving the detective standing there in the rain, bewildered and indignant.

As he mounted the steps at headquarters, he was surrounded by men in plain clothes and blue uniforms. Mr. Hobson himself pushed through the pack, his ordinarily set features working with excitement.

"For the luvva Heaven, Gilbert, where you been all night?"

"I've been out of town," Gilbert growled.

"What did you run away like that for?"

"Because I got tired of being laughed at."

"But, great gosh, Gilbert, nobody was laughing *at* you. They were all laughing *with* you."

"One kind of laugh is just the same as any other kind, as far as I'm concerned," said Gilbert. "You thought you were doing a pretty funny stunt, didn't you, Mr. Hobson, when you palmed off that dog-gone correspondence school detective badge and that cap pistol on me."

"Not so loud, Gilbert."

"I might have been killed."

"Aw, shucks, let's let bygones be bygones, Gilbert. All that is in the past now, isn't it? Of course, you've seen the newspapers, so why cry over spilled milk that's all dried up and forgotten?"

"No, I haven't seen the newspapers," Gilbert snapped, "and I don't want to see the newspapers. I am sick and tired of being laughed at."

Mr. Hobson and the other men around him stared at Gilbert unbelievingly.

"Has anybody got a copy of the *Star?*" asked one of the men.

"There isn't time to bother with that now. The commissioner is up there, getting madder and madder by the minute," said Mr. Hobson in tones of authority. "Come on, Gilbert."

And he escorted Gilbert up the stairs to the police commissioner's office.

Police Commissioner Hayes was, as Mr. Hobson had stated, pacing up and down in the little square room which served him as office. He was chewing a cold and extremely ragged cigar. He had not slept a wink, and he looked it. His eyes were bloodshot and yellowish; he needed a shave; his skin looked oily from lack of his matutinal water and soap. He had, in short, the air of a very tired and very irritable old fox.

"Well!" he half snarled, half roared when Mr. Hobson steered

Gilbert inside and closed the door. "Well, where in the name of eighteen suffering fiends have you been all night?"

"I went back home," said Gilbert, looking him square in the eye, and not caring what happened.

"What did you go home for?"

"Because I got fed up with this dog-goned police force and everybody's sense of humor."

"Why did you come back?" the commissioner snapped.

"Because I—"

"Never mind. I know why you came back. You saw the morning papers. Just try and keep you away from Steel City after that, huh? Well, let me tell you something, young fellow. If you are nourishing any ideas that you are about as important as the Prince of Wales or somebody, you'd better put them on a starvation diet right away, do you get me? I don't know how you got that gang last night, but I know that head-work didn't have much to do with it, and if you begin taking all this apple-sauce literally that the papers are serving out, why—"

"I haven't seen any papers," said Gilbert crossly.

"What?" said Mr. Hayes faintly.

"I haven't seen any papers," Gilbert repeated, "and I don't want to see any papers. I am sick and tired of being the hick sleuth who slams guns, and cap pistols, and so on down on people. I am sick and tired of any kind of kidding, and I want to tell you that the next fellow who tries to play a practical joke on me—well, honest, Mr. Hayes you might just as well send for the janitor with a dustpan, or a good, first-class, reliable undertaker maybe—"

"Nobody is going to play any more practical jokes on you," the commissioner irritably stopped him, "and what is more—I hope you are paying close attention to me, Hobson—the next man on this force who I find playing practical jokes on anybody—on *anybody*, I said, Hobson—is going to find himself going rapidly down the street with a big tin boiler tied to his coat-tail.

"He is going to be fired, canned, bounced, and given the bum's rush in such a thorough manner that the next time he hears the very words practical joke he will become violently nauseated. Now as for you, young fellow, there is a lot of work cut out for you. But first of all, if you haven't seen the papers, you had better glance over the *Star*."

"I don't want—" Gilbert began, slightly dazed, but angrily determined. But the police commissioner had thrust into his hand an opened copy of the paper that contained Fogarty's brilliant story.

MASKED MASTER MIND NETS
12 CROOKS IN COUP!

The headline fairly slapped Gilbert Dollow between the eyes. Gulping, trying to concentrate, trying not to fall over backward in a faint as his instincts at first wanted him to do, Gilbert read the article. His head swam. His ears roared. The room wheeled about him. The commissioner became a very blurred old fox. Gilbert read:

> If there is one thing a crook fears more than anything else, it is the unknown, the mysterious. The man in the black mask, backed up by this brilliant and daring exploit, instantly obtains a power to inspire awe that verges closely on the supernatural. If is safe to say that every evildoer in Steel City is at this moment shaking in his boots.

Gilbert's first sensation on reading of the masked master mind was one closely akin to shell shock, as we have witnessed; following that first stunning, bewildering blow, was a feeling almost of ecstasy. The pressure of ridicule upon this downtrodden young man so suddenly lifted, the consciousness of ridicule's reversal to a public attitude of awe and worship, shot a dizzying glow through every nerve in his body. Gilbert's mental machinery was not one that adapted itself rapidly to startling transitions or changes, but for once in his life he grasped the essentials of a situation without any appreciable delay.

It was struck upon him with delightful violence that he was, after all was said and done, not so bad. In fact, he was pretty good. Again, in fact, he was pretty dog-goned good. He was mighty good. He was all right. He was fine. He was a master mind. So it happened that when Gilbert lifted his eyes from those delicious lines of print, he was a changed Gilbert.

He was no longer the butt of a police force's practical jokes; he was a person of real distinction and undeniable power. He was the man in the black mask; he was the masked marvel. His perceptions and deductions were comparable to those of *Sherlock Holmes, Lecoq,* Flynn, Burns, et al. His intellect was a piece of polished, brilliant machinery. It said so in the paper.

When he looked up, the first thing the police commissioner said was:

"Do you think you'll need to send for a hat maker?"

"A hat maker?" Gilbert repeated, dazed.

"Yes, a hat maker. I was just wondering if your present hat hadn't probably shrunk."

"Oh, I don't think so," said Gilbert, picking up the headwear in question and examining it. "Hats don't shrink, do they? And I wasn't out in the rain much."

"Let us hope," said Mr. Hayes, "that you won't have to have a larger one. Now, my boy," he went on kindly, "you can plainly see that no one has kidded you, is kidding you, or will kid you for your arrest of those men last night. Nobody knows how it was done. Not one soul will breath to another soul that you pulled off that coup with a cap pistol, and a spurious badge.

"The policemen and detectives who assisted you in the arrest are too ashamed to breathe what happened, and so are the prisoners. The only possible danger is that you may, in a moment of forgetfulness, tell your story to some reporter. You won't, will you?"

"I should hope not!" Gilbert gasped. "Gee, Mr. Hayes, I wouldn't dream for a minute of whispering it to a soul. It's a secret with me all right. But, look here, I do sort of wish I had been here last night when these reporters were around."

"It was your fault you weren't."

"I know it, Mr. Hayes; but it seems to me that you have taken a lot of credit for something I doped out all myself."

"What did you dope out all yourself?"

"That black mask and everything. Why! The whole idea was mine."

Mr. Hayes, who was seated at his desk, leaned forward, placed his chin upon his hands and his elbows upon the blotter, and looked up at Gilbert with his cold smile.

"Would you mind telling me where, when, and how you got the idea? It's one of the things I am curious to know about."

"I will never tell," said Gilbert firmly. "But I do think I deserve credit, instead of you taking it."

"Don't forget," said Mr. Hayes, "that you will receive every penny of the rewards."

"How much are they?" said Gilbert.

"Altogether they total seventeen thousand dollars."

"Good gosh!" Gilbert breathed.

"And Mr. Hobson tells me the check for five thousand for your arrest of Carter, the counterfeiter, will be here for you in another day or two."

"Why!" said Gilbert. "I thought you were only going to let me have five hundred of it, Mr. Hobson."

"Did Mr. Hobson tell you that, Gilbert?"

"Look here—" began Mr. Hobson hoarsely.

"Yes, he did," said Gilbert.

"Well, Mr. Hobson, like all the rest of us, has his greedy moments, but he is at heart a most generous fellow. You are entitled to receive the entire reward, Gilbert. You agree to that, don't you, Mr. Hobson?" asked the commissioner politely.

Sundry and mighty emotions were employing Mr. Hobson for a battlefield. He had already pledged his end of the reward by having signed a little dotted line that made him the owner, when paid for, of a snappy little Misler roadster. It pained him exceedingly to give it up. Indeed, anything and everything connected with Gilbert pained him exceedingly.

The lucky blunder of Gilbert with his paint-smeared face had taken from him and his department credit and fat rewards which they would have, he firmly believed, received eventually.

His department had gobbled up Gilbert, so to speak, and it was now finding him impossible to digest. And now Gilbert was spilling bean after bean.

"What you say goes with me, commissioner," Mr. Hobson said with his most gracious smile.

Gilbert smiled too. He was more than delighted with the way things were working out. Seventeen thousand dollars, and five thousand dollars! Why! He would be a rich man! And the paper said that he was the greatest detective who had ever been in Steel City. The men—those smart aleck reporters—who had less than a week ago made fun of him for the way he had slammed down his gun on Carter, the flannel-money king, were now chanting his praises.

Overnight he had become a great detective, a master mind. Well, it all went to show you that that early training of his had been a pretty wise thing, after all. Not for nothing had he laid on his back under telephone pole after telephone pole, studying the mysteries of woodpeckers, and so on. Twenty-two thousand dollars! Gee, if he could only find Annie May and tell her that news! Wouldn't she be proud of him! Wouldn't she love him!

"I wonder," he said eagerly, "if there is any way I could get a thousand dollars of that money now?"

"I am sure it can be arranged," said the commissioner.

There was another thing Gilbert wanted. Here at last was his chance to realize that gnawing ambition of his.

"And can I be taken on the force?" he asked.

Mr. Hayes thoughtfully considered him. He really didn't want Gilbert on the force, because he was reasonably sure that

Gilbert's run of luck was over. It didn't stand to reason that any man could accommodate more luck than Gilbert had already had; but Mr. Hayes thought that because he didn't realize Gilbert's capacity. Gilbert on the force would be a nuisance, and Mr. Hayes had enough troubles already.

"I don't expect to be made a captain right off the bat," Gilbert said modestly, "but I do think I am entitled to favorable consideration."

"You are certainly entitled to favorable consideration," Mr. Hayes granted.

"All I want is to wear a uniform and carry a night stick," Gilbert explained.

"Gilbert," said the police commissioner, "it hurts me to have to refuse this request, because it certainly is reasonable, after the way you nabbed Carter, and then got yourself up in that clever mask and engineered the round-up of those twelve."

"I think I would be a pretty valuable man to have on the force," Gilbert added.

"Priceless," agreed Mr. Hobson heartily.

"The fact of the matter is," said Mr. Hayes, "that you are *too* valuable for the force."

"What do you mean, Mr. Hayes?" Gilbert gasped.

"Do you think I would let a man with your ability wear a uniform and carry a night stick? I am surprised, Gilbert, that a man with your intellect would suggest such a thing."

"Then you'll put me on the detective force?"

"Oh, no," said Mr. Hobson hastily. "You are much too valuable a man to waste in my department."

"True," said the commissioner. "You are so valuable, Gilbert, that I am going to create a special department for you. It will be the department of the black mask, and I am going to make you chief of the department."

"Will I wear a real badge?"

"Certainly you will!"

"Can—can I start wearing it now?" the handsome lifeguard asked eagerly.

Mr. Hayes nodded. He opened a drawer of his desk, and tossed a black object on his desk. A hasty glance identified it as a domino—a black mask. There were holes for the eyes and a black elastic to hold it in place.

"Good gosh!" Gilbert exclaimed. "That isn't any badge! Why, I used to wear one of those things on Halloween when I was a kid."

"This," Mr. Hayes explained, "is the badge that is worn by the head of the black mask department."

"Look here," said Gilbert, "are you kidding me?"

"My Lawd!" groaned Mr. Hobson.

"No, Gilbert," said the commissioner gravely. "It is a new department, and we have had to create a new badge, and this is it. You are to report to my office for duty every evening at six o'clock. A great deal of important work is cut out for you, Gilbert, but the most important thing to bear in mind is that you must not tell a soul who you are.

"You must not let any one know that you are the man in the black mask. If you do, the whole idea is spoiled. With your help, I think we can clean every crook out of Steel City inside of a week. If any one should look you square in the eye and say, 'Are you the man in the black mask?' what will you tell him?"

"I will say no," said Gilbert.

"You are a young man of *exceptional* intelligence, Gilbert. You can go now, but you must report here by six this evening—to my office."

"Yes, sir—and can I ask just one more question?"

"Fire away, Gilbert."

"I want to know if the night work I am going to do is going to take me into low dives—places where a girl who went wrong might be found?"

"Dives and such places are the only ones you will visit," said

Mr. Hayes "Why? Do you know of some girl who has gone wrong?"

"Well," said Gilbert cautiously, "I heard of one."

He had decided to say nothing to Mr. Hayes of Annie May. Now that he had read what Fogarty, of the *Star*, had to say of his last night's exploit, his faith in his own ability as a detective had returned, and he had quickly built in the field of his fancy a dizzy structure.

He saw himself finding Annie May in one of these low dives. He would be wearing the black mask. He would rescue her from her life of shame and he would forgive her, of course.

"This time," he said to Mr. Hayes, "I will carry a real gun, won't I?"

"No, Gilbert. I have been thinking it over. A man without arms is bound to think more quickly and more shrewdly than a man who is armed. So I don't want you to carry a gun. Now, if you will come down to the cashier's office I will fix it up for you to get that thousand."

They went downstairs. Presently there were ten fresh, new hundred-dollar bills in one of Gilbert's pants pockets, and in his upper breast pocket was a fresh, new cigar, a present from his admirer, Mr. Hobson.

It was a petty trick, that cigar, but after all Mr. Hobson was a petty man with his little or no imagination; in short, a mean man.

Gilbert lit the cigar as he left headquarters. It exploded with a great deal of noise, smoke and excitement on the corner of Elm and Myrtle Streets.

Gilbert was dazed for a few minutes, but presently he recovered his equanimity, and brushed off his clothes with his hands. His smile over the incident was contemptuous. "Pure jealousy," said Gilbert with a sniff.

CHAPTER XX

THE KIDNAPED KID

THE RAIN HAD stopped, and presently a gay and smiling summer sun was breaking through the clouds. Gilbert strode briskly to an automobile renting station, and, so strange is fate in the pranks she plays, a few minutes later he was riding in the same Buick touring car with the same driver that Annie May had hired only a few days before in her search for Mrs. Sullivan.

Gilbert sat up in the front seat with him, smoking a cigar, but it was not an explosive cigar. It burned smoothly, evenly, and with a delightful aroma, as a Corona-Corona usually does. The driver was an amiable young fellow, and soon the two were chatting away with the perfect lack of restraint which characterizes youth.

The driver advanced several theories concerning last night's sensational round-up of criminals, and Gilbert sat beside him, smoking his costly cigar and enjoying himself hugely. What a shock it would be to this affable young chauffeur did he but know that the man in the black mask was seated beside him! In anonymity of this kind there is a certain excitement, but to Gilbert was denied the climactic thrill of announcing, as he craved to do: "I am the masked marvel. Laugh that off."

They chatted about this and that, as they drove out of town, and presently they were rolling along the State Highway at a comfortable forty-five.

"A funny thing happened the other morning," the driver said

as he stepped on it. "A girl—cute-looking kid, she was—came to the office and wanted to rent a car for the day. I got the job. Well, she wanted me to do nothin' but drive here and there all over town. All of a sudden she spotted a yellow Minerva roadster—"

"A yellow Minerva roadster?" Gilbert gasped.

"Ayop—yellow Minerva roadster, only one in town. She yells at me, 'Follow that car, and don't lose it.' Well, Alice Sullivan was drivin' the roadster—it's her car, I mean—and so I followed. Well, what d'you s'pose? The kid had been in Steel City two or three days tryin' to find this Sullivan dame, and she'd been snoopin' around the streets all that time for a sight of her, when all she would had to do would be to ask any cop and he would have told her! Ain't that a laugh?"

"Ha, ha, ha," said Gilbert, but his mind was off on a tangent. He would have to look up Mrs. Sullivan one of these days. It occurred to him then that a few days ago he had been passionately in love with Mrs. Sullivan, and he smiled a little sadly now. Now no other girl in the world existed for him but Annie May.

His expression changed to one that was hard and determined, and a little bitter. He would find Annie May! He would rescue her! No matter what she had done, he would forgive her. After all, any harm that befell her was his own fault, just as Grandpa Prine had said. Gee, but she was a sweet girl!

"This kid was certainly a good looker," the driver was musing. "She had big brown eyes and curly hair, and the kind of skin you love to touch."

"Yeah," said Gilbert dreamily.

"And she had the prettiest dog-goned legs. You know, the thin straight kind, but kind of plumpish. I took a good look when she got out. I could have et that girl with a wooden spoon, no kidding."

"Yuh," Gilbert sighed.

They rolled along, chatting of this and that, but mainly of

girls, crime, automobiles, travel, and personal achievements, and presently they rolled into Maple Hollow. Gilbert directed his new friend to Constable Dench's house, and the constable himself came to the door to greet him. How old he looked! Well, that was reasonable. The constable was well in his eighties.

Constable Dench stared at him, then seized his hand.

"Well, well, well! I don't see no uniform or brass buttons on you, Gilbert. Ain't you got on the force yet?"

Gilbert made a grimace indicative of mystery.

"I'm doing a little special work, constable."

"What d'ya mean, a little special work?"

"Oh, the police commissioner and I are working along together on a little special stuff."

"You mean Mr. Hayes?"

"Sure, sure. There's only one police commissioner."

"You can't talk about it, huh, Gilbert?"

"No, constable. It's absolutely secret stuff."

"Well, well, well! Tell me, Gilbert, what do you know about that man in the black mask who pulled off that big round-up of criminals last night?"

"Well, that's a pretty secret matter around headquarters, constable."

The old man chuckled. "I'll bet I could pick up a rock and throw it at somebody who could tell a hull lot about it, Gilbert."

Gilbert only smiled. "It's inside stuff, constable. Read the papers and draw your own conclusions."

"You seen this masked marvel, Gilbert?"

Gilbert remained silent.

The old man leaned toward him, whispering:

"In the lookin' glass, mebbe?" Then he burst into laughter. "Oh, I knew you'd start things in that smart aleck town, Gilbert, once you got down there. You can't keep a good man down. I didn't have to have three guesses who the man in the black mask was. I knew none o' them city cops had the guts to pull off a round-up like that."

What, Gilbert wondered, was happening? Somehow Constable Dench, without the slightest effort, had possessed himself of the information that Gilbert was the man in the black mask. How had it happened?

"Now, look here!" said Gilbert sternly. "Look me square in the eye, constable, and ask me if I am the man in the black mask."

The old fellow grinned. "Aw, stop foolin', Gilbert."

"Do what I tell you!" Gilbert snapped.

Constable Dench, a little startled at his tone, obeyed. He looked Gilbert square in the eye, and asked him if he was the man in the black mask.

"No!" said Gilbert decisively.

"Well, you needn't get sore about it, Gil. I was only funnin' anyhow. You on some special case out here?"

"I came out here," said Gilbert, "to buy this house. Annie May has always admired it a lot, and so have I, and we'd like to buy it to set up housekeepin' in. You told me one day last week you'd take forty-five hundred for it. Well, here's five hundred to bind the bargain, and the rest I'll mail out to you in a few days."

"Huh! Where'd ya git all the money, Gil?"

"I earned it."

"In this little bit o' time?"

"I'm doing special work that pays high, then I'm getting the reward money for nabbing Carter—all of it, constable. It isn't going to be split."

"Oh," said the constable, "I thought I was goin' to git fifteen hundred of it."

"You aren't entitled to any of it, so the commissioner said. I get it all, but," Gilbert added quickly, relenting before the look of pain in his old friend's eyes, "you're goin' to get a thousand of it anyway."

The constable's smile returned. "That's right good of you. So you want to buy my house?"

"Yeah-ap. It's right on the lake, and Annie May has always been crazy about the view and all."

"But ain't ya goin' to stay on and do this special work with th' commissioner?"

"Yes, and no," said Gilbert. "I have not quite made up my mind just what I'm going to do. It's a sort of a struggle between my ambition and Maple Hollow. I know my place is in the outside world, but I sort of like a place to come back to, and Annie May feels the same way."

"Well, I'm mighty glad you've found Annie May. The whole town's been worried over her. Not a word from her, and old man Prine says you came out here last night, thinkin' she was here, and everybody figgered you and she was together."

"I haven't found her yet," said Gilbert, "but I'm going to. What I wanted to make sure of, first of all, was—you will sell me the house, won't you?"

"Sure I will. Come on down to the town hall and we'll fix up the papers."

"Can I take a look at the kitchen first? Sort of want to get an idea about it."

They went into the large, sunny, spotless kitchen. It was a delightful old-fashioned kitchen, and in his fancy Gilbert could easily see Annie May standing at the big wood stove in a pink dress and a blue gingham apron—his favorite combination. She was cooking quantities of delicious food, stopping from time to time to throw her arms around his neck and kiss him. Gosh, how he loved her!

"What?" said Gilbert.

"I said, I know dumb well *you'll* find her all right, Gil. I ain't worryin' none about that. After what you pulled off last night, findin' Annie May is goin' to be child's play for ya."

"After what I pulled off last night?" Gilbert echoed.

"Listen, Gil," the constable said in a low, cautious voice, "it's been stickin' up out of your pocket all this time. You want to be more careful."

Gilbert quickly glanced down. One end of the black mask was protruding from his upper left hand vest pocket.

"Don't you worry, Gil," the constable hastened to assure him. "Your secret is safe with me. Now let's go down to the town hall."

It was almost four o'clock when Gilbert returned to Steel City, and he paid off the driver and went up the steps to headquarters. He smiled as he recalled what painful associations those steps had had a few days ago. Once he had been brutally-thrown down those stairs. Now he was a department head!

He thought he would drop in and see Mr. Hobson and lord it over him a little, and perhaps tell him how much he had enjoyed the fireworks cigar, but just inside Mr. Hobson's door he stopped, almost overwhelmed by sounds that met his ears.

A woman sat in a chair beside the chief of detectives' desk; and she was wailing and wringing her hands, and Mr. Hobson was saying: "There, there, now, madam, everything will be all right." Other detectives were gathered about her.

Gilbert walked hesitatingly toward the group, and asked one of the detectives what the matter was.

"Kid's been kidnaped," the detective informed him.

"You don't tell me," said Gilbert.

The man turned away from Gilbert with a grunt, and Gilbert went to Mr. Hobson.

"Hello, Hobson," Gilbert said briskly. "What seems to be the trouble?"

The chief of the detective bureau looked up at Gilbert for several seconds as if he did not recognize him. His nostrils trembled a little.

"Were you addressing me?" he asked.

"Sure!" said Gilbert breezily. "What's up? What's doing? A little kidnaping case, eh?"

Mr. Hobson took a long, deep breath. His hands, which had been lying limply on the desk, were now formed into fists, but these gradually relaxed.

"Yes," said Mr. Hobson, "just a little kidnaping case. This lady's baby disappeared from in front of a down town store about three hours ago, and practically every man on the force is on the case. Merely a little kidnaping case, Gilbert—too small a case for a man of your talents to waste his time on, so if you don't mind moving along and giving us a—"

"Of course," said Gilbert modestly, "this sort of thing isn't exactly in my department, but I wonder if I mightn't be of some assistance. I have nothing to do for the next couple of hours."

"You—help?" said Mr. Hobson, looking at him.

"Why not?" Gilbert inquired, stiffening a little.

"Gilbert," said Mr. Hobson sternly, "have you been drinking?"

"Indeed I have not."

"Well, I don't think you ought to take your mind off the big cases it's on, Gilbert. I don't think you ought to bother with such a trifling case as this."

The woman beside him stopped sobbing. "Trifling!" she repeated, having entirely missed Mr. Hobson's fine sarcasm: "Do you consider the kidnaping of my baby a trifling matter? Take him off the big cases he is on, and see if he can find my baby! My poor baby!" and she began to sob hysterically.

"Go ahead, Gilbert," said Mr. Hobson cordially, "and find Mrs. Randall's baby for her. To a man of your talents it ought to be as easy as rolling off a log. The facts in the case are simply these. She parked the baby in his carriage on the sidewalk out in front of the five-and-ten-cent store on the corner of Elm and Myrtle."

"Woodworth's," interrupted Gilbert.

"Brilliant fellow! Yes, Woodworth's. She left the baby there at 1 p.m. approximately. Then she went out another door, to do some shopping in another store. She had the baby on her mind, and she was a little confused. Mrs. Randall hasn't been in Steel

City very long, and she suddenly got panicky or something. Anyhow, with the baby on her mind and all, she got lost; and when she got back to the five-and-ten, the carriage, baby and all, was gone, see?

"She is pretty sure she saw a dark-faced, ragged-looking woman of about forty-five or so pushing a white baby carriage down the street, but she was so distracted, and confused, and so on, that she didn't pay much attention until she got back to the five-and-ten and found her baby missing.

"It looks like a clean-cut case of kidnaping. There aren't any clews to go on, except the dark-faced woman. Every man on the force has been looking for a dark-faced woman pushing a white baby carriage. That happened three hours ago, see?"

"No other clews?" said Gilbert briskly.

"No," said Mr. Hobson in a patient voice, "no other clews, Gilbert. You might go up to the five-and-ten and see if you can find any."

"I was thinking of that," said Gilbert.

"At least eight other men have been up there looking for the same thing, but that doesn't mean anything. A man with your intellect would probably find clews that Flynn himself would overlook."

"Are you kidding me?" asked Gilbert coldly.

"My good heavens, Gilbert, do you think I would try to kid a man of your genius?"

The conversation was interrupted by Mr. Soppel who threw down a copy of the *Evening Bulletin* on Mr. Hobson's desk. A glaring black headline on the front page inquired:

TINY TOT IN CLUTCHES OF FIEND?

And in smaller type under the headline, Gilbert quickly read that nine-months-old Bobbie Randall had been spirited away from in front of the five-and-ten-cent store, and that the police had so far had no success in following any number of clews. Demands of a ransom were expected hourly.

The sensational sheet cried:

> Here is a case to test the wit and genius of the man in the black mask. Police Commissioner Hayes, when questioned, declined to state that the out-of-town detective would be assigned to this baffling case. The masked marvel, he stated, was in seclusion until nightfall, when another sensational raid might be anticipated upon crookdom.

"My Lawd!" said Mr. Hobson.

> At the minute of going to press, the child's father announced that a reward of two thousand dollars would be given for the return of the child unharmed.

The woman was sobbing again, sobbing as if her poor heart would break.

"Oh, do something!" she wailed. "Why don't you do something?"

"Madam," said Mr. Hobson, "we are doing everything in our power. Practically every man on the force is hunting for your child. Don't worry. We'll find him."

"I have decided," Gilbert announced, "to assign myself to this case."

"I don't want you on this case," said Mr. Hobson irritably.

"You have nothing to say about it, Hobson," said Gilbert. "I am the chief of my own department. Tell me, madam, are there any distinguishing marks on this baby carriage?"

"Ask him," the woman sobbed. "I've answered that question a thousand times."

"It is a white carriage," said Mr. Hobson wearily. "And the only difference between this one and the hundreds of other white baby carriages in town is that one of the front wheels is new—the left one, isn't it, madam?"

"Oh—oh—oh—I don't know! I want my baby! My poor baby! My poor little Bobbie!"

"Anyhow," Mr. Hobson went on, "one of the front wheels is

new, and it doesn't match the others. They are white, and this new wheel is a sort of cream. Go right out and find it, Gilbert."

"Thank you, Mr. Hobson," said Gilbert gratefully. "I will do the best I can. You say it was left out in front of the five-and-ten on the corner of Elm and Myrtle."

"That's right, Gilbert. Elm and Myrtle."

"I wonder," said Gilbert, "if there are any bloodhounds in Steel City."

Mr. Hobson made some answer under his breath which Gilbert took to be a negative one. It should be a simple matter, he reasoned, to trail a lost baby with bloodhounds. And his mind went on revolving the various facts in the case. Two thousand dollars. A white baby carriage. One of the front wheels a cream color, the others white. Elm and Myrtle. The corner of Elm and Myrtle.

Gilbert left headquarters, and started in the general direction of Elm and Myrtle. He was concentrating on the problem, his mind so absorbed with it that several people bumped into him, and one man even cursed him picturesquely, but Gilbert did not hear, so preoccupied was he.

A bright red façade suddenly arrested his attention. It was a five-and-ten-cent store, and it occupied a corner. Six or seven baby carriages were lined up along the front of it. Several of them were white, one was blue, and the other one was painted black.

Gilbert went slowly down the line, and on the second white baby carriage his eyes were suddenly riveted. Three of its wheels were white; the fourth, the right hand front wheel, was cream color.

Gilbert looked inside. A child was asleep on the pillow, and it might have been five months or three years old, as far as Gilbert's ability to guess ages was concerned.

Grasping the handle of the carriage, Gilbert wheeled it out of the line, and started pushing it down the sidewalk. He felt rather silly, as most men do on their first adventure as the motive power of a perambulator, and he felt that every one was looking at him. He blushed and his actions were those of an exceedingly self-conscious man. A woman looked at him, then darted a glance at the wheels of the carriage. She turned pale, and suddenly she seemed to reel.

Other people were now staring at him. He was vaguely aware that a small crowd was beginning to follow him. He walked more rapidly. Presently, he was almost running down the sidewalk. Three blocks he traversed at a high rate of speed, then he turned left, and a block in that direction brought him suddenly in front of another red façade. In gold letters on a long sign above the windows he read:

WOODWORTH'S 5 & 10 CENT STORE

Filled with misgivings, Gilbert glanced up at the street sign. He was at the corner of Elm and Myrtle! He had, he hastily realized, taken the carriage from in front of the five-and-ten-cent store on the corner of Main and Maple! The wrong store! The wrong baby! What was he to do?

Suddenly some one, a man, shouted: "That's that kidnaped kid!"

Glancing hastily behind him, Gilbert perceived that a crowd of men and women were walking along briskly behind him.

"Grab that guy!" another man yelled.

"Where's a cop?" a woman shouted.

People appeared from all sides. Gilbert's path was blocked. He thought rapidly. He must let them know that he was a member of the police force.

A man grabbed his elbows.

"Hold on there, you!" the man panted.

"Let me go!" Gilbert cried. "I'm on the police force!"

"The hell you are!"

"The hell—I am!"

"Show me your badge!"

In a twinkling, Gilbert snatched the black mask from his

pocket. Without pausing in his stride, he clapped on the black mask.

A muttering roar went up from the crowd. And the word sped swiftly.

"The man in the black mask!"

Suddenly the jam was so thick about him that Gilbert could not move. Then he caught the gleam of brass buttons, and heard loud voices. Three policemen fought their way through the pack to his side.

One of them stared at him and saluted.

"Clear me a way through this crowd!" Gilbert panted. "I've got the Randall kid!"

"You bet we will!" one of the policemen snapped, and he roared: "Clear a way, there! Stand aside! Move along! This ain't no side show!"

And through a wide lane suddenly formed, Gilbert pushed the carriage. The baby was now awake. He was sitting up, laughing and waving his hands at the babbling bystanders, quite as if he were a prince royal being gazed upon by his loyal subjects.

Gilbert, full of doubts, bent over the hood of the carriage as he strode along, and demanded:

"Hey, kid, is your name Bobbie Randall?"

The child turned its head and looked up at him, its pink mouth full of bubbles and laughter.

"Blah!" said the child.

"My Lord!" said Gilbert. "With all this commotion, supposing it isn't the right one? It isn't the right one! It can't be the right one!"

The tiny unknown, fascinated by the black mask, was laughing up at him, clapping its chubby little hands.

"Oh, my Lord!" Gilbert groaned.

The man in the black mask, pushing the perambulator, finally reached headquarters. There was a cheering procession, a block and a half long, trailing it by that time. Many hands seized the carriage at the foot of headquarters' steps, and it was passed along to the corridor. Policemen, rapidly assembling, held the crowd back.

Gilbert, clutching the handle, pushed the perambulator down the corridor to Room 112. Fifteen policemen and detectives tried to open the door for him. Eventually he was inside. He saw Mrs. Randall leap up and come stumbling down the long room toward him. His heart was beating frantically.

"Madam, is th-th-this your ch-ch-child?" he stuttered.

But the question was needless. Mrs. Randall had seized the child in her arms and was straining it to her bosom, covering it with tears and kisses, laughing and crying.

Then she looked up and saw the man in the black mask. She uttered a faint cry.

"How—how—where—?" she gasped.

Gilbert lifted his hand.

"Madam," he said quietly, "I never reveal my methods."

Mr. Hobson was looking over her head at Gilbert. His face was working, and it was very pink, almost purple, in fact.

"Clear out of this room, all you guys," he roared. And when the room was emptied of all but himself, Gilbert, the joyous mother, and her new-found darling, Mr. Hobson said:

"Gilbert, I can guess what happened. I guessed it just about ten minutes after you started out. You are wonderful, Gilbert. No kidding, you are absolutely marvelous. If it was raining hot dogs, Gilbert, you would be caught out in it with a dozen rolls in one hand, and a jar of mustard in the other!"

CHAPTER XXI

TRACING HIS SWEETHEART

OF COURSE, THE papers made the most of it. The kidnaped child had furnished one sensation. The man in the black mask had, by his mysterious and startling rounding up of twelve dangerous criminals, furnished another. The morning papers had been full of his exploit. The afternoon papers had been full of the mysterious kidnaping. And the evening papers were full of the kidnaped child, and the man in the black mask.

Gilbert, under orders from the police commissioner, was hidden away in a reading room on the top floor at headquarters, where no prying reporter could find him. The commissioner gave the story to the newspaper men. And what a story it was!

The masked marvel, Mr. Hayes told the reporters, had been assigned to the kidnaping mystery late in the afternoon. With his unique ability to make miraculous deductions, he had secured the missing child within fifteen minutes. Where he found the child, Mr. Hayes refused to state. The methods employed by the man in the black mask were brilliant, but mysterious, and they were going to remain a mystery.

"The promptness with which our detective of the black mask," said Mr. Hayes, "found the child can be taken as an illustration of the quickness with which the evildoers of Steel City are to be brought to the bar of justice. We are sick and tired of the criminals in this town, and with the aid of our expert in the black mask, who is working in conjunction with myself, we expect in a short time to make Steel City a spotless town. 'War on the criminals!' is our slogan."

And while the presses of the city were grinding out this thrilling account, Mr. Hayes was closeted with Gilbert in the reading room upstairs.

"Every reporter in town is fairly itching to interview you," the commissioner told Gilbert, "and if one of them once gets you in his clutches, our goose is cooked. You shouldn't have put on that mask this afternoon, Gilbert, but luck was with you; a reporter wasn't in the crowd, and the descriptions of you that the crowd have given to the papers make you out to be tall, short, stout, thin, old, young, beardless, bearded, with mustache, without mustache. It is just what I want people to be saying. It makes you a phantom. You exist, and you don't exist. It was an extraordinary piece of luck. I think the time is ripe for a real killing."

"Are we going to visit the dives to-night?" Gilbert asked.

"We are. But you are not to leave this room until I give you the word. By the way, here is a check drawn to bearer for two thousand dollars. It is from the father of the Randall brat. It is yours, Gilbert."

"Thank you," said Gilbert, folding up the check and stowing it away.

"And now," said the commissioner, "I would like to know just how you found that Randall kid when every man on the force had been looking for him for three solid hours."

"I do not," said Gilbert, "reveal my methods."

"All right, Gilbert, keep those big, scientific secrets to yourself, but for Heaven's sake, don't reveal your identity. That's all I ask. I am going to have your dinner sent in to you. You will stay here until about ten o'clock. Then we are going to stage a little raid."

"I wonder," said Gilbert, "if I can have a talk with Mr. Bayliss."

"Of course you can, Gilbert. I'll send him right up."

Mr. Bayliss, who had charge of the Rogues' Gallery, was the

only man Gilbert had so far met on the force whose interest could by any stretch of the imagination be described as kindly. And Gilbert was sorely in need of a friend. In spite of his brilliant success as a detective, he hadn't the slightest idea of how to go about finding Annie May, and if he did not find her, he would soon lose his appetite, and that would be disastrous.

His dinner, which came in a few minutes before Mr. Bayliss did, consisted of a large pot of soup, a fish course, a thick sirloin steak, French fried potatoes, spinach, carrots, peas, hearts of lettuce salad, and a segment of coconut custard pie. Gilbert ate nothing but the soup, the fish, the steak, the potatoes, the salad, and the pie. At this rate he would soon begin to lose weight.

Mr. Bayliss came in with a question in his eyes, and Gilbert plunged at once into the heart of his problem.

"Mr. Bayliss," he said, "you have been on the force for a good many years, and you know how things are done. Well, I'm up against a kind of difficulty. My girl—I mean, the girl I am going to marry if she will have me, came to Steel City a few days ago, and she hasn't been heard of since. I know what happens to pretty, innocent girls from the country when they hit a big town like Steel City. I know she's just been swallowed up. I mean, I know that finding her means combing through every dive in town."

"How do you know that?" Mr. Bayliss wanted to know.

"Why, I—I deduced it."

"Oh, you deduced it. How do you know she hasn't been hurt and isn't in some hospital?"

"Because she would have had the hospital authorities notify her folks, Mr. Bayliss. What I want to know is, how do you go about looking for a person when they are lost like that?"

"Well, how did you go about looking for the Randall kid?"

"That was different," said Gilbert. "I want your expert advice."

"Well," said. Mr. Bayliss, "it oughtn't to be so hard to find a girl in a town no larger than this. If you walked the streets long enough, you would be almost bound to bump into her sooner or later by the law of averages. What sort of a looking girl is she?"

"Well, she wears a pink dress, Mr. Bayliss."

"Do you think she would wear a pink dress, coming to Steel City? Wouldn't she be more apt to wear a suit or something like that?"

"I hadn't thought of that," Gilbert admitted.

"That isn't so very important, anyhow," said Mr. Bayliss. "Supposing you describe her. What does she look like?"

"Well, she's terribly pretty. She's the prettiest girl in Maple Hollow. She's the prettiest girl I ever saw in my life. Honest, Mr. Bayliss, when I think of her and her face comes up before me, like it's doing now, I sort of hurt—she's so pretty."

"You can see her face pretty clearly, can you?"

"Oh, yes."

"All right. Supposing you describe it for me. What color eyes has she got?"

Gilbert pondered.

"Are they blue?" Mr. Bayliss prompted him.

"Gee—" Gilbert faltered.

"Or are they brown?"

"Gosh darn it, I don't seem to remember. Are they blue or are they brown, now? That's important, isn't it?"

"Well, we've got to know what she looks like, Gilbert. What sort of hair has she got? Is it brown, or light?"

Gilbert frowned. "Gee, Mr. Bayliss, you've got me there. Is it dark, or is it light? It seems to me it's dark, and then again it seems to me it's blond."

"Does she wear it long, or is it bobbed?"

"Why, she wears it—let me think. Dog-gone it, I've looked at her hair a million times. I think it's long. No; I think it's bobbed. No—wait a minute. Gee whiz, I don't remember."

"But we've got to have something to go on, Gilbert. How tall is she?"

"Oh, she's—" Gilbert began, and faltered. Only a few days ago she had told him her height, and her weight. If his memory had only served him, Gilbert would have recalled that Annie May's height was five feet one inch, and that her weight was one hundred and two pounds. But his memory was faithless to Gilbert.

"She's sort of kind of tall," he expressed himself.

"Say about five feet seven?"

"Oh, she's taller than that. That isn't tall. Why, she must be around five feet nine. Let's see. I'm six foot two. Yeah; she's just about five feet nine or maybe ten."

"Is she thin or stout?"

"She's kind of plump."

"Well, that gives us something to work on. She's about five feet ten, and rather plump. That would put her weight at, let's say, a hundred and forty. No, fifty. A hundred and fifty pounds. And you aren't sure about her hair, or her eyes?"

"No," said Gilbert.

"I'll tell you what let's do, Gilbert. Tomorrow morning, if things aren't too busy, we'll take a walk, and you can pick out a girl who looks like your girl. That's always a big help. Maybe we'll stumble on your girl."

"I hope we do," said Gilbert. "I know it sounds like a foolish thing to say, but, honest, Mr. Bayliss, I love that girl so much I just can't get the picture of her out of my mind a minute!"

"It ought to be easy finding her," said Mr. Bayliss dryly, "seeing her so clear as you do."

While this conversation was taking place, one a little more spirited was occurring in the commissioner's office. At least, one end of it was. He was talking into the telephone, and at the other end of the wire sat Mrs. Silas Bainbridge, who was the acknowledged society leader of Steel City.

"You have no doubt read in the papers, Mr. Hayes," the wife of the steel magnate was saying, "that I am giving a mask ball Saturday evening. A great many priceless jewels will be worn, and I do hope you can spare a man who will come in some fitting disguise and watch things."

"That can be arranged easily, Mrs. Bainbridge," Mr. Hayes answered. He was afraid of Mrs. Bainbridge. Her husband, one of the richest men in Steel City, could make or break a police commissioner with a snap of the finger.

"I was wondering," the lady went on in her velvety, ingratiating voice, "if you couldn't spare me the man in the black mask. He would be so thrillingly appropriate."

"I am extremely sorry," said Mr. Hayes, "but I am afraid it is quite impossible to grant that request, Mrs. Bainbridge. As you've no doubt read in the papers," he said with sly malice, "the man in the black mask engages his attention only upon the most dangerous of our mysteries."

"But finding a kidnaped child was not so dangerous!" she illogically protested.

"That, madam, was nothing but a stunt. We turned him loose on that case simply for publicity—to prove to the criminal element how readily he can ferret his way through any mystery. To-night and Saturday—and this is *entre nous*, Mrs. Bainbridges—he is planning to execute a raid on the crooks even more brilliant than his coup of last night. He is an extremely important person, Mrs. Bainbridge."

"I understand that perfectly," said Mrs. Bainbridge, and her tone was a little less velvety and a little less ingratiating. "There will be a number of extremely important persons at this ball I am giving Saturday. He will not have to stay long—just as short a time as he wishes. The unmasking will take place at midnight—twelve sharp—and I had thought it would be thrilling and amusing for my guests to have the masked detective present. He will, of course, not be required to unmask. I am sure you won't disappoint me."

Mr. Hayes did some rapid thinking. He was afraid to risk Gilbert out of his sight.

"I don't like to disappoint you," was his answer, "but our great risk is that his identity will be revealed. The whole purpose of this scheme will be lost if he is again seen in public. We ran a great risk this afternoon when he appeared, first unmasked, then masked. We were taking a great risk, but it was necessary."

"This is equally necessary," Mrs. Bainbridge said firmly.

The police commissioner was perspiring.

"Perhaps," he said, "I can spare him for a little while—say a half hour. From eleven thirty to midnight. Will that do?"

"It will do nicely—very nicely. Thank you *so* much, Mr. Hayes. I was sure you wouldn't fail me."

"Not at all. It really gives me the greatest pleasure," said Mr. Hayes sweetly into the mouthpiece, whereupon he hung up the receiver, threw a telephone directory across the room, and cried shrilly: "Damn her hide!"

The door burst open. Mr. Soppel came trotting in. He was out of breath. He panted. He was purple with some recent violent exertion.

"Commissioner," he gasped.

"Spout it, Soppel, spout it!"

"Just been tryin' to plug in on your line, commissioner!" the detective panted, "Line was busy. Cal just came in from the Third District. Four men went into the office of the Barlow Mill, stuck up the cashier; got to-morrow's pay roll! Officer Harlinger chased 'em. They ran down into Mop's. He fol-followed 'em in.

"There was nearly a hundred people in there, eatin'. These birds are down there, but Harlinger didn't see 'em close enough to identify 'em, and you know how easy it is to get that gang to spill the beans."

"Wait a minute!" snapped the commissioner. "What was the Barlow Mill office doing open this time of night? It's almost seven o'clock."

"Makin' up the pay roll for to-morrow, commissioner. Hobson told me to run up and tell you. He's on the way out there now to surround the place, and says he'll keep anybody from goin' in or comin' out. But how in Sam Hill are we going to find out who those four are?"

Mr. Hayes drew a deep breath.

"Get Gilbert!" he snapped.

CHAPTER XXII

SAFE FOR A WHILE

WHEN GILBERT ENTERED the commissioner's office, Mr. Hayes was hurriedly loading two revolvers. He was loading them with blank cartridges. "Yes, sir?" said Gilbert affably, "Mr. Soppel said you required my services, Mr. Hayes. If there is anything I can do, I will gladly render any assistance that is in my power."

Mr. Hayes finished loading the revolvers. He thrust them, butts forward, at Gilbert.

"Shove these into your hip pockets," he snapped. "They're loaded with blanks. Open that door and lead the way down the hall."

Gilbert leisurely dropped the revolvers into his hip pockets, and leisurely started down the hall. He had taken only a few steps when a pain shot through him in the rear. He indignantly turned.

"Did you kick me?" he demanded.

"I did kick you!" the commissioner snarled. "Do you think we are going to a funeral? Will you kindly show some signs of life, Gilbert?" Run! Don't walk! Run to the nearest exit. Have you got your mask?"

"Yes, sir!" Gilbert bleated. And ran.

At the foot of the steps, the commissioner's black Marmon roadster was waiting. He seized Gilbert by the arm, and the two men ran down the steps.

"Are we going to a dive?" Gilbert feebly inquired.

"We are going to a dive called Mop's," the commissioner explained as he stepped on the starter. "I will tell you what you are to do as we drive along." The roadster seemed to leap. "You are to go into Mop's with your mask on. Upward of a hundred people are eating there."

"Is—is it the sort of place where a ruined girl might be taken?" Gilbert interrupted.

"Will you kindly keep what we laughingly call your mind upon what I am saying?" the commissioner snarled. "You are to go into Mop's with your mask on. You are to draw both guns and cry out: 'You four who just came from Barlow's Mill—stick 'em up! I'm going to count three and begin shooting!' And if four men don't stand up, you are to begin shooting. Get me?"

"But why should I start shooting?"

"Will you kindly do what I tell you?"

"Sure, I will do it gladly, Mr. Hayes. But it seems pretty mysterious to me."

"Oh, does it?" said Mr. Hayes.

"Yes, it does," said Gilbert with spirit. "It seems a mighty queer thing to do, if you want my opinion of it."

"I don't," said the commissioner, and the Marmon roadster rushed around a corner, almost knocking a man down.

"Well, all this is contrary to my methods, Mr. Hayes," said Gilbert. "I have a certain way of going about these arrests and so on, and I have to have the situation well in mind before I can do my stuff. Kindly explain everything to me, or I am afraid that I must refuse to help you, Mr. Hayes."

"Oh, my suffering aunt!" moaned the commissioner. "Very well, Gilbert. These four men just held up the pay roll clerk at Barlow's Steel Mill, and they got into Mop's before the officer who saw them could identify them. They are in there now, do you understand?"

"I don't see why you have to call in anybody whose time is as valuable as mine on a case as simple as that," said Gilbert. "Why can't a few ordinary detectives go in there and make everybody hold their hands up. It isn't much of a job to search a hundred people, and the ones who have the pay roll on them will be the ones you are after."

"It evidently hasn't occurred to you, Gilbert," the commissioner patiently explained, "that, in going over fences and through back yards, these holdup men could have easily cached their loot, and that it would no longer be on their persons. If you had just executed a holdup, and ran into a public place, don't you think such a thought would have occurred to you?"

"Well," said Gilbert, "that is a matter I would like to give some thought to, Mr. Hayes. These arrests I make and so on I always like to plan out very carefully beforehand."

"Gilbert, I don't want you to tire your poor mind so. If you will simply follow my instructions, although I will grant that they are not nearly as brilliant as the instructions you would give if you had plenty of time, I am sure we will get good results. Now here we are. Hop out. Put on that mask! Get your guns ready!"

In a daze, Gilbert climbed out of the roadster. It had stopped on a dark street on both sides of which were brick houses, common to all the streets of that section. Rather bewilderedly, Gilbert put his mask on and adjusted it; then he removed the two revolvers from his hip pockets.

Dazedly, he perceived that elaborate preparations had been made for this raid. Across the street, uniformed policemen were loitering under the trees. A group of men—all detectives—were lounging about near the doorway. And if he had looked up, he would have seen several uniform caps protruding over the edge of the roof. Every avenue of escape was cut off. And, some distance down the street, two patrol wagons were parked.

At a shove from Mr. Hayes, the *prima donna,* that is to say, Gilbert, stepped upon an elaborately set stage. He strode through the door that was suddenly opened for him, and he found himself in a dimly lit place, smelling heavily of garlic and cooking food, of saffron and acidy wine.

The low-ceilinged restaurant was crowded. Every table was full. Every eye in the place was upon that door when Gilbert, black-masked, strode in; and it is safe to say that every face in the room paled.

He lifted the revolvers and cried:

"You four who just came from Barlow's Mill—stick 'em up! You're under arrest! I know who you are. I'm going to count three and begin shooting, and when I shoot I shoot to kill. One—"

Mop's was suddenly filled with an excited babbling.

"Two!" Gilbert shouted.

At a table not ten feet away from Gilbert a man turned and aimed at Gilbert a huge square black box, on the front of which a large lens glittered. Across the table another man lifted above his head a queer, spidery apparatus. From a slender trough at its uppermost extremity there suddenly leaped a blinding magnesium glare. A mushroom of soft white smoke bounced upward to the ceiling and clung tenuously to the lighting fixtures.

Gilbert did not flinch. He knew the newspaper men had taken a flash light photograph of him: but he did not mind.

"Three!" he roared.

Each revolver blazed once.

In the rear of the restaurant four men sprang to their feet with hands reaching toward the ceiling.

"Don't shoot!" one of them cried. "We give up!"

The quartet shambled toward him, their faces white, their eyes rolling with terror. One of them was muttering:

"Didn't I tell ya this guy would nail us sure? Whyinell didn't ya take my word for it, ya flatheads, and pull outa this lousy town while the pullin' was good?"

Commissioner Hayes was standing beside Gilbert. Four detectives were ranged behind him, all with guns drawn, and behind them policemen were massed.

"Well," said Gilbert modestly, "I got them, Mr. Hayes."

"When," Mr. Hobson muttered under his breath, "are you going to reveal your methods, Gilbert? How you pull off these brilliant, masterful coups is a big mystery to us plain, ordinary, low-brow detectives. Hold 'em up there by your ears, you saps!"

A young man with penetrating gray eyes had risen from the table where the news photographer sat. It was Fogarty of the *Star*. He strode, almost ran, to where Gilbert and the commissioner stood, and he seized Gilbert's right hand.

"At last!" said Fogarty.

"Come out of this!" hissed Commissioner Hayes into Gilbert's nearest ear.

But Gilbert stood his ground. He was not in the least opposed to publicity—the right kind of publicity.

"We know, sir," said Fogarty rapidly, "that you are one of the world's great detectives, and the newspaper reading public is demanding to know who you are."

"I cannot tell you," said Gilbert brusquely.

Fogarty was staring at him, trying to read the secret that lay behind the black mask. There was a puzzled look in the reporter's eyes.

"I've seen you somewhere before," he said.

Gilbert coldly smiled. He had recognized in Fogarty the reporter who had written that cruel account of his arrest of Carter, the flannel-money king, for the *Star*.

"Where could it have been?" said Gilbert.

"Are you one of the Pinkertons?" asked Fogarty.

Gilbert shook his head.

"Are—are you Sir Basil Thompson, of Scotland Yard?"

"No," said Gilbert, still smiling that cold smile.

"Are you William J. Flynn?"

"Nope; I'm not Flynn."

"Not Goron, of Paris!"

"Nope."

"Who, then, are you, sir?"

"Well," said Gilbert affably, "I guess the time is ripe for telling you who I am."

"The reading public is getting quite nasty about it." Fogarty pointed out. "They insist on knowing."

At that moment several burly detectives shoved their way between Gilbert and Fogarty. Gilbert did not realize that this was a human wedge designed to pry him loose from reporters and publicity. He was turned about by the pressing men so that he faced another quarter of the long, low room.

His roving eyes fell upon a distant spot of pink. It was surmounted by the face of a girl. A girl in pink! Annie May wore pink. The smoke from the flash light and the blank cartridges had formed a thin fog through which he saw her face dimly, but his ready imagination supplied the girl with the familiar features of his dearest beloved. Here, in a low dive, he had found her!

"Annie May!" he shouted.

The press about him thickened. He was now hemmed in on all sides, quite as much a prisoner as those four desperadoes he had captured.

A hand was inserted roughly between the back of his neck and his collar band. With sickening speed he was jerked backward by this invisible hand and ignominiously hauled out upon the sidewalk. He gasped and almost strangled.

He was hauled across a grass plot like a bag of beans. Some one lifted him and thrust him roughly into an automobile, and by the time he had caught his breath the car was racing through the night, and his blurred eyes presently made out the foxy profile of Police Commissioner Hayes.

Back in Mop's, Fogarty was likewise caught in a ring of detectives. Mr. Hobson was soothing him.

"Where did he go?" Fogarty demanded.

"He's got another job on," Hobson said. "And the commissioner and he just beat it, Fogarty."

"Hell!" said Fogarty. "What was that he yelled just before he left? Wasn't it 'Annie May?' Who in the devil is Annie May?"

"Naw," said Hobson. "He was just yelling at you, and what he said was 'Any day.' He meant any day would do for you to interview him."

"I know I've seen him somewhere before," said Fogarty.

"Your guess about Sir Basil Thompson, of Scotland Yard, wasn't so bad," said Hobson. "Keep on guessing, Fogarty."

And in the roadster Gilbert was so angry that tears smarted in his eyes.

"Look here," he growled, "what was the idea of jerking me out of there that way? How do you get that way, anyway? I want to go back to that place."

"Gilbert," said the commissioner gently, quite as if he had not recently subjected Gilbert to a humiliating indignity, and quite as if Gilbert had not spoken, "I consider this the most brilliant arrest you have made so far."

"But why did you grab me away like that?" Gilbert wailed. "I want to go back. Dog-gone it, that girl I'm looking for was—"

"Gilbert, you were on the verge of disobeying orders. Your entire success as the man in the black mask depends upon your remaining unknown. You were spilling the beans, Gilbert, and it was necessary to employ stern measures."

"But that girl in the pink—"

"Gilbert, we have no time to think of love when we are conducting a raid."

"But I wasn't going to spill any beans," Gilbert moaned. "I was only going to kid him along, to get back at him a little bit for the way he kidded me when he wrote up my arrest of Carter."

"I think you'd better leave all the kidding to me," said Mr. Hayes. "Now I want you to promise me that you won't say a word to another reporter without permission from me."

"All right," said Gilbert. "I won't say a thing to the reporters, but I am going back there and look for that girl."

The roadster had pulled up before the steps at headquarters.

"I am going to assign a man," said Mr. Hayes, "to guard you from reporters, girls in pink dresses, and other dangerous influences."

"But," Gilbert protested as they mounted the steps and entered the dingy old building, "I don't need a guard."

"I don't think you realize, Gilbert, that literally dozens of trigger fingers in the underworld are itching for a chance at you. They are in deathly fear of you, and it is the way of criminals to destroy the thing they fear."

"I'm not afraid," said Gilbert.

"I am," said Mr. Hayes. "And I don't think you understand how vitally important you have become to me and to the force, Gilbert. Walk down this way with me. I want to see the warden a moment."

They were approaching the "vestibule of sighs," a cubicle with double doors at either end, which connected headquarters with the Steel City jail.

"I want to go back to Mop's," said Gilbert.

Mr. Hayes said nothing for a moment; then:

"Have you ever been through the jail, Gilbert?"

"No, sir," said Gilbert, "and I'm really not very much interested in seeing it. I want to get back to Mop's and see if that girl is the one I'm looking for."

Mr. Hayes urged him through the vestibule of sighs. Beyond it was a corridor, and on both sides of the corridor were steel bars.

A warden met them.

"I want this young man to see that new bank of solitary confinement cells," said Mr. Hayes.

"I haven't time," Gilbert panted. "I want to get back to Mop's and see if that girl in the pink dress—"

But quite as if Gilbert were not speaking at all Mr. Hayes

was pushing him gently along, one hand on Gilbert's elbow, toward a steel stairway.

"I want you to see where we keep the dangerous criminals you capture, Gilbert. These are new cells, and they are absolutely the last word in cells. We keep only the most dangerous men in them. They are padded and sound-proof, and they would defy the jail-breaking genius of a Dutch Anderson or a Gerald Chapman. This way, Gilbert."

Sullen faces peered out at them as the three men walked down the corridor toward a cluster of bright new cells.

But Gilbert's mind was not on bright new cells. He wondered if he hadn't better break away and run. That glimpse of the girl in the pink dress had made his heart beat frantically, and now he felt almost sick. Every minute was vital.

"Mr. Hayes—" he began desperately.

"Now, here," said Mr. Hayes, "is one of the cells. I want you to look it over carefully, Gilbert. See how nice and clean it is? And you will note that the walls are padded, in case a prisoner might get desperate and start throwing himself around. So many prisoners hang themselves that we have taken every precaution against things of that kind. Wouldn't you think that cot would be comfortable to sleep on? Go on in and take a look, Gilbert."

"Really, Mr. Hayes, I'm not especially interested—"

Mr. Hayes gave him a push, and Gilbert found himself inside the cell. Then the door slammed upon him.

"Hey!" said Gilbert.

There was a sort of shutter in the steel door, and through the shutter he saw Mr. Hayes's foxy face.

"It's all right, Gilbert."

"Let me out!" Gilbert wailed.

"Gilbert, please listen to me. I have decided that the time is ripe for you to disappear for a little while."

"But I've got to go back to Mop's!" Gilbert wailed.

"Not to-night, Gilbert. I want you to be well protected, and—"

"Look here!" Gilbert protested, and he choked back a sob. "I think this is a pretty rotten way to treat a fellow, after all I've done for your police force."

"I'll do anything within reason for you, Gilbert, but you must stay in this cell to-night. No other place in Steel City is safe for you to-night."

Gilbert thought rapidly.

"All right," he said. "Go up to Mop's, and bring that girl in the pink dress down here. She's sitting on the left side as you go in. She's wearing a pink dress, and she's got dark hair."

"I'll bring her," said Mr. Hayes.

Mr. Hayes left, and Gilbert sank down on the edge of the cot with his head clasped in his hands. Hot tears burned in his eyes. He supposed that this was the commissioner's idea of a practical joke.

"Oh, my Lord!" Gilbert groaned. "Why did I ever leave Maple Hollow?"

And he fell to thinking of the pleasant life he had led in that sleepy old town, What a fool he had been to leave!

A clinking at the door presently caused him to look up. The shutter opened, and he leaped up. Through the blur in his eyes he saw a girl standing in the corridor—a girl in a pink dress. On one side of her stood Mr. Hayes, and on the other stood Mr. Hobson.

The girl was pale with fright, but she was not Annie May. Nothing about her resembled Annie May except the pinkness of the dress. She had a thin, mean mouth, and shifty eyes. She was not even pretty.

"Can you see her?" Mr. Hayes wanted to know.

"Yes," said Gilbert faintly.

The girl seemed to reel.

"I know that voice!" she cried huskily. "It's the man in the black mask!"

"Is this the girl?" asked Mr. Hayes.

"Listen!" cried the girl. "I give up! I admit it! I swiped all that stuff! You'll find it all stowed away in my room! You don't hafta give me no third degree. Fer the Lawd's sake, don't put me through that!"

"Well," said the foxy commissioner, "if you want to come through clean, I guess we won't have to."

"He knows what I been doin'," the girl snarled, flinging a jeweled hand toward the padded cell.

"Sure he does," Mr. Hobson said soothingly; "but we want it in your own words, girly."

She hung her head sullenly. "I beat it outa New York because every department store in town was wise to me. I thought it was goin' to be easy pickin's here. He knows who I am. I'm Maggie More."

Mr. Hobson uttered a muffled exclamation. So did Mr. Hayes. Then he called the warden.

"Lock this girl up," said the commissioner, and he came to the shutter behind which was Gilbert's pale, unhappy face.

"Gilbert," he said, "this is one of the cleverest arrests you have made so far. Do you know who this girl is? She's Maggie More, and in the underworld she's known as the Queen of the Shop-lifters. We've been looking for the shoplifter for months who's been looting the big department stores. We've got her, thanks to you, Gilbert."

"Now will you let me out?" Gilbert whimpered.

"I'm sorry, Gilbert, but we can't—not yet. You stay here and think. I want you to think things over very thoroughly. Saturday night you are going to the mask ball that Mrs. Silas Bainbridge is giving. Now get a good night's sleep and bring all your facul-ties to bear on the ball. You can have anything you want within reason. Is there anything I can have sent up for you?"

"Well," said Gilbert, "if it isn't too much trouble, I'd like another piece of that coconut pie I had for supper."

"You shall have your pie," the commissioner promised.

"Thinking always makes me hungry," Gilbert explained.

When Mr. Hayes had left, Mr. Hobson came over and looked through at Gilbert.

"Honest, Gilbert," he said, "you are wonderful. I am not kidding you. You are just marvelous. The more I see of you, and the more I see of your arrests, the more marvelous I am sure you are. If it was raining silk socks, and you got caught out in it, you would turn into a centipede."

CHAPTER XXIII

MORE MURDERERS!

GILBERT THREW HIMSELF down on the cot with a sob. He wanted Annie May. Maggie More, Queen of the Shoplifters, did not interest him in the slightest. Somewhere in this awful city was the girl he loved, and if he did not find her soon he would die. Without Annie May life would not be endurable. Where, oh, where was Annie May Prine?

A warden brought him a large piece of coconut-custard pie, and Gilbert, sitting on the edge of his cot in the padded cell, slowly devoured it. Presently he lay back, and soon he was asleep and dreaming that he was once again a simple lifeguard on Maple Hollow Beach.

When he awoke, sunlight was streaming in past the thick steel bars of the little window set close to the ceiling. The first object on which his gaze fell was a newspaper. It was lying flat on the floor. Some time while he slept his cell door had been opened, and the newspaper had been tossed inside.

He picked it up, and was startled by a large photograph which seemed to leap out at him from the center of the front page. It was the photograph of a man with a black mask on. In his hands were two revolvers. There was something sinister, something frightening, in the photograph. Above it in brilliant black type streamed the headline:

MASKED MASTER MIND
MOPS UP MORE MURDERERS!

And underneath that, in smaller black type, was the statement:

Four Pay Roll Bandits and Queen of Shoplifters Netted in Raid Last Night. Two Bandits Are Murderers Wanted in Eastern Cities—*Star* Reporter Obtains Exclusive Interview With Man in Black Mask—*Star* Photographer Secures Exclusive Photograph of Masked Marvel in Low Dive at Moment of Making Arrest.

Below that bank of black type was still another bank, set in somewhat smaller-sized type:

Supernatural Qualities Hinted at in Methods of Master Mind. Refuses to Divulge Identity but Admits He is Not Member of Steel City Force. Smiles When Asked If He is Sir Basil Thompson of Scotland Yard, Wm. J. Flynn of New York, or Goron, The Great Parisian Crime Hound.

Then came Fogarty's article:

There is absolutely no question but that the unknown genius who is working in collaboration with Commissioner of Police Reynold D. Hayes to rid Steel City of its criminals is succeeding in a most brilliant fashion.

Last night at eight seventeen the pay roll clerk of the Barlow Steel Mill was held up at the point of revolvers by four men, who seized the twelve thousand dollar pay roll and vanished. It was reported to the police that they had gone to Mop's, a notorious dive on Broom Street. At eight thirty photographers and a reporter from the *Star* seated themselves at a table near the door. Three minutes later, Commissioner Hayes and the unknown genius in the black mask entered the dive.

Pointing his two pistols directly at the table at which the four bandits were seated, the man in the mask called on them to surrender or he would begin shooting at the count of three. At the count of three the bandits leaped to their feet, and surrendered.

They were promptly seized by police and detectives, and manacled.

It was at this juncture that the reporter from the *Star* obtained the only interview that has so far been secured with the Man in the Black Mask—the detective genius who is so swiftly wiping Steel City clean of its criminal element.

The man in the black mask appears young. He is brown of skin, and the eyes shining through the slits in the mask were of a clear, deep blue, and they were blazing with almost religious fervor. To rid the world of its criminals is this man's passion to which he has dedicated himself religiously.

The *Star* reporter shook hands with the masked genius. He speaks brusquely, but pleasantly. He refused to reveal his identity, and smiled when asked if he might be either Sir Basil Thompson, of Scotland Yard, William J. Flynn, of New York, or Goron, the great French criminologist.

At the point, perhaps, of revealing his identity, he was whisked away by Police Commissioner Hayes, and all attempts at finding him have been in vain.

Certainly, the man in the mask has struck terror into the heart of Steel City's criminal element. He seems possessed of a sixth sense. It is doubtful if he was aware, last night, of the identity of the four pay roll bandits before he captured them. Yet, when he strode into Mop's to make the arrest, he leveled his revolvers at the four without an instant's hesitation.

No wonder the criminals of this city are trembling in their shoes!

A brilliant example of his almost clairvoyant powers was given shortly after the arrest of the four bandits, when Commissioner Hayes and Chief of Detectives Hobson, acting under orders of the Masked Master Mind, later visited the Mop's and arrested Maggie More, the most notorious shoplifter in this country.

The woman was seated at a table in the rear of the restaurant. The man in the mask only glanced briefly in her direction. Fifteen minutes later, she was behind bars. Has the masked marvel a sixth sense that enables him to divine the presence of a criminal?

"Have I"?" said Gilbert, as he read, with glistening eyes, the account of his last night's triumph. After reading Fogarty's account he felt a great deal better.

Mr. Hayes paid him a call while he was eating his breakfast, and brought in the other morning newspapers, and some additional information which appeared in no newspaper.

"Gilbert," said Mr. Hayes, "we have got them on the run. I have been getting reports from every police district, and the number of people who moved out of this town between midnight last night and six o'clock this morning would take your breath away. You have got them buffaloed, Gilbert. I take off my hat to you."

"All I want," said Gilbert, "is to get out of this cell. I want to go home. I don't want to be a detective any more. I'm fed up with your police force."

The commissioner regarded him thoughtfully.

"There is a brilliant career ahead of you, Gilbert."

"I don't want a brilliant career. I want to find my girl, and go home. I want to get out of this dog-goned cell. How much longer are you going to keep me locked up in here?"

"Gilbert, I am sorry that you have to be made a martyr to this cause, but there is no way out of it. Your presence terrified criminals, but your absence is going to horrify them.

"What I am doing, Gilbert, is taking advantage of the weak link in every criminal's make-up. They are in deathly fear of the unknown, and you personify the unknown. You seem to have supernatural powers. They commit a crime, and you reach out of nothingness and grab them. I don't think there's a criminal left in Steel City this morning."

"I don't care if there is or if there isn't," said Gilbert. "I've done a lot for you; now you do something for me. I want to get out of here and look for my girl. Please let me look for my girl. Gee whiz, Mr. Hayes, I'll die if anything happens to her, and I'll promise not to say anything to a reporter or tell anybody who I am."

Mr. Hayes looked at him dubiously.

"If I let you go, Gilbert, somebody will have to accompany you."

"All right," said Gilbert eagerly. "Let Mr. Bayliss watch me."

Mr. Hayes opened the door, and Gilbert stepped out.

"There won't be any work for you to do until the mask ball at Mrs. Silas Bainbridge's on Saturday night. Keep away from headquarters, Gilbert, but call me up every night around six, in case I should need you. Between now and Saturday go to some tailor's and have a dress suit made. Drossberg's is the best tailor in town. I will phone him and have the dress suit charged to me."

Gilbert left headquarters with Mr. Bayliss, and that was the beginning of the interrupted search for Annie May. They tramped the streets all that day and all the next. They visited every store in town, following Mr. Bayliss's suggestion that she might have found employment in some such place.

In the evenings they hung around the lobbies of motion-picture theaters. Several girls they saw who, Gilbert insisted, resembled Annie May. Some of them were tall and slim; some were short and plump; others were blondes, and still others were brunettes—and each of them wore a pink dress.

Some days Gilbert was certain that Annie May was tall and slender and fair, and on other days he was as certain that his sweetheart was short and plump and dark. He was not of much assistance to Mr. Bayliss.

On the day following his release from the padded cell Gilbert had a genuine scare, and so did Mr. Soppel, who was following Gilbert and Mr. Bayliss. Mr. Bayliss and Gilbert were passing a drug store, when who should step out of the crowd but Fogarty of the *Star!*

His face lighted up instantly with delight and recognition; and Mr. Bayliss walked on, quite as if he and Gilbert were not together.

"Well, well!" cried the gray-eyed reporter. "And so we meet again!"

"Oh, yes," said Gilbert, his heart beginning to thump.

Mr. Soppel was edging up, his face working.

Fogarty had seized Gilbert's hand and now he was pumping it.

"Been making any more arrests lately?" asked the reporter.

"Me?" said Gilbert.

"Sure! You! You got off to a flying start, but I haven't been hearing much of you lately."

"I've been laying kind of low," said Gilbert.

"I suppose you're just looking them over."

"That's about all," Gilbert agreed, forcing a hollow laugh.

"Going to be in town long?"

"Well, it all depends."

"Thinking of joining the force?"

"No," said Gilbert. "I wouldn't join the force in this town if I was starving."

Fogarty had started to go on. Now he planted his hands on his hips and looked at Gilbert.

"Why not?"

"I don't like this town—that's why!"

"What's the matter—somebody been passing you some more flannel money?"

"Nope. I like the country better."

Mr. Soppel was edging closer and closer. Mr. Bayliss had stopped a few feet farther on and was looking back with anxiety.

"You ought to join the force," said Fogarty with a twinkle in his gray eyes. "They need men of your caliber. You've got a real competitor here, Mr. Dollow—the man in the black mask. What did you say you were doing in Steel City?"

"Just looking around."

"Well, so long. Watch out for the horse cars."

Gilbert, flushing, watched him striding down the street. How he had longed to fling the truth in that upstart, smart aleck's face! He could hear himself saying it:

"You think you're real funny, don't you? Well, do you want to know who I am? I am the man in the black mask, you big slob!"

Mr. Soppel and Mr. Bayliss had pounced upon him.

"I'm the man in the black mask!" Gilbert snarled.

"Good Lawd!" Mr. Soppel moaned. "Did you tell him that?"

"No, but I had a darned good mind to! The smart aleck!"

"What," Mr. Bayliss panted, "did he say?"

"What did you say?" Mr. Soppel burst out.

"Aw, he recognized me from the time he wrote that funny article about me when I pinched Carter up in Maple Hollow. I suppose he's going to his dog-goned newspaper now and write another."

Gilbert's surmise proved to be no less than correct. On an inside page of the *Star* next morning there was a short but very amusing article, purporting to be an interview with Gilbert. It was headed:

BOY SLEUTH CONDEMNS STEEL CITY FORCE!

And in language that made out Gilbert to be even more ridiculous than he had been painted in the previous interviews he was quoted as saying that he wouldn't join the Steel City police force if they presented him with an invitation on a silver platter. The interview ran:

> "Up in the great open spaces where I come from, where men are menacing, a Steel City cop wouldn't last a minute. We don't have to wear black masks up there to round up our criminals. We catch them young, treat them rough, and send them packing."
>
> "Have you slammed down your gun on anybody lately?" the sleuth of Maple Hollow was asked. "Or did you wear it out slamming it down on Carter, the Flannel Money King?"
>
> The boy sleuth disdained to reply, and indignantly denied that the gun used for the arrest of Carter was now pickled in alcohol in the Maple Hollow museum.

Gilbert's ire at this almost libelous article was soothed by what he read on the front page of the same edition. It was stated there, almost with reverence, that the Masked Master Mind was in seclusion, planning another sortie on the remaining criminals in Steel City.

And on the editorial page he read:

Commissioner Hayes is to be congratulated upon the wisdom he displayed in bringing the great unknown detective to Steel City. Our city was fairly crawling with every known species of lawbreaker. Since the masked genius's spectacular and sensational capture of the four pay roll bandits and his later arrest of the notorious underworld character, Maggie More, the queen of the shoplifters, the very air of our community has seemed purer and sweeter.

Once again our little children can play in the streets without fear of kidnaping; our society matrons give parties without fear of robbery of their jewels; our merchants display their wares without fear of shoplifting; our bankers lock up their vaults at night without fear that, ere dawn comes, their strong boxes will be pilfered. It is a startling fact that not one arrest of importance has been made in Steel City since the night of the raid at Mop's.

The *Star* has found occasion many times in the past to criticize the laxity of the police administration. These criticisms, we felt at the time, were deserved. Now, from hearts brimming with gratitude and relief, we extend our most honest congratulations to the Steel City police administration. We commend Commissioner Hayes for the shrewdness and imagination he has displayed; we heartily applaud the brilliant feats that his unknown detective has executed.

May Steel City remain pure, and honest of heart!

"Gee!" said Gilbert.

"Well! Well!" said Commissioner Hayes. They were seated in the commissioner's office, each with his copy of the *Morning Star,* and Mr. Hayes looked at least fifteen years younger than he had on that painful morning when Gilbert had gone in with instructions from the two "German" policemen to bang on his desk.

"To-night," said Mr. Hayes, laying his paper aside, "Mrs. Silas Bainbridge is giving her mask ball. Is your dress suit ready?"

"I have just one more fitting, commissioner."

"The plan of procedure is simply this, Gilbert. You will go with me in my car to the Bainbridge mansion at eleven thirty. At twelve the guests will unmask. You are not to remove your mask. It is a ridiculous thing to do; but Mr. Bainbridge is one of the most influential men in town, and when he makes a request, we usually grant it.

"Mrs. Bainbridge wants to give her guests a thrill. She is going to spring you as a surprise on them. Remember, you are not to remove your mask. And do not, under any condition, permit any one to tear it from your face. Watch out for the flappers."

"I don't want to be laughed at," said Gilbert warily. "I am sick and tired of being made a joke of."

"My dear boy, you will be adored. You will be the lion of the great event of the Steel City social season. You are the man who has cleaned out the criminals of Steel City. You are now a celebrity."

"Wait a minute," Gilbert interrupted. "Supposing somebody tries to snatch my mask off. Everybody is so dog-goned curious to know who is the man behind the mask, somebody is almost sure to do it—just in fun."

"I have arranged for that," said Mr. Hayes. "You will be guarded by Mr. Soppel and Mr. Hobson. One of them will stand on each side of you. They will forestall any attempt on anybody's part to reach you. The press does not know that you will attend the ball; so you need have no fears on that score. You will go, you will be stared at, and you will depart.

"As I said, Mrs. Bainbridge, like all rich women, is a lion hunter, and you are the lion—or the goat. It is the price you must expect to pay for being so much in the public eye. After to-night, if you wish, you can gradually slip out of the public eye.

"There is no more crime in Steel City. There hasn't been a robbery, or a holdup, or a reported case even of shoplifting, or pocket picking, or purse snatching since the night we raided Mop's. Steel City is a spotless town. We deserve to congratulate ourselves, just as the *Star* says."

Impulsively the commissioner shot out his hand, and grasped Gilbert's.

"We're pretty good," said Gilbert.

"We're damned good!" said Mr. Hayes.

Some one banged heavily at the commissioner's door. It flew open. Mr. Hobson came staggering in. He was hatless. His bow tie was undone, and hung in crinkly strings. The hair of the chief of detectives was disheveled. He was breathless. His eyes were staring.

"Commissioner!" he panted. "Commissioner, there's been a double murder up in Elmhurst Avenue! And there isn't a single, solitary clew!"

CHAPTER XXIV

THE MURDER TRAIL

"GOOD GOSH!" GASPED Gilbert.

"Oh, hell," said the commissioner, and sank wearily into his chair. "Just when we, and the newspapers, and everybody in town got through congratulating the police force on how spotless the town was— Oh, well. Give me the gist of it, Hobson."

Mr. Hobson mopped his beaded brow.

"This taxicab was found by Officer Doyle, over on Elmhurst Avenue, only a few minutes ago. That's Hawley's beat, but he admits he wasn't near that spot from four in the morning on. The bodies are both cold, and Doyle figures the murders must have been committed some time shortly after four o'clock. People passing the cab thought the driver was sitting there asleep—him with a bullet inside his brain! There's a girl crumpled up on the floor, inside the cab, with a bullet in her heart."

"And no clews?" snapped the commissioner.

"Not a sign of a clew, sir."

"Maybe," Gilbert put in briskly, "I might be of some use in untangling this case."

Mr. Hobson wheeled on him with a snarl. "Gilbert, will you kindly speak when you are spoken to?"

"What have you done?" Mr. Hayes wanted to know.

"I've sent out Soppel, Gaines, and Harvel, sir. The bodies are on the way to the morgue."

"Did Soppel take finger-print apparatus along?"

"Yes, sir."

"Very well. I'll go with you."

The two men started from the office at a run, and Gilbert trotted after them.

The commissioner and the chief of detectives piled into the commissioner's roadster, and Gilbert started to climb in, too.

"No, Gilbert," said the commissioner, "I'm afraid we can't use you just now. Have the final fitting of your dress suit, and report to me some time before eleven o'clock to-night."

They were off in a cloud of gasoline smoke before Gilbert could voice a protest, and the details of that gruesome murder he secured from the newspapers, edition by edition.

The story broke upon Steel City with the force of a bomb. It was from the outset a baffling mystery. The facts in the case were simply these: John Gormley, taxicab driver, had been shot through the brain from behind while sitting at his wheel. The girl, whose identity was soon established, was Clarice Waring, a manicurist, employed in the barber shop on the ground floor of the First National Bank Building. She had been shot through the heart. Death in each case must have been instantaneous. The murderer left absolutely no clew.

All of this, and more, came dribbling, edition by edition, as the day waned. The girl was known to have many men friends. She was not in love with any of them. Where she and the murderer had spent the evening—for it was presumed that she had spent the evening with some man—could not be learned.

Every detective and uniformed man on duty was called upon. None had noticed this particular taxicab. And, as the day wore on, no information came to headquarters from any source.

It was maddening. Just when Steel City had been freed of crime, the police force had to be saddled with the most baffling of murder mysteries.

"Call in the man in the black mask!" screamed the afternoon papers.

Gilbert, with nothing to do all afternoon but to follow the murder developments, edition by edition, fell to wondering how a detective went about scenting out the murderer in a case as baffling as this one. How would *Sherlock Holmes* have gone about it? How would he start?

On a news stand, whither he went for the latest edition, he saw a magazine with a blue cover. The name of it seemed to leap out at him:

FLYNN'S WEEKLY
Detective Fiction, With the Thrill of Truth

Gilbert bought a copy of the magazine, found a deserted bench in a park, and was soon absorbed in a story entitled, "The Puzzle Lock." It was written by an Englishman, and it dealt with a shrewd, scientific gentleman named Dr. Thorndyke, who made deductions so brilliant that they almost took one's breath away.

"He is just like I am," Gilbert presently announced to himself. "He never misses a detail. It's just exactly the same as the way I studied out the habits of the woodpecker. He knows how to use his eyes."

The story was told in the first person, and one of its early scenes was in a London restaurant. The sharp-eyed Dr. Thorndyke, and the man telling the story, had dropped in there for dinner. Dr. Thorndyke suddenly took notice of a man sitting at a near-by table, who had just dropped his monocle into his soup the second time. Gilbert read:

> Following the direction of his glance, I observed the man with the waxed mustache furtively wiping his eyeglass; and the temporary absence of the monocular grimace enabled me to note a resemblance to the familiar features of Badger, the detective officer.
>
> "If you say that is Badger, I suppose it is," said I. "He is certainly a little like our friend. But I shouldn't have recognized him."
>
> "I don't know that I should," said Thorndyke, "but for the little unconscious tricks of movement. You know the habit he has of stroking the back of his head, and of opening his

mouth, and scratching the side of his chin. I saw him do it just now. He had forgotten his imperial until he touched it, and then the sudden arrest of movement was very striking. It doesn't do to forget a false beard."

"No," said Gilbert, enthusiastically, "it doesn't do to forget or to overlook the least little detail. Now, supposing I was sitting face to face with the murderer of Clarice Waring and John Gormley, just how would I go about deducing that it was him?"

A little farther along in the story of "The Puzzle Lock," Gilbert came upon this bit of wisdom uttered by the penetrating Dr. Thorndyke:

"And yet, Jervis," said he, "it was an essentially simple case. If you review it, and cast up the items of evidence, you will see that we really had all the facts. The problem was merely to coördinate them and extract their significance."

"It's a cinch," said Gilbert, emphatically, "once you learn the trick. Gee, I certainly wish I could meet that murderer."

By dinner time that night the double murder mystery was as much a mystery as ever. No one in Steel City had, so far, been clever enough to cast up the items of evidence and make out a case against any one, largely because there weren't any items of evidence to cast up. The murder remained clewless. Every young man who had known Clarice Waring had presented a good account of himself, a perfect alibi. No one had seen Clarice Waring since the minute she had left the barber shop.

And every edition of every afternoon paper cried for the man in the black mask.

Gilbert dropped in at headquarters at six, and again at seven, but, on both occasions, Commissioner Hayes sent out word that he was too busy to see him.

Gilbert returned to his boarding house, bathed, shaved, and leisurely dressed. At eleven o'clock he entered headquarters, and found Mr. Hayes ready for him.

The commissioner was haggard and gray from his worrisome day. The fifteen years he had lost in the past few days had all returned, and a few more years had joined them. The commissioner looked like an old man—an old and weary fox.

"Well, Gilbert," he said, as Gilbert entered, "you look simply beautiful. Have you your mask?"

"Yes, sir. It's in my coat pocket, here, under my handkerchief."

"Very good. Mr. Soppel will take you to the ball. Mr. Hobson will be unable to go, and I am going to be too busy. Remember this: don't let anybody snatch off your mask. You and Mr. Soppel will take my roadster. Come back as soon after twelve as you possibly can. I need Soppel, and if we have any suspects in the murder case by that time, we may need you. Run along, Gilbert. Don't drink any liquor. Don't talk. Be as aloof as you know how. Good luck. You'll find Soppel waiting in the roadster."

Gilbert went down the stairs, and found Mr. Soppel waiting for him. Mr. Soppel was irritable and touchy. He wanted to follow some imaginary clew in the murder case, and he resented being Gilbert's chauffeur. He drove recklessly through town, ignoring Gilbert's friendly attempts at making conversation, and presently the roadster rolled into a crushed stone driveway at the farther end of which stood a stately white mansion blazing with lights.

The lilting strains of dance music came through opened windows. And above the music came a babble of voices and laughter.

It was Gilbert's first ball, and he was both awed and thrilled. How he wished that Annie May might be here! He put on his mask.

A butler met them at the door.

"Kindly tell Mrs. Bainbridge," said Mr. Soppel, "that the men from the police department are here."

The butler glanced at Gilbert with an expression compounded half of awe and half of fright. Beyond him Gilbert's devouring gaze encountered costumes that made him blush. There was a girl in a red domino, and practically nothing else. Beyond her was a girl in a pink dress, and if Mr. Soppel had not restrained him, Gilbert would have rushed over to her.

Every one he saw was wearing a mask of some description; men dressed as frogs, as soldiers, as pirates, as Pierrots; girls dressed as South Sea islanders, as ballet dancers, as Pierrettes. Every one was laughing and talking. Never had he seen such gayety.

Presently a tall, heavily built woman came fluttering over to them, and Gilbert quickly guessed that she was supposed to be *Juliet,* although he as quickly decided that she was much too old for that romantic part.

She rushed up to Gilbert with eyes that glittered behind a white satin mask.

"You are the man in the black mask?" she breathed.

"He is," said Mr. Soppel heavily.

"I am," said Gilbert.

Mrs. Bainbridge looked at him and sighed.

"Oh, I think it is wonderful—wonderful—the way you have driven the criminals from Steel City! Let me be the first to shake your hand? Do you mind if I introduce you to a few people?"

"It is the commissioner's orders," said Mr. Soppel, "that he be introduced to no one."

"Well," said Steel City's society leader, "supposing we slip away to the balcony above the ballroom. At twelve sharp, according to my plans, every one will assemble there to unmask. I should like to have your entrance very dramatic, Mr.—Mr. Man in the Black Mask. Will you follow me?"

Mr. Soppel and Gilbert followed her through several rooms, and up a flight of stairs to the balcony above the ballroom. There was a flight of stairs from the balcony to the ballroom floor, and across the room Gilbert saw another balcony with a companion flight of stairs.

They seated themselves, and Mrs. Bainbridge did not for a

moment remove her fascinated eyes from Gilbert's face. "Tell me," she whispered, "are you working on the murder mystery?"

"I can say nothing," said Gilbert.

"He positively must not talk about his work or reveal his identity," said Mr. Soppel. "Those are Mr. Hayes's orders."

Mrs. Bainbridge looked nervously at her wrist watch.

"It is five of twelve," she announced. "At twelve sharp, the orchestra will stop, and the drummer will give a long roll on his drums. Every one knows there is to be a surprise—"

"I hope you haven't told any one," put in Mr. Soppel uneasily.

"Not a soul, but they expect a thrill, and oh, what a thrill they are going to get! When the drums roll, every one is to unmask—every one but Mr. Man in the Black Mask. If you will take your place on the floor below, Mr. Soppel, I think his entrance will be much more effective. I will accompany you, and I will make the announcement from the floor. Then the man in the black mask will walk down this stairway. You can join him on the floor, Mr. Soppel, although I am sure there will be no need for your protection unless some of the younger people decide to play pranks. There is a door just behind the orchestra. It gives directly upon the garden. You can make your escape through that door—if you leave in a hurry. You see, I have anticipated every contingency that can possibly arise. Let us hurry down, Mr. Soppel; there is just one minute left!"

Gilbert watched them descend the stairs. The orchestra was playing, but the dancing, except for a random couple here and there, had stopped.

Suddenly, in mid-beat, the music came to an end, and the drummer commenced to beat upon his snare drum in a long crescendo roll.

"Oh," said Gilbert as he arose from the chair, "if Annie May could only see me now!"

Below him in the huge ballroom men and girls were removing their masks. Every one was laughing and chattering. In the midst of this hubbub, the drummer brought a drumstick down upon the cymbal with a crash.

Mrs. Bainbridge strode out to the middle of the waxed maple floor. She raised her hands for silence. And about the large room silence gradually fell.

She cried: "Who wants a thrill?"

All about her voices rose.

"I do!"

"We all want a thrill!"

"Trot out your thrill!"

"Hark!" cried the hostess. "In our midst to-night is a man who has become famous for his deeds of daring, who has become celebrated for his brilliant deductions—the man who has swept Steel City clean of its criminals! If you can name him, you can see him in the flesh!"

"The man in the black mask!" a dozen voices shouted.

"Where is he?" a dozen other voices cried.

"He is coming down the stairs!"

Every one in the crowded ballroom looked up. Some looked at one end of the room, at one flight of stairs; others looked at the other end, at the other flight of stairs.

There was an excited babble of voices, a ripple of laughter.

At the head of each stairway was a man in a black mask!

CHAPTER XXV

ON WITH THE DANCE!

MR. SOPPEL STARED from one stairhead to the other. Mrs. Bainbridge stared from one stairhead to the other. Her several hundred guests stared from one masked man to the other.

It was hard to say who was Gilbert, and who was not. They were of almost the same height. Each had curly blond hair. Each wore a perfectly fitting dress suit.

Step matching step, the two men in black masks descended toward the ballroom floor.

One man was smiling. The other was not. The man who was not smiling was Gilbert Dollow. But both were pale. Both were wary, or so they seemed.

Mrs. Bainbridge turned angrily on Mr. Soppel.

"Do you know what this means?"

"Madam, I think somebody is playing a little practical joke. You must have tipped it off to somebody that our man was to be here."

"I didn't tell a soul—oh—oh—oh!"

"You did tell some one," Mr. Soppel sternly accused her.

"Only my husband!"

"And he told somebody else!"

"I am perfectly furious!"

Everybody about them was beginning to laugh. It was a joke.

It was a good joke. They thought so until they saw their hostess's face. Some began to wonder.

But there were enough who did not wonder, who continued to laugh, to make Gilbert grit his teeth with rage.

He was being ridiculed again! He was being made the butt of just one more practical joke!

"Which of them," Mrs. Bainbridge demanded, "is our man— the real one?"

"I am blessed," said Mr. Soppel bewilderedly, "if I can decide myself? Which side were we on?"

"That side," said Mrs. Bainbridge, ignoring the book of etiquette by pointing, "but there is that connecting balcony. He could have gone around. Which is which?"

Step by step the two masked men descended the stairs. A great path was formed in the crowd so that, when they reached the floor, they were face to face.

In the middle of the floor they met.

"Take off that mask!" snarled one of them.

"Take off that mask!" snarled the other.

"Well, I'll be damned," muttered Mr. Soppel.

"So will I!" gasped Mrs. Bainbridge.

"Which of you," Mrs. Bainbridge demanded, "is the real man in the black mask?"

"My Lord," said one of the masked men to the other, "are you the real man in the black mask? Ain't this a little joke?"

"Stop!" Gilbert shouted, as the man, now as pale as pale could be, turned and started for the nearest exit.

The masked pretender started to run, Gilbert ran after him, and tackled him as vigorously as Red Grange ever tackled a flying opponent.

The spurious masked marvel came to the floor with a crash. Women screamed. Mr. Soppel's revolver came out of his pocket.

Gilbert ripped the mask from the face of the pretender.

"I surrender!" the man yelped.

"Jewels!" Mrs. Bainbridge screamed.

Her sensational announcement was verified in a glittering, twinkling, spilling mass which emerged from the unmasked man's pockets to the floor.

"My jewels!" she screamed.

"Phew!" said Mr. Soppel. "If it ain't Gentleman Joe!"

"Handcuff him!" Gilbert snapped.

Gentleman Joe, that notorious Raffles of the underworld, came to his feet.

"I knew I was a damned fool to come to this party," he whined, "with you in town. What chance has a crook anyhow? Oh, why didn't I pull out of town when the pulling was good?"

"Stop your squawking," Mr. Soppel growled, "and slip on these bracelets. Ladies and gentlemen, kindly stand back. We have a dangerous criminal here."

The chattering that now filled the room was almost deafening. Every one was crowding around Gilbert.

"The big stiff." Gilbert was saying indignantly to Mr. Soppel. "Trying to steal my stuff that way! Dog-gone him, anyway!"

"Shut up, will you kindly?" said Mr. Soppel in a venomous whisper. "What has that got to do with the price of onions?"

A lane was cleared for them. The masked marvel led the way, with beautiful girls and envious young men staring at him as if he were, say, the Prince of Wales, or *Beau Brummel* returned to life.

The jewels that Gentleman Joe had stolen from the little round safe in the wall of Mrs. Bainbridge's boudoir were returned to their owner, and the notorious thief was led out of the house and into the Marmon roadster.

"How did you know I was goin' to pull this job?" Gentleman Joe angrily demanded of Gilbert. "Who spilled it, I want to know?"

"I've a good notion to bust you a good one," said Gilbert no less savagely.

"Aw, you two guys quit quarreling, will you?" Mr. Soppel growled. "How in hell can I drive this bus when you two think you are a cat and a dog, will you tell me?"

"He spoiled my entrance," Gilbert muttered.

"Huh!" said the Raffles of the underworld after a thoughtful pause. "If you're the masked marvel, then I'm the Queen of Sheba."

"Is that so!" Gilbert snapped. "Ask him whether or not I'm the masked marvel!"

"Is he?"

"Sure he is. Now shut up and let me drive, will you?"

"Masked marvel, my eye!" muttered the captive.

"One more crack out of you," Gilbert snarled, "and I'm going to wear my knuckles out on your nose!"

"Banana oil!" Gentleman Joe sneered.

The roadster's arrival at the foot of headquarter's steps interrupted what might readily have become a distressing scene.

Mr. Soppel pushed Gentleman Joe ahead of him, and the three men entered the commissioner's office. Mr. Hayes was seated at his desk, looking even older and wearier than when Gilbert had seen him last.

"Well, Gilbert," he said with a tired smile, "did you have a nice time at the party?"

"He landed another one," said Mr. Soppel glumly.

"This fellow!" exclaimed Mr. Hayes.

"It's Gentleman Joe. He was getting away with the Bainbridge crown jewels, commissioner." And Mr. Soppel related what had taken place.

The telephone rang just as he finished.

"Yes. Yes?" said Mr. Hayes. "I'm quite sure he would. Just a minute, sir. He's in my office. You can talk to him."

The commissioner handed the telephone to Gilbert.

"It's Mr. Bainbridge," said Mr. Hayes. "He wants to have a word with you."

Gilbert put the receiver to his ear, and the mouthpiece to his lips.

"Hello?"

"I will regret to my dying day," said a rich, cultured voice at the other end, "that I was denied the pleasure of meeting you, sir. And I wish to congratulate you upon making one of the most brilliant arrests that has ever come to my attention. You would be conferring a distinction and an honor upon me if you permitted me to compensate you for the—"

"Oh, that's all right," said Gilbert.

"No, indeed, sir. I wish to mail you my check for five thousand dollars, and I positively will not take no for an answer. In whose name shall the check be made payable?"

"Mine will be all right," said Gilbert.

There was a soft chuckling in the receiver at Gilbert's ear.

"But your name is unknown, sir."

"My name," said Gilbert, "is Gilbert Dollow. But you mustn't tell a soul!"

"I won't—upon my word! Let me write it down. And where shall it be sent?"

"To Maple Hollow," said Gilbert firmly.

"Good Lord!" cried Commissioner Hayes.

"It's all right. That's quite enough," said Gilbert. "Thanks very much. Good-by!" He hung up.

"Bonehead!" shouted the commissioner.

"Dumb-bell!" boomed Mr. Soppel.

"Sap!" joined in Gentleman Joe on principle.

"Sticks and stones will break my bones," Gilbert chanted mockingly, "but words will never hurt me!"

"Bah!" said the commissioner.

"He promised not to reveal my identity," Gilbert explained.

"What's a promise to a magnate?" growled Mr. Soppel.

"You've absolutely ruined yourself for further use on the force," said Mr. Hayes.

"But I'm not on the force, I've never been on the force, and I don't want to be on the force."

"Hah! You said you did!"

"I changed my mind. I hate it. I hate the force."

"You can't do it. You can't leave us cold. You've got to be the masked marvel until I say you can stop. I have the power to deputize any citizen to be an officer."

"I resign," said Gilbert.

"You can't until I let you. Your secret is safe until morning, and between now and then I want you to work on this murder case. Now go out and look for that murderer."

"How? Where?"

"Listen," said Mr. Soppel, "just go out and slip on a banana peel, and you will fall in his lap."

"Ha, ha," said Gilbert hollowly. "You think you're funny, don't you, Soppel?"

"That will do, boys," said the commissioner. "Run along, Gilbert. Remember! You are looking for the murderer of Clarice Waring and John Gormley. Soppel, lock this fellow up and put him where nobody can talk to him. He knows too much."

"Yes, sir."

"So this is the masked marvel!" breathed Gentleman Joe with a final withering look at Gilbert. "Well, nature is just wonderful."

Gilbert went. At the top of the steps that led to Spruce Street, he encountered Mr. Hobson.

"Oh, hello," said the chief of detectives. "Who've you been arresting lately?"

"I just got Gentleman Joe, the Raffles of the underworld," said Gilbert modestly. "Caught him running off with the Bainbridge jewels."

"Say, for the love of Pete, Gilbert, leave us somebody to catch, will you? How did it happen?"

"Well, I went up there to give Steel City society a thrill," Gilbert obliged, "and Gentleman Joe was there in my disguise. I got sore at him for stealing my stuff. We had a tussle, and he fell down and all the family jewels spilled out. It was pure luck—this time."

"This time!" Mr. Hobson moaned. "Are you working on anything now, Gilbert?"

"Mr. Hayes just put me on the murder case."

"Oh, no!"

"Oh, yes!"

"Oh, my Lawd! What chance has a guy who was born on Friday, the thirteenth, with a black cat under the bed just as somebody was opening an umbrella in the next room? Say, Gilbert, be a real sport and lay off this murder case, will you?"

"Sorry. Can't. Gave the commissioner my word that I'd work on it, and you know what my sense of duty is. It comes before everything else, Mr. Hobson."

"Yeah, I know all about that sense of duty of yours. If you caught your own mother swiping a peanut in a grocery store you'd have her run in for grand larceny. Where are you going, Gilbert?"

"Before I go to work on this case I'm going to get something to eat."

"You're always getting something to eat."

"Where's a good place to get a bite this time of morning?"

"Gilbert, listen! I almost forgot to tell you something. You can kill two birds with one stone. Did you know there was somebody else in town stealing your thunder?"

"How do you mean?" said Gilbert.

"I am telling you the unvarnished truth, Gilbert. They have a take-off on you up at one of the night clubs. If you want to have a good old-fashioned laugh at yourself, go up to Idaho Alice's. You can get elegant scrambled eggs up there later on, and Idaho Alice has this girl who is doing the masked marvel act, and they say she's a wow! They call her the girl in the black mask, and she's a pip."

"Is that girl making fun of me?" Gilbert demanded.

"Is she? It's the biggest laugh in town!"

"I'll show her!" Gilbert snapped.

He was tired of being laughed at. Oh, how tired he was of being laughed at!

CHAPTER XXVI

WAITING FOR THE "BUTTER-AND-EGG GIRL"

THE FIRST EDITION of the Steel City *Star* had been, as newspaper men say, put to bed, when Fogarty returned to the city room from midnight lunch to find Blaine, his city editor, pacing up and down the room, puffing vehemently at a cigarette, running his right hand through his hair and exhibiting symptoms of nervousness.

At sight of Fogarty, Blaine uttered a bellow of relief.

"I thought you'd gone home," the city editor exclaimed. "Listen, Fogarty, the masked marvel has come to life again. He showed up at the Bainbridge mask ball in full dress, wearing his mask, at about a quarter to twelve. I suppose the old hen got him up there by putting the screws on Hayes. Anyhow, he went, and when the time came to unmask, he made his entrance down the ballroom stairs. You know, there're two stairs, one at the north end of the ballroom, the other at the south end. What do you suppose happened, Fogarty?"

"He nabbed the murderer of Clarice Waring!" guessed Fogarty.

"No, no, no! When he starts down the stairs, another guy in a black mask starts down the other stairs. Great excitement! The two meet in the middle of the floor. Everybody else's mask is off, see? The real man in the black mask makes a flying tackle at the imitation—and saves the family jewels!"

"Huh?" said Fogarty.

"It was Gentleman Joe, and he'd been looting the safe in Mrs. Bainbridge's bedroom."

"Good story," said Fogarty. "Pure luck."

"Pure hell! That guy has got a sixth sense, whether you believe in supernatural stuff or not, Fogarty. He knew that bird had those jewels on him."

Fogarty's gray eyes were large and round.

"Do you want me to write the story?"

"Nope. Mack is handling it. I've got a hunch. My sixth sense is working, too, and my hunch is that the man in the black mask is going to find the murderer of Clarice Waring if he hasn't beat it from town. I've had a man down at headquarters all evening, but he reports nothing doing. I want you to play my hunch. Use your own judgment. Hop to it! A photographer, and a flash light man are down there just hanging around. Take them along, and follow your well-known nose."

Fogarty departed. He reached headquarters just as Gilbert was saying good-by to Mr. Hobson, but he did not recognize Gilbert. The reporter stopped beside Mr. Hobson, tipped back his hat, and thoughtfully scratched his left eyebrow.

"Hello!" said Fogarty.

"Hello!" said Hobson.

"Anything doing yet in that murder case?"

"Not a thing, Fogarty. We've followed every tip that's come in. We've had every man who's been going around with the Waring girl on the mat, and there isn't a clew to work on."

"About time," said Fogarty, "that you turned loose your man in the black mask. I hear he turned another trick up at the Bainbridge ball."

"The guy is clever," said Hobson.

"Have you sicked him on this murder case?"

"Ask Hayes. Well, I guess I'll be ambling along. Good night."

"Good night," said the reporter, and he watched Mr. Hobson start briskly down the street. Under a street light a block away he saw the man who had just left Mr. Hobson walking rapidly. It occurred to Fogarty that Mr. Hobson was trailing this man. He tingled as another idea struck him. Hobson was generally present when the man in the black mask made his sensational arrests. Who was the man with whom Mr. Hobson had been talking, and was now shadowing? Why had Mr. Hobson been so anxious to get away?

Fogarty stopped thinking, and acted. He ran into headquarters, rounded up the photographer, and the flash light man, and with them trailing behind him started off after Mr. Hobson. He saw the chief of detectives about a block distant, but he no longer could see the man who Mr. Hobson was trailing.

Fogarty had all the eagerness of a bloodhound on a hot scent. Another exclusive interview with the man in the black mask, another beat for the *Star*, and he would have the confidence he needed to go in and ask the managing editor for a raise.

Gilbert had meanwhile reached the portals of Idaho Alice's Night Club. Two uniformed doormen blocked his way.

"Your card, sir?" said one of them, speaking respectfully, because of Gilbert's dress suit.

"My card?"

"Your membership card," said the other doorman. "No one is allowed inside without a membership card, sir."

"But I'm from headquarters."

"Police headquarters?"

"Certainly," said Gilbert with mounting impatience.

"I beg your pardon, sir, but is this, by any chance, a raid?"

"A raid? Of course, not! All I want is a plate of scrambled eggs."

They let him in, and Gilbert blinked as he went in. The first appalling sight that met his eyes as he handed his coat and hat to the hat-check girl was a long mahogany bar. Behind it stood two men in white coats, and both were industriously agitating cocktail shakers. In front of the bar stood at least fifteen men, smoking, talking, drinking.

What would Mr. Hayes say, Gilbert wondered, if he knew that a bar was in existence within four blocks of headquarters?

People were going up the stairs, and people were coming down. Gilbert followed the upbound crowd. He heard a man droning: "Place your bets," and he wandered into the room from which that cold, level voice emerged. Gilbert had never seen a roulette wheel, but he recognized this one from pictures he had seen. Almost by accident he had stumbled into a gambling hell in the very heart of Steel City! He must report all this to Mr. Hayes.

He watched the gamblers for a few minutes, and then withdrew and descended to the second floor where the restaurant was. He felt guilty, and somehow furtive and stealthy. Should he go and make his report to the commissioner without delay? He wanted to go, but he was fascinated. He had been in low dives in his search for Annie May, but this was the first gilded temple of sin that he had visited.

Here was the kind of sinning that he had read about in the more lurid magazines, the sort of thing that was destroying the stout moral fabric of America. He was thrilled, but frightened. If he stayed, if he ate food in this place, he was as great a sinner as the rest of them. No, that was not true. He was fortunate in having stumbled upon this den of iniquity. He would stay. He would watch. He would collect evidence. In due course he would leave, and make his report to Mr. Hayes. But he would not touch the food.

Gilbert sauntered into the restaurant. It was a fascinating place. The walls were done in black upon which writhed dragons of gold, and upon which sailed barges of scarlet, and blue, and silver propelled by pink oars in the hands of green men. Gilbert thought these decorations were beautiful but wicked. All about the room were small tables, each with its own cozy pink-shaded light. In the middle was an oblong area of dance floor, and upon this couples were swaying and wheeling and skipping.

"They are probably all doing the Charleston," he said, and

shuddered. He himself was used to a slow, graceful fox trot. The Charleston had not yet come to Maple Hollow. Nice people, he was sure, weren't doing it.

A girl with drooping black eyes and short black hair, which vaguely identified her with the seal family, looked up at him from a near-by table and gave Gilbert a slow, seductive smile. Gilbert blushed, and hastily looked away. Here, indeed, was sin, hot, perfumed, untrammeled!

The muted music of the orchestra did something to his heart. He felt guiltier and more thrilled than ever. He pictured himself throwing himself into this wickedly lurid life, being mad and wanton and abandoned for a night; patronizing the bar, losing as much as ten or fifteen dollars on the roulette wheel, dancing with some of these vixens. Just raising the devil!

He started when a man in a dress suit that fitted him even better than did Gilbert's spoke to him:

"A table for how many, *m'sieu?*"

"I'm all al-alone," Gilbert stuttered.

"Have you a reservation, sir?"

"What do you think I am," said Gilbert, "an Indian?"

"I cannot give you a table alone, *m'sieu,*" said the head waiter with equal coolness. "If you do not object to sitting with some one else—"

Gilbert stiffened. His heart leaped. His face paled. A sudden singing began in his ears. He knew how they worked it in these places. A man coming here alone was seated with a young woman alone, a girl who lost little time in luring her victim into some compromising situation. She would lure him into dancing with her; she would cajole him to drink with her. And then—and then—he knew that he should refuse.

He cared for no girl in the world but Annie May. He was a one-woman man. He didn't want to meet a siren. Temptation and conscience waged battle on the point. Should he adhere to the strict line of duty, or should he be mad and wanton and abandoned?

No, no, no! And again no, no, no! He was on duty. He had come here to eat scrambled eggs, then to go forth and seek the murderer of Clarice Waring and John Gormley. He must not falter, must not give in to temptation.

"Wait!" he said hoarsely, but the head waiter was weaving in and out between tables.

Gilbert saw himself irresistibly drawn into the meshes of a net from which there was no escape. Which of the girls seated alone would he be placed opposite? A blond girl with tangerine lips looked up at him, and pouted provocatively. A girl with red hair looked up at him and grinned.

"Wait!" Gilbert choked.

But the waiter did not hear. He had stopped. He had stopped beside a table for two, one seat of which was occupied by a man in a gray business suit.

"Here?" Gilbert gasped.

"Yes, *m'sieu.* It commands an excellent view of the floor—" He said more, but Gilbert was not listening. He was furious with indignation.

"How about—how about—" he spluttered. He was going to say: "How about that table over there where that little blonde is sitting?" But the words died at his tongue.

"This is all right," he said. "This is fine."

"*Oui, m'sieu.*"

Gilbert sat down, and smiled distantly at the man across from him. He had paid Gilbert's arrival no more of a compliment than a brief frown, and now he was looking out across the dance floor. Gilbert followed his eyes and encountered the provocative blue ones of the blond girl with the tangerine lips. What a close shave he had had! He shivered with relief. His soul was still unsullied.

A waiter appeared at Gilbert's elbow. He had that insolent look which some waiters have, the look that makes a patron want to kill the waiter and that, when the meal is over, results in his receiving a much larger tip than a noninsolent waiter would have got.

"I want some scrambled eggs," said Gilbert.

"Perhaps *m'sieu* would prefer to wait for the butter-and-egg girl," the waiter suggested.

"The what?"

"The butter-and-egg girl. She will appear shortly, *m'sieu*, and prepare the eggs for *m'sieu* while he sits here."

"All right," said Gilbert, "I'll wait."

"Something to drink in the meantime?"

"No, nothing to drink. Water was good enough for my grandfather, and it's good enough for me."

The waiter smiled politely, and withdrew. Gilbert's remark had served one purpose. It had attracted the immediate attention of the man across from him. He stared at Gilbert unbelievingly with large misty brown eyes; then he looked quickly away again.

Gilbert examined the man's profile. He appeared to be about forty. He had dark-brown hair which was graying about the temples and thinning on top. His nose was rather small, and his chin was rather weak. He was wearing a gray business suit, and a rather flashy red and black necktie.

Something about him attracted Gilbert's interest, although he did not know what it was. Gilbert could not look at any object very long without speculating about it, and it suddenly occurred to him that here was a very good opportunity for him to use his powers of deduction, as that clever Dr. Thorndyke had in the story he had read that afternoon in *Flynn's Weekly*. Dr. Thorndyke had gleaned so much about a man by merely looking at him.

"I will dope out all I can about him," said Gilbert to himself, "and before he goes I will get up enough nerve to check up with him, and find out how near I am to guessing the truth."

The man's complexion was dark.

"He probably spends most of his time in the open," Gilbert

guessed. "That suit has a sort of rough-and-ready look about it. Right off, I would say he is a cattle rancher from Texas, maybe."

The more he thought of it, the more this fancy appealed to him, and he decided to proceed on this assumption.

"How's business?" he asked abruptly.

The man turned his brown eyes on Gilbert.

"What?" he growled.

"I said, how's business?"

"I find," said the man rudely, "that I manage to get a lot more business done by minding my own than by butting into other people's."

"Are you kidding me?" said Gilbert indignantly.

The man looked at Gilbert long and earnestly.

"No," he said finally, "I was just answering your question."

"Oh," said Gilbert, with relief, "I thought you were kidding me. I hate being kidded. I am very sensitive about it."

"Are you?" said the man dryly.

Gilbert nodded amiably. "Everybody tries to kid me, but they are usually pretty sorry for it before I get through with them." He hesitated. He wanted the man to talk more. His accent puzzled Gilbert. "Nice weather, isn't it?"

"Perfect," said the man, and ignored Gilbert again.

"Do you think we'll have any rain?"

"That's a question," said the man, "that really requires some serious consideration. What do you think?"

"Well," said Gilbert, "there was a sort of a haze in the east when the sun went down, but maybe it was only smoke."

"I'm sure it was smoke," said the indifferent stranger, and again ignored Gilbert.

"He's a Southerner, all right," Gilbert told himself.

"Texas!" he exclaimed sharply, and smilingly watched the man's reaction.

"What?" said the irritated stranger.

"I said the taxes are certainly unfair," Gilbert said slyly.

"Yes, yes, they certainly are."

Again his interest in Gilbert evaporated as does the dew on the rose when it is smitten by the hot rays of the sun.

"How did the ball game come out this afternoon, do you know?" Gilbert persisted.

"I don't know. I didn't notice. I'm not interested in baseball. I don't read the sport page, ever."

"I usually do," said Gilbert, "but to-day I was too busy reading about the taxicab murder mystery."

The man had looked away from him again, even more quickly than before.

"It certainly is a mystery," said Gilbert, "I wonder who did it?"

The dark-skinned stranger gave him a queer look from his misty eyes.

"I'm not interested in it," he said.

"Not interested in that murder?" Gilbert gasped. "Say! That's the most baffling murder mystery that's been sprung in months. Why aren't you interested?"

The man was gripping the edge of the table.

"Murders don't interest me. I think they're gruesome. Let's talk about something pleasant. How are crops?"

"Crops?"

"I said crops. You're a farmer, aren't you?"

"A farmer?" Gilbert repeated. "Well, no, not exactly. No, I wouldn't exactly say I was a farmer."

"Will you have a drink?" the man demanded. "This is pretty good Scotch. It really isn't bad Scotch at all."

Gilbert was suddenly suspicious. He had heard of smooth city men luring fellows from the country to bars and speakeasies, getting them drunk, and robbing them. He looked sharply at the man.

"No, thanks, I won't drink. By the way, what's your name? Mine's Brown."

"Mine's Smith."

"Brown and Smith," said Gilbert. "Smith and Brown. Hah!"

"What's so funny in that?" the man asked sharply.

"Nothing, Mr. Smith. That," said Gilbert to himself, "is a fake name. He's just kidding me. Well, I can kid him, too."

Aloud he said: "You said you were a Texas cattleman, didn't you?"

Mr. Smith gave him another look, a sharper look.

"I said nothing of the kind. I am the paying teller in the Elmville National Bank."

"Oh," said Gilbert, disappointed. "I thought you said you were a Texas cattleman."

"You know very well," the man said angrily, "that I said nothing of the kind. Say! What's your game, anyway?"

"I'm not playing any game," Gilbert replied earnestly. "I was just wondering who you were. You guessed I was a farmer, and I guessed you were a cattle rancher from Texas. We were both a long way off, weren't we?"

Small beads of perspiration had appeared on Mr. Smith's forehead. He started to leave the table, apparently thought better of it, and, reaching for his highball glass, gulped down its contents.

"It's funny," Gilbert rambled on, "that you aren't interested in that taxicab murder. The papers are so full of it."

"I don't pay much attention to the papers."

"It seems funny," said Gilbert, "that the driver could have been shot and the girl killed that way, and no important clews left behind."

"Were there any clews left behind?" Mr. Smith eagerly demanded.

"A finger-print," said Gilbert. "That's all."

"A finger-print!" the man burst out. "Are you sure? Where was it found?"

"Don't you know?" Gilbert said.

"I? How should I know?" the man demanded hoarsely. "Say! Look here. What's the—"

"I forgot," Gilbert hastily explained, "that you don't read the papers. Why, the finger-print was found on the side of the taxicab door."

"Hell, it might have been left there by any one of a hundred people."

"It might," Gilbert agreed, "and it might have been left there by the murderer. Say, Mr. Smith, you look awfully warm."

"It's hot in here. I—I think I'll go out and take a walk."

"I think I will, too," said Gilbert. "I'm tired of waiting for that butter-and-egg girl. Shall we go for a walk?"

Mr. Smith had gripped his hands in his lap. His shoulders were shaking. He stared across the room, but his eyes returned irresistibly to Gilbert's handsome, tanned face, and his healthy sapphire-blue eyes.

"After all," said Mr. Smith, "I guess I'll stay. I've been troubled with insomnia lately. Can't seem to get to sleep."

"I'll bet that murderer has insomnia," said Gilbert.

A waiter was passing. Mr. Smith motioned for him.

"Bring me another highball," he said. "A stiff one."

At this juncture Mr. Hobson arose from the table where he was sitting, and strolled leisurely into the hall. He entered a telephone booth and called headquarters.

"Commissioner?" he was saying presently in a low voice. "This is Hobson. Up at Idaho Alice's. Gilbert is up here, and I think he's fallen into another piece of luck. He's sitting with a guy who looks something like Dan the Dip. The guy is getting as nervous as hell. He looks like he is getting ready to make a break. Do you want to send a couple of men up?"

"Yes, and I'll be up myself. Dan the Dip packs a gun, doesn't he, Hobson?"

"Always," said Hobson, and hung up. As he strolled back he passed Fogarty.

"Stick around," he said, "Something may break. You'll have another black-mask story if it does."

"I'll stick," Fogarty promised.

CHAPTER XXVII

MR. SMITH SEEMS SICK

"AREN'T YOU FEELING well, Mr. Smith?" said Gilbert sympathetically.

"I have a splitting headache," said Mr. Smith. "I—I think I'll take that walk after all."

"Well, I'll gladly walk with you," said Gilbert. "You know, you do look pretty white around the gills, Mr. Smith. I think I'd better sort of look after you."

"Oh, I wouldn't think of bothering you," said Mr. Smith.

"Maybe you'd better sit there for awhile," Gilbert gently urged him. "You don't want to faint, you know. Waiter, hurry up and bring Mr. Smith his drink. He isn't feeling well."

"It's coming right up," said the waiter. "They're pretty busy down there."

Gilbert leaned toward Mr. Smith. He felt sorry for him, and he had developed a sudden liking for him. It was one of those unreasonable and inexplicable friendships that bloom in a moment. He knew that Mr. Smith was suffering, and it always hurt Gilbert when other people suffered.

"I wish there was something I could do for you," said Gilbert.

"You might join me in a drink," Mr. Smith suggested. "Here, waiter! Bring Mr. Brown a highball."

"Yes, sir."

Presently their highballs arrived. Gilbert's sense of duty gave one final struggle and expired. After all, friendship was as important as duty, and if a man wouldn't stand by a friend he wasn't much of a man. Gilbert lifted his glass and smiled a gay, abandoned smile.

"Well, here's to the force!" he laughed.

Mr. Smith put his glass down and stared at Gilbert glassily.

"To the what?" he gasped.

"To the police force!" Gilbert said. "And to their success in rounding up that taxicab murderer!"

Mr. Smith started to say something, and changed his mind. He was even paler than before, and the beads of sweat on his forehead were now large and glistening.

"I've been thinking a lot about that murder," Gilbert said earnestly. "What theories have you got about it?"

"I—I haven't any," Mr. Smith answered. "There aren't any clews. My Lord, I know there weren't any clews left behind. Finger-print? Finger-print? Oh, hell! It might have been anybody's!"

"The police have a way of rounding up a murderer when he thinks he hasn't left any clew at all," Gilbert reminded him.

"What makes you say that?" the other snapped.

"Well, isn't it true?"

"True? What of it? Supposing it is true? They won't catch the man who murdered that—those—"

"Look here," said Gilbert, "I'm willing to make a bet with you that they do. I'll bet you ten dollars that they catch the man who murdered Clarice Waring and John Gormley!"

"I don't want to take your bet. I'm not interested. Look here, I am the paying teller of the Elmville First National. How would it sound to the officials and the bank's customers if they knew I was going around betting on a murder? Ugh!"

"Well," said Gilbert, "I'll bet they do just the same. I'll bet they have him by morning."

"Stop," Mr. Smith begged him.

"Stop what?" Gilbert asked, looking at his friend with deep concern.

"Stop talking about that gruesome murder."

"All right," said Gilbert crisply. "Do you feel like taking that little walk now? I want to stroll down to police headquarters and see a man a moment. Want to come along?"

Practically every trace of color in Mr. Smith's face had by this time departed. He was as white as snow, as white as paper, as white as a ghost. Whiter. His eyes were great brown blurs, and sweat was trickling down his cheeks.

"No—not before all these people. For Heaven's sake. Please! Be merciful!"

Gilbert was a little dazed by the passionate note in his new friend's voice.

"Mr. Smith," he said, "you're a sick man. What you need is to go away somewhere, and have a good long rest."

Mr. Smith was now swaying slowly from side to side in his chair. He was moaning faintly.

"I wish," said Gilbert pleasantly, "that you'd take me up on that bet. Come on! Change your mind. I'll even make it a harder bet than the other one. I'll bet you ten dollars that I'll catch the murderer myself—before morning!"

Mr. Smith only stared at him, while perspiration ran in streams down his face.

"There wasn't a clew!" he burst out savagely. "You know damned well there wasn't a clew! I know there wasn't a clew. You're crazy! You can't hang that murder on— I mean— Did they find the revolver? No! Did they find any evidence of any kind? No! What are you talking about? I'm no fool. I'll hire the best lawyer in America. I'll get Barrow! I'll—"

"I don't agree with you at all," Gilbert interrupted. "You're mighty generous to offer to defend the murderer with your own money, but that fellow deserves to be punished, Mr. Smith. Or don't you believe in capital punishment?"

"No, no. Oh, my Lord, no!"

"Well, I do," said Gilbert warmly, "in a case like this. I think that fellow ought to be hung. I want to see him hung. I'd enjoy seeing him hung. Shooting a taxi driver in the back—shooting a helpless girl through the heart. Hanging is too good for him, the dirty cur! I want to see them put the rope around his neck. I want to hear him howl with fear and chatter with terror. I want—"

"Why are you saying this?" Mr. Smith wailed. "Isn't it bad enough? Will you have a heart? Say, honest, haven't you a heart? Heaven knows I'm repentant. Don't rub it in. Don't paint that horrible picture of the gallows."

"What have you got to be repentant about?" Gilbert snorted. "What sins have you committed? Think of that murderer! There's a fellow who'd better be saying his prayers and asking forgiveness of his Maker—before they slip that rope around his neck and snap it! Huh! I wonder what he's thinking to-night. I'll bet he's thinking of that moment when they drop the trap, and something snaps in his neck, and everything goes black forever and ever."

"Oh, my Lord," moaned Mr. Smith. "When—tell me—when is the ax going to fall?"

"Sometime to-night," said Gilbert.

"What time?"

"Oh, sometime."

"I can't stand this suspense."

"I wish you weren't feeling so faint," said Gilbert. "Do you think I'd better call a doctor? There's a friend of mine sitting over there—it's the chief of detectives. Shall I call him over?"

Mr. Smith stared at him wildly. Perspiration was now running down his cheeks in small rivers, dripping off the point of his chin. Gilbert's heart melted at his friend's plight. Poor fellow. Maybe he was suffering from indigestion. A man in his physical condition shouldn't stay out so late, drinking liquor and carrying on like this.

"Haven't you got a handkerchief?" Gilbert asked.

"A handkerchief?" Mr. Smith gasped. "A handkerchief? What for?"

"Your face is all wet," Gilbert said gently.

Mr. Smith went frantically through his pockets. He hadn't one.

"Here," said Gilbert generously, "use mine." And he tugged at the corner of the handkerchief protruding from his coat. It came out resistingly. It came out suddenly, and with it came the black mask.

The black mask flipped to the middle of the table, and it lay there, the two white eyes of tablecloth staring up.

"I knew it!" Mr. Smith gasped, springing back. "I guessed it from the very first! I knew it was you!"

He leaped up, grasping the chair.

Gilbert stared at him glassily. The faint, pleasant glow that had begun all over his body shortly after he had quaffed at the Scotch highball had suddenly become more pronounced. The lights had become very bright, and rather slippery looking. He could not see Mr. Smith very clearly. In fact, he could not see anything very clearly. He felt rapturously happy. Why was his good friend Mr. Smith standing up?

"I surrender, do you hear? Stop torturing me, that's all I ask! The rope—oh, my Lord—the rope! You diabolical fiend! Take me away, you hounding devil!"

"Say," Gilbert stuttered, "are you kidding me?"

"Stop!" the man groaned. "Stop torturing me! I confess! I am the man who murdered Clarice Waring and John Gormley. Put the handcuffs on! I surrender! I won't offer any resistance!"

"What?" Gilbert gasped.

"I tell you, I confess to it all! She threatened to tell my wife. She wanted me to marry her. She tried to blackmail me. I shot her. I shot her! And then I shot Gormley, because dead men tell no tales!"

"Say!" said Gilbert. "Say! You're under arrest!"

CHAPTER XXVIII

HOW HE FOUND HER

"PUT ON YOUR mask!" snarled a voice in Gilbert's left ear.

"Get that mask on!" snarled a voice in Gilbert's right ear.

He looked dazedly from left to right. Mr. Hayes was standing on one side, Mr. Hobson on the other.

"Who is this fellow?" the commissioner snapped.

"Didn't you hear?"

"No! Who is he? Is he Dan the Dip?"

"Of course not! He's the murderer of Clarice Waring and John Gormley!"

"No!" groaned Mr. Hayes.

"You're crazy!" moaned Mr. Hobson.

"Ask him!" said Gilbert triumphantly. "I grilled him! I tortured it out of him! Ask him!"

"Yes," sobbed the paying teller. "I confess! I confess everything. Only take me away from this fiend—him and his horrible talk of the rope—the rope!"

A detective had slipped up behind the paying teller, and was now fastening handcuffs on his wrists.

"Gilbert," breathed Mr. Hayes, "how did you do it?"

"By deduction," said Gilbert. "I read how to do it in *Flynn's Weekly*. It's easy when you know how."

"Look here," said Mr. Hobson roughly, "did you suspect him when you sat down here?"

"Certainly!"

"You're a liar!"

"Mr. Hobson, be careful! I am not easily aroused, but when I am aroused, watch out!"

"You're lit."

"What? Huh?"

"You're fried! You're pickled! You're skished! You're stewed! You're boiled!"

"I am not," said Gilbert stoutly, and reeled a little. "It was my sixth sense that warned me about him. The Scotch had nothing to do with it."

Mr. Hobson looked at Gilbert for a long, long time. Then he slowly shook his head.

"Gilbert," he said, "you are wonderful. You are the world's tenth wonder. I am not kidding, Gilbert, you are absolutely marvelous. If it was raining pig's knuckles and you were caught in it, you would have a bowl of sauerkraut in one hand and a stein of Pilsner in the other!"

A tall, stately woman came rushing up to them.

"Mr. Hobson!" she gasped. "What is going on here? Good Lord! It's the man in the black mask!"

Gilbert saw her only vaguely through the mists of happiness that steamed through his brain. It was Mrs. Sullivan—the woman he had arrested for smoking nicotine in public, the woman whom he had once thought was the ideal of his dreams.

"They're just taking away the murderer of Clarice Waring and John Gormley," the chief of detectives explained. "We're sorry to cause you so much trouble!"

"No trouble at all," said Idaho Alice. "Perfectly delighted. And there's Mr. Hayes. Heavenly snakes! Commissioner, will you have a drink on the house? Just when I was looking around for another good publicity stunt, you've gone and dropped a jewel right in my lap! And there's Mr. Fogarty of the *Star!* Gentlemen, sit down! The house is yours!"

"No," said Mr. Hayes. "We have to be getting back to headquarters. I want to quiz the murderer. Come on, Hobson. Come on—" He plucked at Gilbert's elbow.

"Oh, let him stay," Mrs. Sullivan pleaded. "Certainly, he has done enough work for to-night. It isn't often that I can entertain such a celebrity. Please let him stay."

"I want to stay," said Gilbert.

"But you can't stay in that mask. Don't be absurd."

"Let him stay. Just for a little while," she begged.

"I'll stay," said Gilbert.

Mrs. Sullivan was staring at him, but she did not recognize him. The restaurant was in an uproar. She ran to the middle of the floor, and clapped her hands for attention.

"Come on, Gilbert," said Mr. Hayes.

"Nope, I'm going to stay. I came here for scrambled eggs, and I'm going to stay for scrambled eggs."

"If you take off that mask—"

"I'll keep it on."

"Look here, Gilbert. If I take you on the force, give you a nice new blue suit with brass buttons, and a badge, and a night stick, and everything—will you come?"

"No, siree!"

"I'll do better than that. I'll make you a detective sergeant."

"Nothing doing."

"A lieutenant!"

"Not interested."

"Don't you want to join the force?"

"Nope. I hate the force. I hate Steel City. All I want is to find my girl and go back home."

"All right," said Mr. Hayes, reluctantly. "But don't stay long. Come down to my office when you get out of here. There's a telegram for you down there."

"A telegram?"

"Yes, it came an hour or so ago. I didn't open it. It'll be there for you."

"All right," said Gilbert. "Good-by! Waiter! Bring me another Scotch highball—a stiff one!"

"Oh, my Lawd!" groaned Mr. Hobson. "He's running amuck. Now nothing can hold him in."

Mr. Hayes and the chief of detectives departed, and Gilbert seated himself at his table. The crowd still surged about him. Fogarty fought his way through, and seated himself in the chair across from Gilbert.

Mrs. Sullivan was shouting.

"Every one in his seat please! The man in the black mask is our guest, and he mustn't be bothered! Sit down, everybody! Now—a nice big hand for the man in the black mask!"

Everybody was clapping, cheering, banging on tables. The orchestra began to play. Some semblance of order was finally restored, but it was a long time before every one was seated.

"I beg your pardon," said Fogarty, staring at him, "but I couldn't help overhearing a curious remark you dropped, sir. You said: 'All I want is to find my girl and go back home.'"

"Waiter!" cried Gilbert. "Bring this gentleman a drink." He addressed the reporter. "I said it," he agreed, "and it ought to make a good story—lots of laughs."

"Laughs?" repeated Fogarty.

"Sure! Laughs! Don't you specialize in kidding people?"

"Me?" said Fogarty.

"Sure! You! Don't you? And don't you think it's funny for a fellow to come to a city looking for the girl he's in love with, and he can find everybody under the sun without the least bit of trouble that other people are looking for—bandits, murderers, stick-up men, bank robbers, and even shoplifters—he can find all these people, but the one person he wants to find, he can't find at all. Don't you think that's funny?" Gilbert smiled at the reporter.

Fogarty seemed embarrassed.

"I think you must be making fun of me, sir. I know you big

detectives haven't a very high opinion of us small-town reporters, but I—"

"Listen," said Gilbert, sipping his new highball, "I don't
believe in kidding anybody. I know how it hurts to be kidded.
I am telling you the truth."

"You came to town looking for the woman you love and—"

"And I could find anybody that anybody else wanted, but
not her. That's the truth."

"I'd call that tragic—romantic, but tragic, sir," said the reporter gravely. "Didn't it occur to you to let the newspapers
know of this? But I suppose you had some good reason for not
doing that. Will you—will you permit me to write this story,
just as you have told it to me?"

"Go to it," said Gilbert.

"Will you tell me the girl's name?"

"It is Annie May Prine."

Fogarty frowned. "Somewhere I have heard that name before.
Where could it have been? Well, no matter. Annie May Prine.
Rest assured, the story will be on the front page. I suppose you
do not yet care to reveal your own identity."

"Not yet," said Gilbert.

"It's very strange. By your brilliant deeds, I know that you
are one of the greatest and most famous detectives of the age.
But I can't seem—"

"Ladies and gentlemen!" a strong contralto voice rang out
from the middle of the dance floor. "Everybody give a big hand
to my little butter-and-egg girl. She is coming on early to-night
as a treat for our guest of honor—the man in the black mask!
A hand, a great big hand, ladies and gentlemen, for my little
butter-and-egg girl!"

The large room fairly shook with hand-clapping, and table-
thumping. The door into the kitchen opened. Two waiters appeared wheeling a sort of cart.

Following the cart was the girl, and at sight of her a shout
of laughter went up. She wore a black mask.

Gilbert stared at her as she approached. So this was the girl who was stealing his thunder! He began to blush. He turned redder and redder. All about him people were laughing. Once again he was the butt of a practical joke. Once again he was being made ridiculous so that people might laugh!

In a veritable gale of laughter, the cart was wheeled directly to the table at which Gilbert and Fogarty sat.

He did not observe how nervous the girl was. Her smile, beneath the mask, was fixed. Annie May had never been so frightened before, except on the night when she had first carried the cigarette tray. Now she was terrified. She had been reading the newspaper accounts of the man in the black mask, and she pictured him, as did every one else, as a brilliant, ruthless intellect, a harsh man.

His hair was blond and curly, and his features were young, but she could not overcome her shaking knees.

"Buttered rolls, and scrambled eggs, sir?" her sweet, frightened voice chanted.

"Do your stuff," ordered Gilbert. That voice—where had he heard that voice before? Where had he seen those incomparable legs?

A waiter was removing the lid of the chafing dish. With a shaking hand, the girl placed butter in the silver pan, broke eggs, poured in milk, stirred the sizzling mass.

"Who ever taught you to scramble eggs?" Gilbert demanded.

The girl stared at him through the slits in her mask. Her eyes were golden brown.

"My—my grandmother," she stammered.

"I've got a girl," said Gilbert, "who can scramble circles around you. When she scrambles an egg, she scrambles it."

"I am scrambling these the best I know how," said the frightened girl.

"You'd better make it a double order," said Gilbert.

Annie May selected another egg. She could hardly pick it

up, her hand was trembling so. And her chin was trembling. In a moment she would be crying.

"I don't like burned eggs," the man in the black mask growled.

And suddenly poor little Annie May lost her temper. The eggs were not burning. She had selected especially large eggs and especially fresh ones in honor of the celebrated detective. Now he was ridiculing her. He was adding insult to injury.

"You call those scrambled eggs!" he jeered.

It was too much. Something snapped in Annie May. She seized a large white egg, and she hurled it at him.

A girl sitting near by screamed. A man, leaping up, tipped his chair over.

The egg had struck the man in the black mask squarely between the eyes, and it had splattered. Both slits of his mask were covered with the flowing yellow stuff.

With a faint scream, Annie May fled to the kitchen. The man in the black mask leaped up. He dashed after her.

Fogarty, pushing cocktail glasses, table silver, and a pink-shaded lamp off his lap, hastened after.

Gilbert found her crouching behind the large waste can in the corner of the big kitchen.

"Take off that mask!" he shouted.

He had removed his when he left the table.

"Gilbert!" she bleated, and snatched off her mask.

"Annie May!" he groaned, and staggered.

Then the girl's arms were about his neck, and he was pawing her, and she was clasping him as if she would never let him go. He kissed her, and he kissed her again.

"Oh, Gilbert, you've been drinking!"

He had slightly recovered from the rapturous shock, too.

"Yes," he agreed, "I've gone to the dogs myself. I'm wanton! What are you doing here?"

"I came here because I knew you—"

"Oh, my Lord!" he groaned. "I'm to blame for this. I'm responsible for dragging you down into a low dive like this. Annie May—darling—I can never forgive myself. Never, never, never! You were a sweet, pure, innocent girl, and I reduced you to this!"

"But, Gilbert, honey, I'm all right."

"I'll make you all right," he declared hoarsely. "I'll marry you to-morrow. I'll make a good woman of you, Annie May!"

"But I am a good woman, sweetheart!"

"Then I'll make you a better woman!"

Everybody in the restaurant was trying to get into the kitchen, but Fogarty got there first, got there and found the united lovers clasped in each other's arms, making up for all those lost kisses.

Fogarty stared at Gilbert. He stared, and stared, and stared.

"For Pete's sake!" Fogarty gasped. "Are you—you aren't—no. It isn't possible. There's been some mistake. This is all a joke. It's a put-up job. The commissioner framed me. You can't make me believe that the hick sleuth who slammed down his gun on Carter, the Flannel Money King is—is—"

"The man in the black mask!" said Gilbert. "It is! I mean, I am! I'm the guy who made all those deductions, and all those brilliant arrests! Go ahead! Write it up! Make them laugh! I'm used to it! I love ridicule! I eat it up! Tell them I'm going back to where I belong. Tell them I've found my girl at last, and that we're going back to Maple Hollow!"

"Say it again," she pleaded, "say it again, Gilbert!"

"Maple Hollow!" he chanted. "Back to Maple Hollow, and the woodpeckers, and the beach, and—we're taking the early morning train. Come, Annie May, we've just got time to make that train!"

"But I want my clothes, darling."

"No," said Gilbert emphatically. "I won't let you be contaminated by the atmosphere of this dive a minute longer."

"Dive?" said a deep contralto voice. It was Mrs. Sullivan. She stared at Gilbert. She turned pale. She gasped. "Why! It's Gilbert! It's Gilbert! He's come for you at last!"

"Yes—dive!" snorted Gilbert. "A gilded temple of sin—that's all it is. And I've come to take her away from it—and out of your clutches!" And he held Annie May protectingly to his breast.

"Good-by, Annie May," said Mrs. Sullivan gently. "I won't say what I'd like to say to Gilbert for calling this clean, wholesome, respectable night club of mine a dive. Well, after all, any man who would arrest a woman for smoking a cigarette in public would call it a dive, wouldn't he?"

"Dive! Gilded temple of sin!" Gilbert hissed.

CHAPTER XXIX

A HOME OF THEIR OWN

FOGARTY SECURED A taxicab for them, and the three of them went down to headquarters. Mr. Hayes, as he had promised, was waiting.

"I've found my girl," Gilbert announced, "and I want to hand in my resignation as the head of the black mask department. I am going back to Maple Hollow."

"Can nothing persuade you to stay, Gilbert?" asked Mr. Hayes.

"Nothing," said Gilbert.

The commissioner shook his head sadly.

"Gilbert, it breaks my heart to see you go. You have swept Steel City clean of its criminals. And here is Fogarty, ready to leap to his typewriter and inform the world that the man in the black mask was, ten days or so ago, only a simple lifeguard on Maple Hollow Beach. You will be ridiculed, Gilbert—and I will be ridiculed. And the entire force will be ridiculed."

"If there is one thing I especially don't like," said Gilbert, "it is being laughed at. Commissioner, let me make a suggestion. Why not put Fogarty in that padded cell where I spent the night?"

The reporter was scribbling on a pad. Now he looked up.

"I have a better suggestion than that," he said. "The good of the community must come first, and the community cannot be served best by making the police force a laughing stock. All that I ask is that you pledge yourself to secrecy regarding the identity of the man in the black mask—secrecy until the grave!"

"What a delightful solution!" said Mr. Hayes.

"We must be going," said Gilbert. "We must not miss our train. "You said you had a telegram for me, sir."

Mr. Hayes turned over the papers on his desk.

"Your mother!" gasped Annie May.

The commissioner found the yellow envelope, and gave it to Gilbert. He tore it open.

"Good Lord!" he gasped. "Constable Dench is dead!"

"Oh, Gilbert, no! Poor old Mr. Dench!"

"This is from the town council," said Gilbert. "They want to know if I will accept the position as constable of Maple Hollow. Will I?"

"You will!" said Annie May, and she clung to him.

Every one shook hands. The united lovers, arm in arm, descended to Spruce Street, and under a golden moon walked to the depot.

Fogarty returned to his office, and in the morning, just as the train in which Gilbert and Annie May sat, asleep in each other's arms, rolled into Maple Hollow, the city edition of the *Star* came sweet-smelling from the roaring presses.

A headline across the front page announced:

MASKED MARVEL BAGS
TAXI MURDERER AND VANISHES!

And under that a bank of type went into details:

Eugene P. Smith, Paying Teller of Elmville National, Arrested in Night Club by Masked Genius.—Murderer Confesses All.—Masked Marvel Vanishes.—Identity Still Shrouded in Mystery.—Romance with Beautiful Girl Hinted At.—In Exclusive Interview with *Star* Reporter Declares He Will Return if Crime Wave Does.—Steel City Is Spotless at Last!

It was a gallant gesture, a beautifully woven fabric of white lies and golden truth. And on the strength of it, Fogarty was granted his raise.

ABOUT THE AUTHOR

THE DECISION TO become a writer of fiction was made for me by fate. In 1914, in Panama, where I spent a week when I was a wireless operator on a little steamer that creaked up and down the Central American coast, I met an author who painted the joys of free-lancing so vividly that I could not resist the call. We were drunk. I was twenty. Since then, I have been trying to catch up with all of those joys he mentioned.

Starting to write stories in 1914 and, four years later selling my first one, marks up, I suppose, a very poor batting average. But in those years I was getting experience, seeing the world, and acquiring knowledge. I "punched brass" as a wireless operator all over the Pacific. I entered Columbia University in 1915, and one year later left because I didn't believe in higher learning. I still don't believe in it. I became a newspaper reporter, later a magazine editor.

Then came the war, which I won practically single-handed by writing high-pressure publicity to induce patriotic Americans to send books to Washington for camp libraries for soldiers and gobs. Books came by the carload, by the ton: McGuffy's readers, old almanacs, spellers, arithmetics, out-dated novels and just trash. The soldiers and sailors who read those books soon hated the war so bitterly, that they promptly got busy and ended it. That's how I won the war.

After the war, I wanted another look at China, and was sent

to the Far East by *Collier's* to write articles on China, the Philippines, India and Malaya.

George F. Worts

The first story I sold was written while I was editing a motion picture trade paper. It was bought by the *Argosy,* and it was about a wolf named Murg. Don't ask me why. In the intervening years I have written millions of words. Perhaps it is Murg who sits so patiently at my door!

I started writing fiction under the pen name of Loring Brent, because it would have annoyed the owner of the motion picture magazine to learn that I was writing fiction out of hours. He thought I fell asleep at my desk because I was working so hard for him! When my income from fiction exceeded my salary, I quit the job. Since then I have been free-lancing exclusively, except for a two-year period when I lived in a Florida swamp town and added to my writing the duties of postmaster, game warden and deputy sheriff. Out of that experience came a long series of stories about a Florida town I called Vingo.

I have enjoyed most writing stories about certain established characters. Apparently the most popular of these have been the Peter the Brazen, the Vingo and the Gillian Hazeltine stories. I stopped writing about Peter the Brazen (a swashbuckling wireless operator on ships in the China run) about ten years ago. He was, incidentally, the subject of the only novel I have had published in America. I am now starting a new series about him.

When I am not traveling I live in Westport, Connecticut. My interests are horses, sailing and flying. I took up flying about a year ago to write some articles on how it feels to learn to fly, and was badly bitten by the bug. I can make a three-point landing about five times out of ten.

I like New York, but would prefer to live in Honolulu. I

smoke sixty cigarettes a day. I like murder trials. I have never mastered the noble game of poker, although I once wrote a book about it. In my spare time I study law and medicine. I have two young sons and a still younger daughter; an able crew for my sailboat—except that there is usually mutiny aboard the lugger!

THE ARGOSY LIBRARY ™

SERIES 1 INCLUDES:

* DENT * KETCHUM * KLINE *
* MacISAAC * ROSCOE *
* ROUSSEAU *
* SELTZER *
* TUTTLE *
* WIRT *
WORTS

THE BEST FICTION
FROM THE FRANK
A. MUNSEY LINE

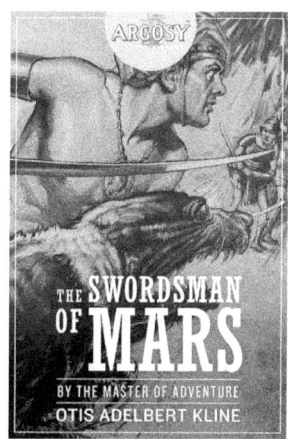

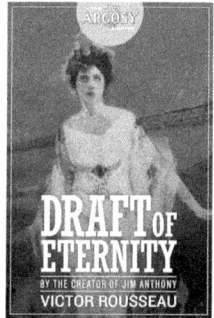

SERIES 1 • AVAILABLE SPRING 2015